Diary of a Half Azzed Father

"Welcome To My Circus"

By Sydney Jones

MCDAN Publishing

Dedication

I dedicate the book "Diary of a Half-Azzed Father" to all my fellow veterans and service men and women of the armed services. What you have faced or are facing now with your service has prevented countless civilians from ever having to face what you have or are going through. Thank you for this selfless act of kindness you willfully gave to others that you don't even know personally. No matter what your role in the service was or is, it does matter and it counts. Without you, the world would be a far worse place to live. Whatever you face in the future, no matter what anyone else says or how they act toward you, you mean a great deal to me. As a veteran, I can only say thank you for becoming one of my brothers or sisters. I hope this book will help others understand what many of us face after our services to the country and we try to live a well-earned normal life.

I also want to thank every employee and volunteer with the VA Medical system. No matter how tough things get, how much the funding is short and how bad the media plays off every bad example of what you do; your tireless effort to march on and help us is our beacon of hope. You never make excuses, you never give up and you always help us veterans to the best of your ability. Without you, there is less hope for veterans. Without your expanding knowledge of PTSD, this illness would still be a mystery to the world. Ignore the media, they don't want to tell the whole story which would show your great example of how you truly make a difference in our lives. Thank you for helping us out.

I am also thanking each and every person taking the time to read this story. Mr. Stewart may be a fiction character, but his PTSD is real. The depression and thoughts going through Mr. Stewart's head are very real for many veterans. You don't have to look far to find the Mr. Stewart in your life. A veteran may be living right in your home. Fifteen percent of attempted suicides by veterans are completed. The numbers are way too high. I hope you will take the time to remind the veterans in your life that they are wanted and needed. Their lives matter. The excellent care they receive from medical staff through the VA helps with illness and injuries they suffer from, but we all can help them battle the depression just by being there. Please go to WWW.VA.GOV so you can learn how to help our veterans by volunteering, donations or supporting current projects the VA is working on to improve their lives. We veterans appreciate everything you do to help us out. Thanks for having the courage to take a glimpse into Mr. Stewarts mind by reading his diary.

I also want to thank our true heroes from VFW Post 483 that continue to look out for us. They have helped me in a great time of need just like countless other veterans. I am not a combat veteran, but will never stop me from supporting their post. Their website is: www.myvfw.org/nh/post483

About the Author

Sydney Jones served in the US Army for four years and feel's honored to be a veteran. He was one of the privileged veterans that volunteered so you wouldn't get volunteered through a draft. Like many veterans, Sydney never felt that the commitment to community ended after his four years of service. He had set time aside to volunteer at the local VA hospital. He served as a surrogate parent for a child ward to the State of NH and learned firsthand how heartbreaking it is for a child not to have a family. All these experiences helped him follow his greatest dream to just be the best dad he could be. As he stayed busy raising his children and working to pay bills, he went to college. This gave him the experience to go through the editing process to get published, but more importantly, learn about early childhood development and have a better idea how to guide his children to adulthood.

Just like any other parent, Sydney met some challenges that have to be faced head on. One of his children was born with a disability that required a medical device. An obstacle was put in front of him, the insurance company wouldn't help pay for the device. Times were tough and Sydney's back was against the wall with only one option: sell his car and walk to work so his child could have the medical device needed to benefit from school fully. Looking back, Sydney would have done just that because the early childhood intervention has paid off. His child with this disability is an exceptional student and getting the medical device paid off.

Sydney didn't have to sell his car and walk to work because our veterans from VFW Post 483 helped him out. They paid most of the costs for the medical device so it was affordable for Sydney without losing his car. That car got him to work and ran the kids around for another five years. The VFW Post 483 didn't care that Sydney was not a combat veteran, they helped him out anyways. Sydney found out that the VFW is not just a place for war veterans to hang out. It is a rallying point for them to continue to be heroes for our communities.

He will never forget how they helped him move forward as a parent and they are his inspiration for dedicating his writing career to "pay it forward" and help his fellow veterans. At this point, it is time to give back to VFW Post 483 so they can help other veterans in need like he was. You can find Sydney Jones on Facebook and twitter to keep up to date with new events and books.

Introduction

Diary of a Half-Azzed Father is a fictional family drama novel. Post-Traumatic Stress Disorder (PTSD) can be like a time bomb going off in someone's head. It can wait for years after a veteran's military service to finally strike. It waited for more than a decade to show its ugly head in Mr. Stewart's life. It waited for the worst time in his life to show up, when he started raising children. No matter what he knew was true, the disease kept telling him something different. No matter how hard he tried to be a good father, the disease told him he was a failure. Most of us parents can survive the trials and tribulations of parenting. Mr. Stewart was not able to do that. It didn't matter that he got his child successfully to the point of enjoying college, his mind condemned him as a failure. His biggest joy was to be a fully involved father through all the years his daughter grew up. His worst nightmare was facing adolescent years that most children naturally ignore parents. In his mind, he knew this was normal, but in his soul, PTSD relentlessly condemned him as a failure.

Mr. Stewart faced many challenges successfully such as his divorce and the Gestapo tactics of the Division of Child and Family services (DCF) to remove his parental rights. His story is about a successful battle against over-zealous DCF workers that neglect their duties to protect children from real danger, but harass this innocent man over one simple mistake of falling asleep. They hounded him for over two years just to make a point that he needs to always protect his child. They had made their point to him within a month. Wasting tax payers' money to continue their assault on him damaging his wellbeing forever. He survived DCF, a cruel ex-wife, but couldn't survive the real judge, jury and executioner; his daughter.

For so many of us parents, we feel the pain when our adolescent children don't have the maturity to gracefully transfer from childhood to adulthood. It's just the way it goes. Sooner or later, they come around when it becomes cool to hang out with parents again. Mr. Stewart did not have the ability to cope with those harsh years of parenting. He felt that he was a total failure as a father and his life tragically ended with suicide. He didn't use a bullet to the head, drugs or alcohol like so many veterans are well known to use in the event of suicide. His method was far more common than the general public realizes. Veterans are trained to recognize the biggest danger in combat. It's not the bullets coming his or her way, it's the elements. Mr. Stewart made sure his daughter got everything she needed until he had nothing left to give. Now one question was over with; "did she need him?" She no longer needed anything material. This left only one question in his mind; "did she want him in her life?" It wouldn't be words but her actions that answered his question. Mr. Stewart's story has no happy ending. It is a tragedy, not much different from so

many stories of veteran suicides.

Act 1: Here Comes the Circus

I like a good circus act, don't you? Most people like watching a great circus act, but it's not fun being in one. Well, maybe other people like being stuck in the drama of one, but it's not a good scene for half-azzed fathers. The second a man becomes a father, he is put in a circus act. The deck is stacked and he has no choice what role he plays. Sorry pal, you get to be a clown, and not just any clown. You are the scape goat. It doesn't matter how hard you try to be perfect, you'll never make it. The world is watching for that first mistake and then their entertainment begins. It doesn't have to be a big mistake, but there it is looming in the dark, just waiting for you to entertain the crowd. Whether you know it or not, it's waiting for you. There are no excuses or empathy for the scape goat. Nobody cares that you are a veteran with a disability. The audience must be entertained and you will thrill them at your great personal expense. My mistake was not getting enough sleep.

I hate father's day. Just another rainy Sunday for me; no calls, no texts, nothing. Here I am homeless again for the third time in less than a half decade again! No place for me but this old abandoned tree house way out in the forest. At least my kid has a nice spot. That's what half-azzed fathers do when there isn't enough money to go around. My child is taken care of and I just deal with my situation. That's just the way it is, no complaints here. I'm an army veteran. I'm trained to deal with it, kids aren't. Now you won't hear that side of the story from anyone pretending to know who I am. They'll just tell you how creepy I am and forget to tell you I am a veteran with a disability. They also don't want you to know why I do certain things. The truth kinda makes them have to take a look in the figurative mirror and face their own flaws. This diary isn't about the blaming game. I don't play that because I only have heard of one perfect man that stayed perfect his whole life until some idiots decided to nail him to a steak. Didn't he say something like: "let the perfect man throw the first rock?" He was being sarcastic because he was perfect and he wasn't throwing rocks. I think he was making a point about playing the blaming game; don't do it!

Now here is why I put my diary in the fiction category: you wouldn't believe this stuff if you saw it with your own eyes! It's just weird. There are no real people. None of this ever happened and nobody gets hurt. I'm just a veteran with a disability that suffers from a vivid imagination. Perhaps the only good that will come out of this silly diary is that some other poor fella trying his best to be a father won't fail as miserably as I have. So as the saying goes, "don't try this at home kids, somebody may get hurt" and it's probably you. Whatever I have done, you probably should do just the opposite to avoid problems. First thing to consider is what your biggest ambition in life is. Mine was simple, I just wanted to be a parent. I didn't care what job I held down as long as I could spend a lot of time with my kids. I could have been shoveling manure for a farmer for all I cared, just as long as I could go home to my kids. That didn't work out too well, did it? Perhaps I should have had a different dream.

Now you are probably wondering what disability I suffer from? Well, it's kind of hard to pin down. The VA hospital has tried for years to nail it down and can't figure it out. So, they just stuck a label on me that reads something like "non-specific mental disorder." I think they just can't afford to link my military service to the disability and increase my benefits. I'm not complaining. I'm pleased they are willing to keep me healthy. That's all I need from them. At least they didn't miss-diagnose me with crone's disease and try to gut me like a fish like my civilian doctors tried to do to me! Yeah, that happened. I'm glad I walked out of that surgery room. I don't like being labeled anyways. I think a proper label that would have been pinned on me about a century ago fit pretty well. They would have just called me eccentric. I'm not hurting anyone, I just handle my situation a little different than most people do. You may think I have a touch of dyslexia since I switch my S with a Z. If it eases your mind, then by all means, label me with that too; but do you honestly think they'd let me title my book the way I did if I got my S's right?

One thing the VA has figured out about my disability is that I have a touch of PTSD. So the next time you come up from behind a veteran and he or she jumps out of his or her skin, remember, that's me. So have a heart, don't go sneaking up on veterans. It would be nice if you announced yourself so you don't go scaring the crap out of us. If you truly want to thank us for our military service, that's pretty much all you need to do. It may seem a bit comical to you and we may even be able to laugh about it after the fact, but there is nothing funny about making us jumpy in that moment. Please stop making us that way. I know you don't do it on purpose, but being a little more aware of your random behavior could go a long way. So, the next time you are shopping for your groceries and you notice some clerk looking over his or her shoulder each time you take a turn down the same aisle he or she is going down, that person may very well be stuck with PTSD. Stop making them paranoid! You don't need to blurt out that they are "insane!" like so many people do to me. Just say hi, you may ease their mind a bit. There is nothing worse than having PTSD triggered by inconsiderate behavior.

Yes, for me to be labeled a veteran, I did have to serve in the Army for four years. I was glad to volunteer my time in the army so you wouldn't have to. You won't get any complaints here about that. Without good army training (ha ha) I wouldn't be capable of living without a home. All those hikes across the 115 degree heat in the desert served me well. Spending months in sub-zero winter forests taught me how to stay warm. We learned how to use rocks for a pillow. All that taught me that I have a lot of luxuries as a homeless veteran. It only costs me ten bucks a months to take all the showers I want down at the gym. I have a car with fully functional AC and the seat kicked back is far more comfortable than sleeping on a rock. If you find me hanging out in an old abandoned tree house in the woods, that's my safe place. I'm probably typing away on my lap top drumming up another one of my crazy fiction stories. My doctor said I needed to visualize a safe place to decompress. Maybe I took that advice to the extreme, but it works. I'm a bit of an introvert, so I do need to chill out alone once in a while. For every one hideout I have that you go out of your way to find me at, I have ten more. I just need to decompress alone once in a while so you don't need to go out of your way to hunt me down. If you really need to get ahold of me, just call. That's what cell phones are good for.

So what did I do in the Army? It was classified so if it isn't in my DD214, I can't tell you. I can say that I served honorably for four years and did go overseas. Can't tell you where since they didn't include that bit. You have to contact the department of defense and ask them. If they tell you I was golfing in Alaska, well you just have to buy that story. I can't confirm or deny a thing. You don't have the need to know and there really isn't any story there. I did my job and that was that. There is no silly condition that if I tell you, I have to kill you. That's a Hollywood myth. Nothing will happen to you unless you are a terrorist. What will happen is that I will be tried for treason and shot. Now do you really think I want to go there? What would be the point? There is nothing to tell. You would just be bored with that story. I had to clear the air on that one. Explaining my disability is far more interesting because it takes me down a very strange path in my mind that never harms anyone in the end, it just scares the hell out of them. Unfortunately, that includes my kid, so I don't blame her for being standoffish.

If you are wondering why they don't just send me off to the funny farm, there are several reasons. First of all, they tried that once and I just wasn't wacked out enough to justify the costs. They gave me the boot after thirty five days. Talk about a strange world that one was. Since I don't break the law, I hold down a steady job and pay my child support, there is no reason to keep this half-azzed father locked up. What's the harm in writing a few fiction stories? You won't hear that side of it from my ex-wife, but I will save that part once I've bored you with a bit of my background. You'll just hear from her that I have ten dragon heads and breathe fire into her life and my twins. I never harmed a hair on my kids' heads and I have always been there for them to the best of my ability. Maybe she has a point about my inability as a dad from her point of view, but I always have the truth as a defense. The twins would be teenagers now and it's tough to be a caring dad for teenagers. It's not cool for a teenager to hang with dad. I get it, I was a teenager too. I sure didn't want to hang out with my dad when I was a teenager either. It just makes it more difficult when the mother of my kid encourages her to shut me out. That's a tough one for a half-azzed father.

So where did my disability come from? Other than the mystery trips down the cellar stairs and a few random nose bleeds, I had a normal childhood with perfect parents. You got

to love perfect parents, especially when they screw up. My

"mood disorder" is a bit of a mystery to doctors, but not me.

My grandfather had it, my uncle and my mom, so I pretty much

figure part of it is due to that. If any good can come out of this

mess, maybe my diary can help my surviving twin figure things

out for herself before it is too late. Besides all my money and all

the love I have for the twins, this diary is all I have to give. I'd

give them all the time in the world, but they don't want that

right now. Teenagers will be teenagers. Everyone tells me I

have to wait until they get older, but I can't hold my breath that

long. All I can do is stay focused on what they need from me

right now and that is money and some space.

Now that I have bored you to death with my

background, let me introduce the other circus clown, Satan the

Devil. I'm not especially religious, so how on earth can I

truthfully talk about the ultimate nemesis in everyone's life? I

was married to her for ten years, that's how. So you might say that I know Satan quite well. She was an attractive woman that told me everything she thought I wanted to hear and when I finally gave her the twins, well you know the rest. She had her hooks in me and her true self came out. She started chasing boyfriends. She never worked and was never there for the twins. I thought that since I came into the marriage deal with a house that was fully paid for, she would at least appreciate that point, but she didn't. She used the equity of the house as leverage for her secret credit cards and put us into bankruptcy within four years. We lost everything. No matter how much she hated me, why would she do that to her own kids? Only the Devil could do something like that. She didn't even want to be around them. She could have walked away so they didn't get hurt.

You will probably say I got what was coming marrying her, but my twins deserved better. When we first met, she acted all shy. We were hanging out with mutual friends and one of the girls was bragging how she was staying a virgin until she got married. Hey, that was my line, so I couldn't resist.

"Hey, me too!" I chimed in. The girl bought my BS and started a

conversation with me. The Devil knew I was full of it and sent

me a private nudge to the ribs and cast me a girlish smirk that

only I saw. That's how we began, not right away because I had

things going on as a bachelor, but she pursued it anyways. A

week later, she slipped me a note. "My parents aren't home

tonight. Here's my number. Call me." She was an adult, so that

wasn't a problem. Still living at home with parents was a

problem for me and I should have listened to that inner voice to

leave it alone. I had been on my own since I was seventeen and

never understood why anyone would want to live with parents

past high school, but there it was. It was an open invitation to

have some fun, and we did."

Her dad wasn't stupid and figured out that she was

dating someone within a week. He didn't care that she was

dating, he just wanted her to be a little respectful and introduce

us, that's all. "If you want to date him, I have to meet him" was all he had to say about it. I understood, but she didn't. The sneaky warning signs were there, but I didn't pay attention. Contrary to her wishes, we met and he was a really solid guy. He just wanted a little respect as her father, that's all. The Devil and I were supposed to go out the night her father and I met. It was a very cold winter night and I had to follow him to the cellar because he was busy fixing water pipes that burst from the change of weather. Being the country boy that I am, I helped him fix the damage to get their water up and running again. It was three a.m. when we finished the job. The Devil was asleep on the couch waiting for me. The first impression he got of me went well. He said it was o.k. to stay the night and crash out since it was still snowing like crazy and the plows hadn't cleared the road yet.

Talk about a father and daughter being on two different pages of a book, Wow! He just meant for me to crash on the couch and for her to go up to her room ALONE, and go to bed. She wanted me in bed with her and she started a big argument with him. Only the Devil has enough brass to start that kind of

argument with her dad! I really didn't want to be there listening

to that conversation and I told them I would be fine to just go

home. The Devil's dad gave into her demands and let her sleep

with me. No wonder why her mother calls her "Queen Bee!"

Another warning sign I should have paid attention to, but what

did I know. When a young guy gets the green light from a father

to go sleep with his daughter, well, of course it's going to

happen. Down the road a bit, on our wedding day, her father

said something very simple, "she's your problem now!" He

wasn't kidding. She hated him so bad, when he was dying in the

hospital, she refused to take the twins to see him. I took them

almost every day to see their grandfather so they could say

their goodbyes. That's what half-azzed fathers do.

The biggest warning sign out there that I was marrying

Satan came from rumors that she was the school fluffer for

twenty five cents. That sounded ridiculous to me and I believed

her story that she only had one boyfriend before me that she slept with. That sounded like a much more reliable story and I didn't buy into a lot of crap people liked to spread around about other people. I met a lot of her close friends and they were a real freaky group, so I should have seen it. She always claimed that she wasn't like them, but why would she gravitate to that group? Should have seen it coming, but I remember my thoughts about it. Even if it was true, what did I care about her past? When she was ready, she'd own up to it. I had a friend in the army that married an ex-prostitute. She got it out of her system and is still faithful to him to this day. I thought my life would be the same. What guy wants to live in fear that his wife is going to shut him off from biological needs? If she likes sex and I get the exclusive, things would be great! I was wrong. Satan was just getting warmed up. Once she set things up with me the way she wanted, the boyfriends entered back into her life.

I got my exclusive for a long time and she knew how to please. She was a total freak and had to have it the moment we woke up, usually sometime in the day, every night before we fell asleep and sometimes, I would wake up to her going at it with my sleeping body! We broke in every inch of the house, the garage and the swimming pool out back. When she demanded that we break in the roof of the house, I had to decline. I'm no exhibitionist and I used the excuse that I didn't want to give her chafing from the roof tiles, so we had to settle for a few private places in remote areas outside. A truck driver caught her going down on me once while I drove down the highway. He just smiled and gave the thumbs up. My prudish parents couldn't deal with our night time activities when we visited their home. Mom put in her ear plugs and dad just grinned at us every morning at breakfast. He claims he is too deaf to hear but I call it selective hearing. C'mon dad! You moved us from the guest room with the squeaky old bed and cleared out the library across the hall so we had to sleep on the floor in there. When our activities rattled the door too much, you moved us down stairs. Yeah, I think you heard us. That exclusive lasted for seven years, only because I made Satan wait that long for children.

I could have waited seventy years to make sure Satan wasn't a cheater, but even that wouldn't have been long enough. She is the poster child of patience and could have waited that long to finally get the hook in to go on her rampage. She needed children with me to do it and constantly pressured me to give her kids. It wasn't even an issue at the time, I just wanted to finish school first, but I gave in. After all, that's what married couples do, they have kids, but I had an uneasy feeling about starting a family before I finished up school. I should have listened to that voice again, but seven years builds some trust. The argument got so heated one night, I had to leave the house. She was actually ready to start a fist fight over the issue! If she jumped on me and stabbed me in the back with a knife, I would have kept walking. In a way she did stab me in the back now that I think about it. I have never hit a woman and never will, but I was pissed. I just drove away and decided to sleep in my office for a while. It was three in the morning and when the red light turned green, I punched it! A cop pulled me over and asked me what was going on? When I explained the situation, he asked if everything was o.k. back at the house. I responded "yes, that's why I left." He understood and cut me a break since I did the right thing.

My anger lasted for three days. I just stayed down there and minded my own business. I answered her relentless calls on the phone, but said I didn't want to talk. She took herself off the pill that week and said it was time to have kids. I wanted her back on the pill until I finished school and got settled into my career as a lawyer. We were both still young enough to wait, and then money would be no issue with that kind of pay check. She didn't care and wouldn't wait. She promised to get a job with benefits to let me finish school which never happened. She knew me too well. I stuck to my guns and stayed down at that office. By the third night, she showed up and let herself in the office with her key. She shut the door behind her and locked it and stripped naked. I sat there in my ugly beet red swivel chair and watched. There would be no arguing that night. She knew me too well. She unzipped my fly and got right up on top of me in that ugly chair. I was surprised it didn't fall over on us. The twins were conceived that night.

I have a younger sister who is my Irish twin for a day. She is a year minus a day younger than me. Our parents raised us like twins and we have pretty much been inseparable over the years. Why do I mention her here you ask? Because that's all she could ever talk about wanting was twins. I guess our parents put the hook in her raising us like that, but real twins don't run in our family at all. She wanted twins real bad and I got them, not her. Twins run on both sides of the ex-wife's family. Boy did that piss my sister off! She loves her nieces to death, but is very jealous. There have been times that her jealousy has flared up, but I will save that circus act for another time. Think of her as another circus clown that two circus clowns constantly pull pranks on. The only prank my ex and I ever pulled on her was to have twins. It wasn't meant as a joke or done on purpose. It just happened, but the twins came with a price that I suspect was the trigger for my ex-wife flipping on me.

Satan knew the second I knocked her up that night. She insisted she could feel it, that's how I know she is the devil. What woman would know such a thing? I ignored it as wishful thinking until her yapping just got so annoying I bought her a pregnancy test three weeks later and there it was, positive! We got a confirmation of her pregnancy from the doctor and started pre-natal care right away. It's a good thing because they found some complication right away. Satan would have to have surgery within the first trimester if we didn't want to lose the baby (didn't know it was two at the time). I always wonder if not waiting to get pregnant a full month after stopping the pill had something to do with it. The twins were born healthy enough down the road, but that surgery was a nightmare. Some idiot with a title of anesthesiologist gave her morphine for the surgery. Morphine has Sulphur in it and Satan (the ex) is highly allergic to Sulphur. No wonder she escaped hell to come live with me. Maybe god sent the anesthesiologist to remind her about her true home in the Sulphur fires of hell. What a punishment from god, not only does the Devil have to feel the heat, she's allergic to it too!

All kidding aside, it was a very scary moment for the both of us. The surgery went like clockwork; the complication was corrected and a pleasant surprise that we had fraternal twins on the way. Everything seemed fine except that the ex-wife couldn't stop coughing. I wanted to stay with her the night, but the surgeon saw that I was exhausted between working two jobs and having a roof that needed to finish up re-shingling before the rain hit. The surgeon kicked me out of the hospital for the night knowing I needed rest. The ex-wife knew something was wrong and begged me to stay. Once again, the surgeon insisted that I leave, so I kissed her goodbye and said I would be back in the morning. I will regret that decision for the rest of my life. Even though I highly doubt it would have made a difference between the two of us, I will never know for sure. I almost lost three people in one shot with that incident. It is a defining moment in any relationship when a man fails to be there for a wife at a critical moment. Dying is pretty critical. She did pull out of it and so did the twins, but not without her growing totally resentful toward me. It doesn't matter that I was ignorant to the danger. Everything was supposed to be so routine with her surgery. It didn't turn out that way.

I got a frantic call from the surgeon the next morning. "You have to get here right away! Your wife is dying and we need you!" Half asleep and half shocked from what was said to me, I must have thrown my clothes on, jumped in the car and sped down the road in under sixty seconds. What could have gone wrong? I got my answers as soon as I got in her hospital room. I'm a veteran and I knew the moment I looked at her and saw her colors that she was bleeding out. There was no visible blood, so I knew it was internal. I pulled the surgeon out of the room to chew her out in private. "My wife is bleeding to death! Why isn't she back in surgery?" "We want to give her a blood transfusion, but she refuses!" "Doctor! Don't you know you don't fix a leaky faucet by turning up the water pressure? Get her in there and stop the bleeding first!" "She won't let us!" "I'll talk to her." I scurried back into her room and held her weak and cold hand. "You got to let them stop the bleeding or you will die, please!" "I'm afraid I'm going to die if they put me back under. I couldn't breathe before." "They have machines to help you with that, but they need to stop the bleeding or you will die. Please let them!" "O.K." she weakly answered.

That took care of that argument between doctor and patient within seconds. They took her back into surgery immediately and stopped the bleeding. She came out of it and so did the twins. Needless to say, I stuck around for two days until she said it was o.k. to go. I did put a tarp on the open roof, but the rain still got in a bit and destroyed all of my personal stuff and a little furniture. I didn't care. The most important things survived that ordeal, my wife (at the time) and the unborn twins. I don't scare easily, but that was scary. You might think now that I look back on things that I have changed my mind about her survival. Nope! I don't even wish that on Satan. Even if the twins weren't at risk and she could have died, I wouldn't have wanted that. Kids need their mother even if it is Satan. Besides, I know what it feels like to be in a bad spot and everyone that is supposed to care ducks for cover and leaves you hanging. I might be the person Satan hates the most, but I will always be there for the mother of my kids to the best of my ability. That's what half-azzed fathers do.

Every circus has two main clowns and I suppose with mine, that would be Satan and me. One always gives the other a hard time to make everyone laugh at the scape goat. I suppose the scape goat is me. Just the role I got stuck with. You have to have a ring leader too. We have two, and that would be the twins. There would be no story without them pulling all the strings. Any parent that thinks their kids aren't leading the show are fooling themselves. Think about it. Would you work two jobs like the average parent has to just to survive? Would you stick out a horrible job just because it keeps health benefits without kids? Would I be sitting up here in this tree house in between the sixty hours a week that I work and leave myself with less than twenty bucks a week without the twins? The answer is a big fat no! Having my own children completely changed my circus act forever. There is no choice but take the good with the bad. Half-azzed fathers don't walk away from that.

The Millennium, January 1st, 2000 was extra special for me. My twins were born healthy as could be. They weren't the first ones born in that hospital on the big day. Some woman cheated and scheduled her C-section one minute past midnight so she could win all the prizes. Another mother naturally delivered hers after Satan did. Satan didn't need much time in there. She had a craving for crackers and milk so we went out for a midnight run to the store when she broke her water in the car. Good thing I didn't leave her home for that car run. I took a U-turn and brought her straight to the hospital. She originally had told the doctors she would go thru her labor without pain medicine, but by the time we got to the hospital, her tune had changed. "Give me my f...n drugs!" she screamed at them all the way up to her room. Who am I to judge? I'm just a guy and have nothing to compare the pain to and it must have hurt pretty bad! She already had paperwork signed so we got to go straight up to her room. We got lucky. Her doctor was already making rounds and popped his head in the room within ten minutes to give her pain medicine and check her progress. He had more rounds so it only took him five minutes to check her out. By his estimation, she was eighty percent dilated, to he had time to make more rounds and would come back.

The doctor was wrong. Nobody should argue with a woman in labor. If she says she has to push, I think she knows what her body is telling her. Satan looked right at the nurse. "I have to push!" The nurse looked down and saw what I was looking at, a baby's head getting ready to come out. This happened as soon as the doctor ducked around the corner. The nurse looked at me with a scared look. I guess she didn't have anything prepared yet. I said the only thing that could come to my mind. "Unless you want me to deliver, you might want to get that doctor back in here!" "Try to keep her from pushing!" the nurse said as she ran after the doctor. My job was easy. All I had to do was stare Satan in the eyes and keep her slowly breathing until the doctor bolted back in the room about thirty seconds later. I was shoved to the side and three pushes later, my first twin was born. Less than three minutes later, out came my second as I held my screaming first born daughter.

As I held my Millennium baby, I watched the doctor stitch up Satan. Boy, those girls did a number on Satan. She got tore up pretty bad, and all under ten minutes. I'd have to say, my millennium baby did most of the damage. It must have been her feet and fists punching and kicking all those months inside her mother. She was in a hurry to be born; loud, full of energy and very sure of herself. As time went on, it became evident why she was so confident. She learned how to talk quickly. She was very observant and quick to try things for herself. She saw everyone around her walking around and had to try it for herself. Her first steps weren't for walking, she got right up and ran. It didn't take her long to figure out that she needed to slow some things down a bit when she took a flop. It didn't take long for her to figure out that just because her mind knew how to do something, it didn't mean her body could keep up. By the time she was in first grade, results came back that she had a genius IQ. I'm pretty smart, but not that much, and I knew I had my hands full with her.

My double miracle was so much different; quiet and cautious. She let her twin make the mistakes first, and then slowly try things out so she wouldn't get hurt. She always seemed to be shy to everyone else, but not me. She had no problem talking to me, just everyone else. She didn't have to show off what she was learning, she had me for her first steps, learning how to read and all that stuff. Everyone had her labeled as having developmental delays and she got an early start with pre-school and kindergarten. My millennium baby got home schooling other than four days of summer school to see if she was ready for first grade. Nobody could figure out how my double miracle could keep pace with my millennium baby with schoolwork. The two of us weren't fooled.

I gave them both a little advise before the first day of first grade. I wanted them to think before they acted so they didn't have to learn a lot of stuff the hard way. We all know how peer pressure can be and there isn't anything worse than getting dubbed a nick-name from classmates that labels a girl for life. I remember the kind of names girls got stuck with in my school for developing early, or having boyfriends. "Don't be the first girl to kiss a boy. Just sit back and watch the show when someone else does it." They both listened to me on that one. I remembered how tough it was for those kids not smart enough to keep things to themselves that weren't their business.

"Don't be a tattle-tale when you see kids doing something they shouldn't be doing." They both listened to that one too.

Finally, I remembered how tough it was on me for being such a trouble-maker. "I don't expect you to be perfect kids, but stay off the adult radar. If you need to cause trouble, do it at home and not at school." They followed that part of the advice pretty good, but my double miracle took it too far.

Boy, she really knew how to stay off the adult radar! When it came time for her IQ test results, they came back showing that she was barely on the lowest end of average. I'm surprised nobody picked up on the fact that she pulled straight A's in school just like her twin. I wasn't ever fooled, but I had confirmation from my millennium baby what happened. It would seem that she decided to cheat on her IQ test and answered questions wrong on purpose. When I told her to stay off the adult radar, that wasn't what I had in mind, but it worked. There were no high expectations put on her, so she didn't have that pressure. She got to mind her own business without people paying much attention. Her quiet, shy routine didn't fool me. She was just as slick as her old man, maybe more. I knew I had to stay on my toes with her. The way my double-miracle handled herself was the exact opposite of my millennium baby.

Having the exact opposite personalities made it easy for my twins to become best friends right out of the gate. In secret, they had each other's' backs; in front of their mother, well that was a different story. That was part of their game. I'm sure they both craved attention from their mother, but my millennium baby was the one that constantly got in Satan's face about it. Satan was in no mood to give them the right kind of attention when they were young other than ignoring them or screaming at them to go do chores. My millennium baby constantly argued and screamed at her mother all the time just to get Satan to give her any kind of attention she could get. My double miracle stayed silent about the neglect all the time. Satan turned my millennium baby into Cinderella and didn't care if my double miracle helped out or not. She helped her

sister out in secret. Of course my millennium baby got blamed

for everything that went wrong, especially the pranks. Rubber

spiders in the underwear draw, money missing, evidence of

unscheduled snacks, it was always my millennium baby's fault.

The twins let it go on that way, because that was their thing.

I knew my slick little double miracle was usually behind

the mischief. I picked up on the whispers and conspiring the

two of them always did together just before something weird

would happen. She would put an idea into her twin sister's

head and my millennium baby would carry out the deed. My

millennium baby always got in trouble from Satan, even if it was

a physical impossibility for her to be the culprit. Satan's

underwear cut up with scissors, new box of tampons finding

their way in a filled up sink of water, mother's clothes finding

their way out on the front lawn; it went on and on that way.

They would rattle Satan's cage with a prank, she would yell at

my millennium baby and they would giggle about it together

afterward. That's how those two ring leaders ran the circus.

But they couldn't control everything. Like every circus, there's

always a lion or two and you never can truly tame those things.

Satan was just that.

I could always accept the fact that Satan hated my guts.

That just went with the territory, but how could she hate her

own kids too? I know I was no prize as far as it goes as a

husband, but at least I came with a house paid for in cash. I

saved every penny since I was a kid myself, and what I ran short

for money to pay for the house, I got an interest-free loan from

my folks that I eventually paid back. It was supposed to make

life easy, only needing one income to support the family. I

guess she didn't like it much that I never put her name on the

deed, even after I paid back the loan. I was going to give the

house to our children when they were adults and Satan and I

were supposed to earn our retirement home together. She

would yes me to death about the plan, but her actions said a big fat NO! I had the loan paid back before the twins were born, but Satan went to work after they were born.

Having two parents of my own that always saw eye to eye on money did nothing to prepare me for a spouse that was selfish and greedy. She wanted everything for herself and if she couldn't have it one way, she'd get her hands on it another, even my daughters' house. She used the equity of the house to secure credit cards behind my back. I would pay off the loans thinking her word to never do it again was the truth. It was a lie. That just boosted her credit score and she racked up more debt. Who knows what she spent it on because she never brought home anything of value. She did come home one day with a very expensive new pickup truck that brought in another seven hundred dollar a month bill. I figured out what she really wanted that for when she ran over all my orchard trees that I had planted. Even the rare occasions that she decided to try working a part time job never brought in a dime for bills. That was her spending money. I was stuck with all the bills she created.

Like a fool, I kept trying to fix the problem, but she was just given ammunition to make it worse the next time. Within two short years, she had racked up over two hundred thousand dollars in debt. I was so tired and overwhelmed from working two jobs trying to financially survive, but it wasn't just the bills. Satan was never home when I was. I came home from work and she would take off, leaving me to take care of our daughters. She allowed me one hour nap a day and four hours on Sunday before she took off. It wasn't as if she made it a mystery what she was up to. She bragged about every boyfriend she had. I was no carbon, and there was no way I was putting up with that, but I had kids and how was I supposed to find a way out of this nightmare. It was 2002 and fathers' still had virtually no rights as a parent no matter how you sugar coat laws. Satan knew this fact and knew how badly I needed to be a parent.

She used this to have her own way until I could figure it out. Keeping me exhausted didn't help much.

Satan knew exactly how to carve away my self-esteem. First she tied my hands behind my back and kept me busy dealing with her debt. Over time, her plan worked well keeping me so tired from work, I couldn't think straight. She knew I wouldn't neglect the girls when she would take off. They were my world and she knew it, but that's where she really stabbed me. There it was, that name she gave me that stuck for life. No matter how hard I tried, how much effort I put in, I was a "half azzed father!" The insult struck right in the core of my existence and it hurt badly. Here was the mother of my kids telling me how rotten I was on a constant basis. I don't care how strong anyone is, a constant diet of being reminded of being a failure as a parent gets to you. It got to me. The damage was done and I started to believe it. I was just too tired to argue anyways.

Now that I believed that I was unworthy of being a parent, I knew there was nothing to lose. I finally got the courage to talk to someone about my problem. I was no longer going to isolate myself and hide my shame. I told a close friend the problem. He always talked in riddles and it took me a while to figure out what he was talking about. "Having half a loaf of bread to eat is better than no loaf" he would always say. I never understood his saying until that moment. I had done enough fishing around about divorce and even under the worst circumstances, I would only lose half my income to Satan for child support. I would finally get control over my finances and half a check to work with. That was better than nothing. I only had to fight for my rights as a parent, and things were looking a little better than every other weekend for fathers. I just wanted my time with my kids and that was it. I'd work out the rest of it as long as I didn't lose that.

I didn't breathe a word to Satan that I was divorcing her. I didn't have to. She could tell it was coming. She was the master of manipulation and greatly understood how to get her own way with the law. I was going to learn that the hard way.

So, enough introductions of my circus. You know the four main players of the show. I suppose it is time to stop narrating and get to the show. Like every circus, new members of the show get introduced as they play their part. Let my circus begin.

Act Two: Here come the clown cops!

It's amazing that clown cops are the only ones on the planet that don't realize they aren't real cops. No matter how much they truly want to belief they are real, it's never going to happen. They run around trying to arrest some other clown, but it's all just an act. They are just as much the fool as the scape goat. DCF isn't much different. Their intentions are good since they really are out there to protect children, but the way they go about their business can be real stupid. Most case workers are good people just stuck playing a role like the rest of us, but there's always that one bad apple. Yeah, you know the type, someone with an ax to grind. That person may get away with abusing the power given to her for decades. Sooner or later, she faces the wrong scape goat that isn't taking her guff and the consequences entertain the crowd.

I wasn't the only one looking into the law about a divorce, so was Satan. She must have seen that there was no clean way of getting everything she wanted so she played real dirty. She was always a step ahead of me and set me up for a fall real good. She knew how to play the poor abused wife real well. She knew all the resources available to her that I would never gain access to as long as I was the fall guy. It was early spring of 2002 and as usual, Satan had taken off without letting me know. I was dead asleep on the bed and the twins made a bee-line for my neighbor's freezer that had ice cream in it. Now this wasn't any ordinary neighbor. She was a mother who often had an ambulance show up for her panic attacks and had a woman that came to her door knocking quite often. I got to find out who that woman was the hard way. She was the regional manager for DCF (child protective services).

It would seem that my neighbor was not content with being alone facing DCF and their case against her. She needed somebody in the neighborhood to point a finger at to show them she was better than somebody else. Why not point a finger at the half-azzed father across the street. When the twins raided her fridge, that's exactly what she did. Instead of coming over to get me, she called the cops. Strange way to treat the guy who always let her kids have all the popsicles and ice cream they wanted when they came over to play with the twins. The cops came over and were pretty cool about it this time. They lived next door too and already had a pretty good idea what was up with the neighborhood. They knew I was just a hard working father trying to make ends meet that wasn't looking for trouble. They also knew a lot more about my neighbor than I would ever find out for sure. She was a bit of a hypochondriac that was always going to be ducking child protective services. They brought the twins home to me and woke me up. They did suggest putting a better lock on the door to keep the girls from running out, but how does that address the real problem? I had a she-devil of a wife that just walked out any time she wanted without thinking about the safety of my daughters.

There was another problem too. They had to file an official report to child protective services thanks to my neighbor. The cops gave me fair warning and I had nothing to hide anyways. They said child protective services would pay me a visit, and they did. The regional manager didn't send someone else to do the job, she showed up herself. Mrs. SaddleBurr lived up to her name. She was a burr under my saddle. There's nothing wrong with someone doing their job, especially when children are involved, but that woman really hated men. She came by on a typical day that Satan had taken off. "Where is your wife?" "I don't know." "Does she work?" "No." Her comments moved directly to insulting me the rest of the time. She let out a disgusted sigh. "I suppose I have to teach you how to be a parent."

She poked her head in the fridge. "There's no food in here! How do you expect a child to eat?" The fridge was clean as a whistle and had just enough food to make meals for the day. I opened up the freezer which was full of meats. "It is too hot to defrost more than what we need for the day. I don't want it to spoil." She opened up cabinets and saw they were packed with dry goods we needed for food. She changed the subject as she jumped back from a fly that buzzed by her. "This house is disgusting!" I looked around my kitchen clueless. "What are you talking about? I just made breakfast, the dishes are clean and put away and there is not a speck of dirt on the counter, stove, table, or high chair." I gave her a puzzled look. "Your house is bug infested!" She had a serious phobia over one silly little fly that found its way into the kitchen. I wasn't in the mood to get played. "Are you serious? That was one fly that probably found its way in when you came!"

She moved on to the living room. "This is a safety hazard!" "I'm re-modeling and if you notice, I have child gates up to keep kids out while the work isn't finished." "You better hurry up" she said as she looked around the rest of the house. These visits went on for about two weeks so she could find something to nit-pick. Satan was never home until her last visit. That was the last visit I got. SaddleBurr talked to Satan in private so I couldn't hear a thing, but I got to watch both of them smirking as they looked at my exhausted face. SaddleBurr said something that made me know I was being played. "I have a package of resources that are available to you that I will drop off" as she looked right at me. She never did come by with the information or return my calls about the matter. I called every day to leave her a message that I wanted the information. I tried to get ahold of her for about a month without any luck. I was on my own without any help. That empty offer for day care assistance sounded nice, but they don't help out half azzed fathers working two jobs that use sleep time to watch the kids.

I didn't know a thing about abusive relationships. I wasn't brought up that way and had no warning. Satan did a good job of isolating me from the world and keeping me too busy and exhausted to seek help were I could have found it. Mom had passed away before the twins were born and I was too embarrassed to let my dad know what was going on. He hated my wife and I didn't need to hear it from him how bad I had screwed up. I was in a really bad spot and finally realized I needed out. I was on my own and the only hope I had was to pull myself out of this mess somehow. I just needed to keep up the pace I was going for a little longer, just long enough to put the thousand buck retainer on my lawyer. Then I could quit my second job and get a little sleep. It was too late. Satan must have sensed something was up and made her move.

It was late in July and already a hot sticky Sunday morning. I had the money I needed for my lawyer for my Monday morning appointment. I had secretly opened a separate account that my wife couldn't get to. I had finished up my final night at one job on second shift. They already got my notice and I was always welcome back. I stuck out my overnight shift from my regular job. I didn't tell Satan that I was down to one job and would only have to go back to work at eleven p.m. It was no longer her business. It was seven a.m. and I was flat out beat. I just needed Satan one last Sunday morning to take the twins off to church so I could get my four hours of sleep. She liked to pretend to be a Christian and would always take the twins to put on the act. That didn't happen on this Sunday morning. I got played real well.

Satan started right off the gate with that "half-azzed" nonsense about me as soon as I walked in the door. I had picked up donuts like usual for their breakfast and left it on the kitchen table. I was in no mood to put up with her mouth and went straight into my bedroom and locked it. There were three bedrooms; mine, the twins and Satan's. There was no way I was sleeping with her after I found out she was a cheater. I was too tired to hear any more words she was screaming at me through the locked door. I fell asleep right away. Had I not been so tired, I might have heard her final words before she went storming out of the house without the twins. I found out from one of my neighbors what she said and what had happened. "I'm leaving by myself you half-azzed father!" Those words should have alarmed me, but I was dead to the world. It took four hours of sleep for those words to sink in and make me jump up. I looked at my cell phone. It was eleven o'clock. Oh my god! Did she really leave the kids home alone?

I unlocked my door and peeked in Satan's room. Nobody was there. I hurried to the twins' room. Toys were thrown everywhere, but no girls. I began to panic. The trash bucket in the bathroom was dumped on the floor, but nobody was there. Gates were wide open in the living room, house plants and donuts were thrown all over in that room, but no sign of life. As I ran to the kitchen, I really began to get scared. My heart was pounding and almost jumped through my throat. The fridge door was wide open with milk dumped on the floor and condiments mixed in with the mess. My biggest horror had come true; the kitchen door was wide open with nobody inside or in the yard as I frantically looked around. That neighbor of mine saw me and stepped out of her front door with an ear to ear grin on her face. She was so happy that she was the cause of my pain. "The cops got 'em!" she said proudly just before she stepped back inside.

Nobody else was around. Satan's truck was gone.

Before I had a chance to call her, my cell phone started ringing. It was Satan. "I hope you don't think I'm making lunch you half azzed father!" "Are you serious? The neighbor called the cops! Did you really take off alone?" "Yeah! You mean to tell me you were asleep? You are such a half-azzed father!" "Just meet me at the police station." I jumped in my car and went straight to the police station. I was in such a panic as I tried to talk to the police officer at the window. "My children are missing! My neighbor said you took them!" I passed my driver's license through the slot so she could see who I was. "Please have a seat over there. I'll send the sergeant in charge out to talk to you." She passed me back my license. I was shaking real hard and didn't have more than a minute to sit before the sergeant came out. He could see how upset I was and how bad I was shaking. "Sir, please calm down. Everyone is safe. If you would have arrived a little sooner, child protective services wouldn't have taken 'em. You will have to show up at court tomorrow morning to talk to the judge. There's nothing you can do until then, so please go home."

I had never been so dejected and crushed in my life. Satan never even showed up at the house until later. When I got home, everyone in the neighborhood popped back up on the grid. Two of my neighbors came straight to me. "We showed the cops that you were home since your car was there but they didn't care. They peeked in your window and we knew they saw you sleeping by the way they were talking. They walked in the house to take pictures and then left." The neighbor who was talking pointed to the nervous looking woman across the street. "I can't believe she did that to you!" The woman quickly went back into her house and I never saw her again. Her husband came home from work a few minutes later and came over to talk to our group that was gathered on my front lawn. My neighbor who was a cop had pulled his cruiser up next to my house to fill me in on what to expect tomorrow. "They won't have a closed hearing over your case until noon, so show up with your lawyer." My appointment with my lawyer was for nine a.m. I would let her know what was going on.

The husband of the woman who started this mess figured out she was involved. He looked at me with a worried face just as Satan pulled up in that expensive truck of hers. I didn't want to talk to him or her. I turned my back on everyone and walked away, straight into the house and into my room. I locked the door and shut the bedroom window so I could bolt it shut too. After I set my alarm to get up for work, I plopped myself down on my bed to rest. I never realized until that day that depression could make me so tired. Satan was frantically banging on my bedroom door. She found out what happened from the neighbors and was sobbing. "Please let me in so we can talk!" "There is nothing I have to say to you. Leave me alone and never come back!" "I don't know what I'm going to do!" "I don't care! It's not my problem, so just go away!" I don't know how long she stood at my door banging because I fell asleep quickly. I had blocked out any noise coming from her and by the time my alarm went off at 10:30 p.m., she was gone. I was glad because it gave me a chance to take a shower and get dressed for work in peace.

I threw my emergency bag into the trunk of my car and drove to work. I hadn't needed a survival pack in a long time, but it made me feel a little bit more secure having it ready to go from here on out. I drove to work which was just around the corner. I could have walked, but do you really think that I trusted Satan with my car? She trashed my orchard so what would she do to the car? Back when it was the only car we had, I had a job seven miles from home. She would forget to pick me up after my shift and I had to walk home, rain or shine. I spent plenty of winter afternoons trudging through the snow to get home. Nope! I wasn't giving her the chance at that anymore. The car would stay with me wherever I went and both sets of keys went with me too. The first thing I did was fill in my supervisor on what was going on. He said I had personal time and vacation time I could use if I wanted to go home. I turned the offer down which was probably a good thing. I didn't know at the time that keeping as much of my routine as possible was actually helping me out.

That was the longest eight hour shift of my life. Even though I buried my head into my work and stayed busy, time crawled by. I didn't need to look at a clock since the supervisor came to get us for our breaks. We always got two fifteen minute breaks and one thirty minute break, all on the clock. It was overnight, so we could throw on headphones and tune out until customers showed up at six a.m. I wasn't the usual drone from lack of sleep just going through the motions. Getting that extra sleep time helped with that, but the depression was killing me. I had never been separated from my twins and this was absolutely heartbreaking. Customer showed up so I had to lose the headphones and keep working for one more, longer hour. I was so caught up in my thoughts that it took a nudge from my supervisor to let me know it was time to punch out. "Go let the store manager know what's up." He gave me the same offers for time off, but we agreed to save it for when I really would need it. We anticipated the need for court, but that wasn't where I would need it. That would turn out to be something else. I drove the forty minutes to my lawyer's office. I was going to be real early for our appointment, but I needed to be there. I didn't mind the wait. I had a lot of things to think about.

It's amazing who we chose to talk to about our problems. I had no problem talking to my boss and a lawyer who at the time was a stranger about this embarrassing situation. I couldn't talk to my dad though. He would just stick his nose into this and mess things up. His mind was still stuck in the 20th century, a time in history when an honest man could work hard and get somewhere. It doesn't work that way for soon to be single fathers in the 21st century. I didn't know it at the time, but I was about to get schooled on that fact real well. It doesn't matter how well lawyers sugar coat the laws, fathers still have no rights. To survive, a father has to learn how to play the game and have only one agenda; spend time with your kids. Fortunately, that's all I wanted, but the law works real hard to test fathers, and make absolutely sure that's all they want. Otherwise, the system keeps the kids away from fathers as a ransom to get what they want out of him. They push and push and push to break you. I wasn't going to go down like that.

My lawyer's secretary finally showed up to unlock the door at 8:30 and let me in to the lobby as she got my paperwork ready. I filled out the paperwork and wrote the check for the retainer, handed it through her window into the secretary's booth and sat back down. My lawyer showed up ten minutes early to get ready for our meeting. She was always punctual. I liked that about her. She was referred to me by the best lawyer in the state. I originally wanted him, but he no longer handled divorce cases. He said she was the only lawyer that ever beat him in court. I knew his reputation and that meant that she had to be real good at her job if she could do that. Judging by her attractive looks and her soft spoken voice, one would never suspect she had legal teeth that would come out the right way at the right time for a client. I learned a lot from her through this mess, so much that eventually, I could handle my legal affairs on my own. However, at this dark moment in my life, I really needed her. She peeked her head into the lobby and asked me to join her in her office.

Once I sat down, we discussed some end game issues involving my decision for divorce and bankruptcy. "You know I can take care of the bankruptcy too?" "Thank you, but it may be a conflict of interest with the divorce. I'm setting up a lawyer to jointly file with my soon to be ex-wife." "I understand. If you change your mind, let me know." I didn't know at the time, but I would find out the hard way that the court system does everything in it's power to keep parents together. The circle of lawyers really don't care how tough that makes it on parents, as long as kids get the best deal. "I have an immediate problem that needs to be dealt with" I told her as I explained what just happened to my twins. I was amazed that she didn't give me a judgmental look once as I explained the child protective services incidents leading to my twins' abduction. "I will make sure my schedule is cleared so I can meet you at the courthouse." I wasn't used to a person changing their plans for the day just to help me out. I certainly will never forget for the rest of my life that she was the only person that never once judged me. I could tell we were going to get along just fine.

It didn't take long with our meeting; it was only 9:30. I had plenty of time before I had to show up in court. I could actually go home to grab a bite to eat and shower up. I would find out that she was real accurate on her book keeping. What could have been charged to my account as a full hour was kept at a half hour. I turned into her charity case because she didn't end up charging me for a lot of time she put into this case. My new attorney tried to get a smile out of my face without any luck as I left our meeting. She joked about the fact that I had three first names; Paul James Stewart. I was not in good humor at the time, but eventually, she and I would be able to laugh about it, but she got my pokes at her last name too: Burner. What a name for a lawyer, because she sure knew how to burn the opposition. I learned from the best. But at this moment in time, life was as dark as it gets. My children were my entire world and I was stripped of them having any contact with me. My Irish twin often told me that as long as I was living this situation, it would be like trying to get out of a dark forest and I wouldn't see any light until I got close to the end. It couldn't get any darker than this. I pulled up to my home. I was glad Satan was not there. Our neighbor who started this had a moving truck parked in front of her house. It was being packed with all their personals. That was the last time I ever saw that family.

This was all new to me, not just the fact that I was in trouble with the law. Satan was the one that brushed up against the law, not me. She took a short cut from getting her coffee one morning through the breakdown lane to the house instead of going in the proper driving lane one time when she was still pregnant. Some detective followed her to the house and pulled out his pistol on her without showing his badge, all just to give her a ticket. She came in the house crying to me about it and showed me the ticket. It was the most ridiculous act of misconduct by a cop that I had ever heard of before, so I went straight to his captain about it. "Yes, my wife deserves her ticket and will have to pay for it. However, your department doesn't need to gain a reputation of pulling guns on unarmed pregnant women without identifying yourselves just for a moving violation." Needless to say, he got busted back to uniform. Unfortunately, he was the cop that made sure my twins were taken away so he could get some payback. I recognized him. Yeah, being in trouble with the law was new to me, but so was having a clear head. I was no longer a walking zombie from lack of sleep. I could see that people in the system use their power in very bad ways to get revenge over something they had an axe to grind over.

I had taken my shower and was sipping coffee as I thought about how unreasonable that cop was. He didn't know who he was messing with, but fortunately for him, he was a very irrelevant piece of the puzzle for me. I just wanted my kids back and I wasn't going to get caught up in his revenge circle. The buck stopped with me and that part was over. There would be much larger culprits in this fiasco to bring down as I fought to get my girls back. Some people would find out the hard way who they were messing with and I didn't have to break the law to nail them to their own crosses. They really had no idea what world I came from. I was the buck sergeant that got a two star general in hot water for sticking his nose where it didn't belong. My service obligation was long sense over, and I no longer had the clout that I once had, but I knew how the chain of command worked. Everyone has a boss, even the president of the Unites States. We all have to answer to someone and I knew how to work that angle.

The only thing I could do at this moment with the military was to check up on the status of my benefits. As I sipped coffee, I called up the Dept. of Veteran affairs to confirm they sent out my DD214 and military records. They did, and it was just a matter of time before I got it in the mail so I could set up an appointment to start using the VA hospital for my medical. My civilian hospital miss-diagnosed me with Crones disease and wanted to gut me like a fish. I was done with that foolishness. I just had to be patient to gain access to the only medical organization that could understand me. I hung up the phone and would have to wait to get that ball rolling. The state had their ball rolling right over my head and I would have to start dealing with that pretty soon. It was 11:30 and time to head up to the courthouse.

I got up to the courthouse and went through the security routine of emptying my pockets and getting scanned in. I asked the bailiff where the courtrooms were. He pointed to one door. It was a small town and there was only one courtroom. I quietly let myself in to the back of the room without slamming the door and sat in the back. It was a very old style designed room with wooden benches. There weren't many people left inside; just the judge, bailiff, two lawyers, a cop and a defendant. The judge was wrapping up a moving violation case and was chewing out the defendant for being caught speeding in his town for the third time. "I've given you plenty of chances to straighten yourself out, and yet you don't seem to do that. You should have taken the deal that the officer offered you because I am giving you the maximum penalty, license is revoked, thousand dollar fine!" He slammed down his gavel. "All rise!" came from the bailiff and I stood up, everyone else already was. The judge got up and left the courtroom. I was a bit confused. Was I too late?

I was starting to panic. Even Satan wasn't around. I walked up to the clerk's booth and asked if there was a case involving Stewart on her list today. "All the cases got done this morning and I don't see your name on the list. Are you sure you have the right day?" "The cops took my children and said to be up here this afternoon!" "O.K. Please calm down. You don't need to announce it to the world. That would be under a different file and I see it. There is an emergency closed hearing at one. You have time to get lunch. Here is a form you can fill out if you need an attorney." "No, my attorney will be here, but thanks anyways." I was use to "hurry up and wait" from the army, but this was different. There is nothing but boredom waiting like that in the army. This kind of waiting filled me with a lot of anxiety and kept my heart stuck in my throat. I went out to my car to listen to music as I waited.

Satan came rolling up in her truck about 12:30 eating fast food. It would seem that she was better informed than I was. I didn't want to be near her so I went back inside to wait. Satan followed me into the courthouse shortly after and tried to sit next to me but I got up and moved to the other side. It didn't faze her a bit as she kept talking on her cell phone. Four people started showing up that I didn't recognize, but the bailiff did. Two attorneys were let in without being scanned. One turned out to be for the state and one for my daughters. The DCF manager that had gone to my home several times got scanned in and the cop that was behind the mess walked in. They all stood together talking. I couldn't hear much, but the words "permanent removal" did ring out In my ears. It was ten 'til one and my lawyer showed up. She was let in without being scanned too. If it wasn't for her showing up at that point, I probably would have had a heart attack.

My attorney smiled at me and held up her finger indicating she would come over to talk to me in a second. She greeted the other two attorneys and talked a bit. It would seem they already knew each other, knew the routine and had all been to this kind of circus before. She sat down next to me. We won't be let into the courtroom for this. The state has to present its case to the judge and set up a formal hearing. When they come out, we will know when that will happen. "You mean we aren't allowed in?" "No, you have to be formally charged by the court first, or they have to reunite the family." "You think that will happen?" "Not likely. They have two witnesses, an experiences DCF worker and a police officer." "So it's their word against none. How fair is that?" "It's the way the system works." My four opponents were let into a different room than the formal courtroom.

I looked right into the eyes of my lawyer. "They better not be in there lying or stretching the truth. I can't stand a liar." Had she really known me at that point in time, she would have laughed. She had a worried look on her face. It would turn out that most fathers that get to a boiling point like me usually take their anger out in an illegal way. She would learn soon enough that my bite was even worse than hers and I didn't have to break the law to do it. I just had no experience with the courts and needed to figure things out as I went along. I didn't know anything about court except one thing, don't get caught lying to a judge. If they did, I was going to do everything within my power to make them suffer. They all came back out within a half hour and my attorney walked up to the two attorneys as the cop and DCF worker left with huge smiles on their faces. The two attorneys finished talking to mine and left.

She came up to me with a worried look and handed me a document with the formal charges on it. "It doesn't look good. We have to be back here Wednesday afternoon for the hearing." Satan walked up to us to find out what was going on. "Is this your wife?" "Yeah." My attorney looked at her warmly. "You need to get your copy from the clerk over there. If you don't have an attorney, I suggest you fill out the form and get one in here for Wednesday. I need to talk to my client alone. Have a nice day." Satan got the message and went up to the clerk. I was slowly getting a little sharper in the brain since I was finally getting some sleep and could see why my lawyer was so deadly in a courtroom. She was sweet and nice everywhere else, but not there. She was a lot like me, waiting for the right moment to show her teeth.

We looked at the charges together that were formally labeled abuse and neglect. The abuse charges were on the top of the list; mental, physical and emotional abuse. It was very vague and there were no examples or evidence presented other than abandonment. "This is ridiculous! I have three witnesses that saw I was home and the police saw me there. If anyone walked out, it was my wife, not me." Just have the names of the witnesses ready so I can add them to the list. What about this medical neglect charge?" "I was at the pediatrician Thursday. All the shots are up to date and I have a regular routine for checkups." "Bring those medical records in with you. I wouldn't worry about this educational neglect. There are no public preschools or mandatory kindergarten." "I have documents of homeschooling, IEP testing and summer camp through the elementary school. Should I bring that info too?" A big smile lit up on her face. "You definitely want to bring that too, but there may be a problem with the messy house issue. The police have pictures." "Don't they have to have a warrant or something for that?" "No, they had probable cause. They didn't need a warrant." "Should I bring in my own pictures? It took me less than an hour to clean up the superficial mess I found." "Sure, you can do that but I don't think it will help much, it's after the fact evidence. We are all set. See you Wednesday?" "See you then!" It looked like there was some promise to the case, so I felt a little bit encouraged.

All I had to do was wait it out for two days, go to work and get my rest and then show up on time. I let my bosses know what was going on and that I would not miss work. It was a blessing in disguise that I worked overnight. I could show up for court any time they wanted to throw at me. Little to my understanding, this thing was going to get dragged out for a long time. The state is never in a hurry to return kids home and I wouldn't figure that one out until December. All I wanted to do was be with my kids and I hadn't seen them since Sunday morning. Wednesday afternoon finally came as I sat out in the court house lobby. Satan's court appointed attorney showed up and talked to her, then talked to my attorney and then the four attorneys went off to the side and talked together. The bailiff

motioned for the attorneys to go into the courtroom for a

private meeting with the judge. The cop wasn't present but

SaddleBurr was. She went in with the attorneys. Satan and I

were not allowed in. It took a long time before the bailiff came

out to get us.

I had to stand on the defendants' side with Satan and

our two attorneys. The two attorneys stood with SaddleBurr on

the prosecuting side. Judge Kingston looked right at me. My

hopeful smile got ripped right off my face when he spoke. "You

better get your act together by the time I see you again Mr.

Stewart." I looked down at the table in front of me and my

heart sunk even lower. I was being blamed for this whole mess.

"Yes your honor" was all I said. "I'm awarding custody to the

state and I have approved the family plan. We will meet in a

month. What day works for everyone?" My lawyer looked at

me. "I'll show up any day I am told to" I said loud enough for

everyone to hear. Satan just nodded yes to her attorney when asked if any date was good. When it came for the four attorneys to get on the same page and agree on a day, it wasn't easy. They all had busy schedules' and couldn't agree to anything. I watched back and forth as they argued. I finally just crossed my arms and shook my head in disgust. What a sick joke. I couldn't even be with my kids and they were arguing about some pretty silly stuff.

To most people, it would seem like the judge was ignoring the whole thing, but I knew better. He was looking down at the judge's bench pretending to do something else as the lawyers argued on. My grandmother use to do that trick and she was paying better attention to us than we thought when my sister and I were young. Judge Kingston was using his peripheral vision and he must have gotten his que from my crossed arms and stare right at him to say something. "I'll give you about ten more seconds to figure this out or I'll set the date for you." It was amazing how his words helped them find a good day to show up. They picked the last Wednesday in

August. The judge agreed to it and wrote it down in his book. He slammed his gavel on the bench, the bailiff shouted "all rise" even though we were all standing. He left the courtroom for his chambers and we all stayed there for a bit to finish up our business. That would be a long month.

My daughters' attorney came up to us to introduce himself. He was nice enough and explained that he was independent from the state and would assign a volunteer to keep an eye out for us. I liked that idea. The state's attorney was a different story. She was mean as hell. "You need to bring medical cards down to our office immediately. SaddleBurr will meet you there so you can fill out some paperwork." My lawyer had handed me a copy of the family plan with all my conditions and I pointed to the "supervised visitation" part. "It says this is a reunification case. When do I get my visitation." "I'm still permanently taking away your custody so you can find out at the office when and if we give you any visitation." My lawyer grabbed my shoulder to hold be back as the prosecutor and

SaddleBurr left. Satan's lawyer turned out to be a very practical thinker and spoke up. "I'm going to file the usual objections so we have our appeal ready for a higher court. All this for just a messy house case. How absurd. Right now, the two of you need to work together to beat this thing." Satan left with her attorney.

There were over a dozen conditions that the judge signed off on. I pointed to the only one that I had a problem with. I would jump through any silly hoops they made me do, just like a circus dog does, but that one really bothered me. "Why do I have to do marriage counselling? I thought we were moving for a divorce?" "If you want to get your family back, you'll have to wait on the divorce. I'll file it when the time is right. Right now, try to work through this with your wife. The two of you need to go down to sign the paperwork and set up your visitations." "I'm not comfortable signing any paperwork they want without you. Are you meeting me there?" "No, you'll be fine. Just read it carefully first and sign only medical paperwork. Anything else, keep it blank and bring to me. Just make sure you comply with all the conditions and document everything so we are ready for August. Call my office to set up an appointment so we can prepare for court." "All right, I'll see you then." She winked at me. "Keep getting your rest. You're pretty sharp when you aren't tired."

I suppose that compliment should have boosted my confidence a little bit, but it didn't. Nobody ever threw a compliment my way in my whole entire life like that and I wasn't quite sure how to take it. Besides, I was consumed with only the thoughts of being with my girls. I had never been away from them longer than a shift at work. I drove back home to get birth certificates and SSN cards out of the safe so the state could make copies. I already had medical cards in my wallet. Satan was there waiting for me standing near her truck holding the documents in her hands that we needed. "My lawyer said we should show up together. Ride with me, o.k?" I rolled my eyes up as I locked up my car and reluctantly climbed into the passenger side of her truck. "You better not make me walk home when we're done." "I won't do that!" "You've done it before, what's stopping you now that I have a lawyer?" She didn't answer. We rode in silence all the way to the DCF office.

As we walked up to the door, I recognized the guard from Satan's church group. He was friendly enough. "Where's DCF?" "Up to the second floor on the left." Satan was thinking about taking the lazy way out and ride the elevator up to the next floor, but changed her mind and followed me up the flight of stairs. When we got to the window where a clerk could buzz us into the waiting room, the DCF lawyer came up the stairs from behind us. I couldn't resist. "Good afternoon councelor. I didn't know lawyers were invited to this meeting?" When she recognized me, she got a scared look on her face, buzzed herself into the door and disappeared. A very friendly clerk was standing at a tiny window waiting to find out why we were there. "I'm Mr. Stewart and I'm here to fill out paperwork with SaddleBurr." "Come right in and have a seat. She will be right out to get you. I heard the buzzing noise and we went into the waiting room to sit down.

There were five doors in the waiting room. One right next to the clerk window for employees. Two doors were lined up next to that one which were used for parent interview rooms. On the other side were two doors, each leading to a private visitation room for parents. There were several parents waiting their turns to go into a room to spend time with their kids and a state worker. Children were led out of the room and when they were out of the building, the parent or parents were allowed to leave the room. Then the next set of parents were put in the room with a supervisor. When they were inside, a state worker would lead the children into the room. Everything was locked up. One state worker was talking to a mother in the lobby. "This is the third time his father missed his visitation." I guess that dude didn't care about seeing his kids. We wouldn't get a turn in those rooms. SaddleBurr came out into the waiting room and motioned for us to go into one of the interview rooms with her. We sat down at a table facing her, and a one way mirror.

I didn't know much about how DCF messed with people at the time, but I recognized an interrogation room when I saw one. We used them all the time in the army. The rooms and doors were lined up so other officials could watch and film the room from the office area. The picture windows behind SaddleBurr were pretty standard one way glass that looked like tinted glass on a limousine. I might have gotten roped into this mess, but I wasn't a fool. I pointed at the glass and looked at Satan. "Smile for the camera!" She didn't smile one bit. She was scared. SaddleBurr looked a bit concerned about my comment as well. She handed over a stack of papers for us to sign. The medical consent forms on the top of the stack were pretty straight forward and were one of the requirements of my court orders to get signed. SaddleBurr started her interrogation as we filled out the papers.

As Satan and I filled out the top paper and signed it, SaddleBurr went to work with her questions that had nothing to do with the paperwork. Satan remained silent and I could have too since my lawyer did say not to discuss the case without her being present, but I couldn't resist. She started off the conversation as she handed us each a copy of her card. "You should have called me when you felt like you were going to harm someone. We are here to help parents." "No you're not! You use your authority to kidnap children without just cause. I documented all your visits and my phone calls that you never answered. If you were concerned about abuse, you would have done something about it months ago. You can answer to the judge when our pediatrician testifies against you. Here's your copies of all the medical records and ID forms, the doctor appointment for next Tuesday to get scheduled shots and the form we just signed for you. Make sure that doctor appointment isn't missed or I will be filing some complaints of my own." She looked nervously at me as I pulled the insurance and dental cards out of my wallet. "I'll need these back after you make copies and give our copies of the papers we just signed. When's my visitation?" She ignored the question as she took the cards and the papers to make copies in the back room. I knew she did more than that as she disappeared back into the office area.

As Satan and I waited for her to return, I talked to her a bit. "You do realize they are illegally interrogating us and probably taping us right?" Satan just shrugged her shoulders and looked at me with that scared look on her face and watery. "Stop worrying, I've got this handled. You just sit back and enjoy the show. I'll have my lawyer subpoena the tape they are illegally making and start the lawsuit. What lies are we looking at next?" I took the next form from the top of the pile. "Oh, this is cute. They are trying to pin us with educational neglect of a two year old. My lawyer already has copies of the IEP testing we had done in the spring, home schooling records and the summer camp from two weeks ago. I'll give this idiot a copy of the music camp coming up in a couple of weeks. She better not drop the ball on that since we already paid for it." Satan looked at me with those teary eyes without saying a word. "You got' a hang in there until the end of August when the judge can send 'm home." I finished filling out the consent form to allow day care. We both signed it and SaddleBurr came back in with my cards and handed them over with two copies of the medical forms we signed earlier.

I slid the day care form across the table to SaddleBurr with another paper on top of it. She read it and looked at me as I saw more fear spread across her face. "You better make sure band camp doesn't get skipped." I held up the form showing available day care schools in their program with a sliding scale payment plan and then leafed through my daily planner as I spoke up. "Tell me SaddleBurr, how come you never provided this information to me in the—wow—fourteen visits that you promised to give me an information packet. I also have records here that show I left you a message over thirty times to provide the information. You never called me back. All you had to do was call me back and have me pick it up. Looks to me like you'll be answering for that. When do we start visitations?" SaddleBurr finally figured out what I was jotting down in my calendar planning. I put the exact time down each time I asked her about visitation. She ignored the question as her shaky hand picked up the day care form. "I- - I'll make your copies." She left us alone in the room again.

There were only two forms left; one was just a list of approved marriage counselors and the other was a consent form to allow them to take pictures and video of the family. I showed them to Satan. "There's no way we sign this one. That gives them permission to go straight to the press and embarrass us publicly. We are protected under child privacy laws as long as this paper doesn't get signed. I'll call the insurance company to find out which one of these marriage counseling places are covered under our insurance." Satan nodded in agreement. She had stopped crying when she saw that I had things under control. I doubted SaddleBurr ever faced a guy like me before.

I talked to the insurance rep on the phone and they identified

one of the counseling facilities on the list as being part of our

network. Satan nodded her head yes as I confirmed one on the

list that was approved with my insurance. I looked right at the

smoked glass window. "O.K. counselor, send her back in. We

are ready to wrap this up and set up our visitations." I made

sure it was crystal clear through the glass that I looked at the

time and jotted it down in my book.

It took her a while, but a very jittery SaddleBurr came

back in. I spoke first. "Should I bring some clothes and things of

my daughter for the visit?" "We already gave them things they

need. You keep those bug infested clothes out of here!" "There

are no bugs in our house. In fact, I had the state building

inspector come into my home as soon as I knew you filed a

complaint to the judge about that. The inspector will be at

court in August and his story is a lot different than your written

lie. Here's a copy of his report." I handed it to her. Once she

read it and saw how official it was, she looked at me with great fear. "That's right. I had him come into the home before we cleaned up the mess your dirty cop probably made. It was chocolate donuts, not feces! There was no trash, just clutter! Your cop has a documented history of harassing my family! I don't know much about the law, but perjury may be a crime. When is visitation?" SaddleBurr tried to grab the two remaining forms. I pulled them away from her reach. "Oh no! You don't get these. My lawyer is going to show this evidence that you tried to go public with this information and I'll give the clerk the information about marriage counseling. When's visitation?" She answered as she ran out of the room. "Make an appointment!" That was the second to last time I ever saw her.

Act three: Look! Caged Animals!

Don't you like it when a circus brings out a truck with a string of cages behind it? Cop clowns usually drive them in to show off lions and other dangerous animals in their cages that you get to see perform. Dealing with DCF isn't much different. They separate families and bring them out to the audience to show them off before the circus act. They tried to do that to us, but failed because they were wrong. They provided false evidence to a judge, made no real effort to help us out for months and had a lot to do with creating the circumstances that led to the abduction of our children. One thing was for sure, Satan and I could never have any miscommunication about who was watching the kids ever again if we were to get them back. It didn't matter if the unsupervised kids or the cop created the mess in the house, it didn't matter how many government workers broke the law to create an illegal case, we were ultimately responsible for child safety and they were going to make sure we understood that.

I did survive the months of separation from my kids, but it was a very long and stressful court battle. If you are wondering how I could go through all that so I could enjoy seven years of raising my daughters; how did I wind up killing myself now? Everyone has their breaking point. I was in my forties and had more of a fight in me back then. I didn't know I had a disability back then and I was not facing my true weakness. Those were all third party individuals trying to keep me out of the lives of my children. Since I hadn't done anything wrong, there was nothing they could do to stop our relationship. Kids crave attention from parents at that age. It's a great time in a father's life when children want to spend time with him. It's not cool to be seen with parents when they are teenagers. That's what I face now. I'm a month away from being able to collect social security and a teenager in college has no obligation to stay in contact with dad. I'm just too old and tired to face the true judge, jury and executioner. Most adults find a way to handle being ignored from their teenage kids. My disability doesn't allow me to do that.

After ten minutes, Satan and I pretty much figured out that the interrogation was over since SaddleBurr never came back in the room. We got up and left the room and I went up to the clerk's window in the waiting room. I could hear the click of the lock on the door as the interrogation room door shut behind us. I saw the lawyer pass by her with SaddleBurr as they argued. The clerk had a smirk on her face and must have known what was going on back there. I slid the marriage counseling form through the slot at her booth window. "Can you give us our copies of this please?" "Absolutely Mr. Stewart" she said with a friendly voice. She time stamped the form, made two copies and handed the copies back through the slot to me. I asked her my next question. "How do I go about setting up visitation?" She time stamped six business cards and handed them through the slot two at a time. "This is SaddleBurr's office number. I handed one of them to Satan. She passed us two more cards. "This is how you get ahold of her attorney." I gave one of the cards to Satan. The clerk passed two more cards to me and had the biggest grin on her face. "If Mrs. SaddleBurr doesn't make an appointment with you by Friday, call her boss at this number." I handed one of the cards to Satan.

Office clerks are the most powerful gate keepers on earth. If you play nice, they'll hand you the golden keys to the crapper. I learned this routine in the army and I could tell this clerk was on my side. It was if she could read my mind, or at the very least, had a hint of what I would do next. She probably overheard what I told Satan as we left the office, because I heard her giggle. "Call her number every hour on the hour. We are going to get our visits." This was probably the only time in Satan's life that she didn't just yes me to death and do exactly the opposite thing. We both called SaddleBurr's number and left a message right away to start visitation. Of course we used cell phones so we had a record. Every hour, on the hour, we both called and left a message. There was no call back from her and by the time Thursday morning came along, her voicemail was full and we couldn't leave any more messages. We went to work on her lawyer's phone number. Every hour, on the hour, we left our messages. No calls were returned and no visitation was set up. This went on until her voice mail was filled up and we couldn't leave any more messages. It was almost after business hours on Friday. It was amazing how easy cops could get ahold of DCF, but we never could.

I remembered what the courthouse clerk had told me the last time I was there. "You can give me copies of any paperwork you want. I will make sure everyone who needs a copy gets one." I loved dealing with gate keepers. This was the back door to slip the judge a message without breaking the law. We went straight to the courthouse and the clerk gave me a blank piece of paper. "You can write your complaint here." "We don't need an official form?" "No, this will be fine. I'll notarize it and send copies to all the attorneys for you and give a copy to the judge." She had a big grin on her face. There was nothing like adding a little fun to a clerk's life. We were doing everything by the book, and she knew it. She knew we were bypassing our own attorneys and going straight to the boss. I briefly wrote the complaint that DCF was refusing to set up visitation. I added the information of each way I attempted to make visitations happen, visiting the office, phone calls and who was contacted. Satan and I signed it and I stood behind another man talking to the clerk at the booth.

"I'm sorry sir, you will have to come back Monday. Office hours are closed." The clerk pointed to the clock on the wall. It was five p.m. The bailiff watched the angry man storm out of the courthouse. He had already locked the front door behind the man when he came in at 4:59 p.m. I was disappointed that I missed my timeframe and turned around to leave. The clerk stopped me. "Mr. Stewart, please come back. We were already in the process of your request. I'll stay until it's done." She smiled at me as I passed the complaint into her booth. She notarized it and began making copies. Once three copies had passed through the machine, she scooped them up and walked back over to me. She handed me two copies and waived the third in the air, still holding a big grin over her face.

"Those are your copies and don't worry, I'll send out a copy in the mail to the four attorney offices bright and early Monday morning to make this legal. Judge Kingston hasn't left yet. I'll make sure he gets this before he leaves." She winked at me, but I still couldn't find a way to smile. I just wanted to see my girls.

The bailiff walked with us to the door and held the door open for us. "Mr. and Mrs. Stewart, try to have a good weekend. I'm sure you will get a phone call bright and early Monday morning for your visitation." As the door locked behind him, I smiled a weak one at him. It wasn't funny being stuck in the middle of that mess at the time, but looking back, I know they were helping us get some payback. The bailiffs get to hear everything. They talk to the clerks and if you are worthy, the clerk helps you through the backdoor to the judge. Nobody will ever admit the truth, but that's how it goes. If you never disrespect the gatekeepers, you'll always find out with that big grin on their faces that you got your message to the judge and it would be favorable for your case sooner or later. You just had to be patient and accept how a judge goes about punishing misconduct, in his own time and act like you don't know what's going on. That was easy for me. Everyone had me pegged as being stupid, so I just let them think what they wanted.

Satan was no dummy either. She could be a total space shot at times, forgetting something or just ignoring me, but she knew what was going on. As we went back to her parked truck, I pulled out that card with SaddleBurr's boss' phone number. "Ooh, Concord, the main office at the state capitol. Should we get back to work?" Satan and I both left her a message before we got in the truck. We got home and my car was still were I had left it earlier. We kept busy all night on the phones until every voice mailbox was full with our requests for visitation. Even the general mailboxes at both offices were full before I had to go to work. We still called each day to make sure we had records of showing our cell phones called the offices each day, but now we only needed to do it once a day. I went to work Friday night, Saturday and Sunday night. I didn't miss work even though I really wanted to. I never miss work unless I really have to. That was a long weekend, but seven a.m. Monday morning finally came, I had the night off and I went home from work.

When I got home, Satan was there in the kitchen. She had made coffee, bacon, eggs and toast for the both of us. She never cooks, but she did today. Yep, the usual cinnamon was sprinkled in everything for the rare occasions that she did cook and this morning was no exception. Ever since her pregnancy, cinnamon went in everything; coffee, toast, eggs, everything. I was too hungry to refuse. We ate together without saying much. I thanked her and reminded her we only had two things to stay in compliance with the court orders. Everything else was out of our control. All we could do was to keep trying to establish visitation and get the marriage counseling started. I hit the shower and changed into clean clothes. We went in my car this time, to head down to the marriage counseling office. There was no way I was going to trust her with getting me around today. It wasn't even eight o'clock and their office would not be open until nine. We were going to wait. We waited in the parking lot and as soon as 8:30 hit, my phone rang, and so did Satan's. It was the local DCF office.

Some guy named Scott identified himself as my caseworker. From the sounds of it, Satan was on the phone with her new caseworker too. I eventually found out her name; Jennifer. They wanted to go over our family plan and schedule visitation. It was amazing how quick we got the phone call back from that office the minute we started getting their bosses involved. It was two calls at the same time, not one. My attorney often said it was a big system and the ball gets dropped all the time. I didn't want excuses, they didn't give me one. Since Satan and I were married, it didn't matter who did what. We were liable for each other's screw ups. As far as I was concerned, every swinging one of them involved with my case would be responsible for every screw up they made from here on out. First, they outwardly refused to provide any information they had access to that would have gone a long way to help me out. Had I known anything about scaled payments for daycare that I qualified for, I'd have had the twins in there playing and learning with other kids while I got badly needed sleep. Now they were contradicting their own arguments in court. If we were to be tried together and forced to do marriage counseling, why did we need two caseworkers? What a waste of time and money.

It was a good thing I was getting my sleep and Satan wasn't acting up at the time. She needed the visitation just as bad as I did and I highly doubt she appreciated DCF's foolishness any more than I did. Had we been in separate cars waiting at the shrink office, there would have been more scheduling conflicts. I had endured enough chaos and mayhem from those idiots and enough was enough. Satan and I took our time with our individual phone conversations so we could inform each other what was going on. Both case workers were in the middle

of a department meeting until nine. Jennifer was the more

reasonable of the two. She would wait for Satan and then

continue with her busy schedule. Scott wasn't so reasonable. I

was already sick of this good cop- bad cop routine from their

office, so I got real assertive with him without seeming

aggressive. "I would suggest you wait until I get there or I'm

making some phone calls." Evidently, word was already out

with their office what I meant when I said "I was making phone

calls." He backed down and waited. Nine o'clock came. Satan

and I made our marriage counseling appointment for that

afternoon. Mondays worked out good for my work schedule.

We got down to their office and headed up the stairs.

Low and behold, a man and woman were standing in

front of the lobby door holding brief cases and clipboards in

their arms. They definitely were not parents that had to hurry

up after work to go see their incarcerated kids. "Are you

Scott?" I asked. He held out his hand, not to shake it, but hand me his card. "Yes, and you must be Mr. Stewart." "I'm Jennifer, and you must be Mrs. Stewart" she said to Satan. She handed Satan her card and shook her hand. We both wrote down the date and time we got the cards before we tucked them away. They were in a big hurry so they held our brief meeting out in the public hallway so any passerby could listen to our conversation. Any time someone passed by, I stared them down so those two disrespectful case workers got the hint to shut their mouths until we had a little privacy again. All four of us had a copy of the court orders so we were able to quickly go through item by item to make sure everything was in compliance with the judge. Everything was in order except visitation. The case workers were satisfied with who we picked for marriage counseling and Jennifer recommended we go to a parent support group she knew about on Wednesday nights. Where was that offer months ago?

As for visitation, it was simple. We would be supervised in the building and the appointed time had to be arranged with the clerk. DCF was too busy to let us have more than a single one hour visit per week. Satan and I had to share that time. Our case workers didn't have to be there. DCF had plenty of babysitters inside the building for that. This was the only duty on the planet that the foster parents had no choice but show up with the twins on time. I kind of liked that idea. I finally had one identifiable legal right with this crap, and it was the only important thing to me. I did have to pry a little bit and figure out how many strings SaddleBurr was still pulling. "So, is SaddleBurr your boss?" I asked. Jennifer just rolled her eyes up, let out a disgusted sigh and wrinkled her facial expression as if I just held up a dead skunk in front of her face. Neither one of them responded to my question. Jennifer and Scott were done with us, so they buzzed us into the lobby and then took off.

Satan and I marched straight up to a vacant clerk window. The clerk was hanging back a bit, secretly talking to another office worker. They broke away from their giggles to sit back down when they noticed me standing there. "Good morning Mr. Stewart. I take it you are here to arrange your visitation?" "Yes we are. Do I have to confirm this with SaddleBurr or can we handle this ourselves?" The other office worker let out a snorting giggle. "Don't worry about a thing Mr. Stewart, I'm in charge of visitations. I'm going to make sure this works out for you." The clerk managed to keep the best poker face she could as she spoke her next words. "Mrs. SaddleBurr no longer enjoys employment from the state of New Hampshire." The other clerk's giggles stopped abruptly when their lawyer walked into the booth and pretended that she needed to use the copy machine. I could keep a pretty good poker face too as I leaned into the slot of the booth so my voice could carry right over to her ears. "Good morning counselor! Break any laws lately?" The DCF lawyer looked right at me with a scared look before she scurried out of the booth like a rat.

When the coast was clear again, the two clerks were free to giggle some more. I could tell I was going to get along great with those two gate keepers. Satan was clueless with what was going on like most parents stuck in that lobby. Gate

keepers see it all and know how twisted the behavior of their

department's workers can get. Judging from what I was looking

at in that lobby of caged parents, we weren't dealing with the

cream of the crop. Those two gate keepers must have waited

for a very long time to have the wrong kind of parent snared in

the DCF trap. That was me, the guy that was going to get some

payback without breaking the law. I had no problem

entertaining them since they taught me a lot through that mess.

I finished our cryptic conversation about SaddleBurr. "Hmm.

What a shame, and to think how excited she was to be only

three years from retirement." The gate keepers stared at me in

amazement. "She told me herself!" They both laughed pretty

hard at the irony of that statement.

We shifted our thoughts to the more important subject

of establishing my visitation. The clerk looked at her scheduling

book and pointed out available slots for the week. The earliest

available slot was Wednesday at nine a.m. I looked at Satan and she was not paying attention as usual. It took me a couple of tries to get her attention before she responded. "Wednesday at nine o.k.?" She just shrugged her shoulders. "Is that a yes?" Satan nodded and then spaced out again. "Nine on Wednesday it is. That's a good day and time for me because of work. Can we schedule that routine?" "Yes I can and that is a very good idea." She looked around to make sure I was the only one hearing what she had to say next. "You don't really have to do visits with your wife, but... it will look good for you if you make sure you bring her along." We both looked back at Satan. Her mind was still drifted off somewhere. I looked back at the clerk, rolled my eyes up and let out a big sigh. "I understand Mr. Stewart. Hang in there." I responded back to her before I left. "Thank you for being so helpful."

Some impatient guy had dragged himself in behind me and just about pushed me out of the way as I left with Satan. I could hear his rants raging on and the gatekeeper's response back to him. "Mr. so and so, you don't have an appointment so you need to call me and set one up." The gate keeper was giving him a lesson on manners, and judging from what I saw quickly bounding its way up the stairs, I would say that she already hit the panic button hidden in her booth. The guard was already on his way into the parent lobby to help escort the raving lunatic out of the building. He was just another caged parent that didn't have the skills to manage his anger properly. I was just as pissed off as he was, but I was going to take my anger out the right way. I had all the evidence I needed that there was gross misconduct with our case. SaddleBurr was the head honcho of the whole district and was immediately fired over our case, but the lawyer insisted on playing hard ball. My lawyer informed both of us that the judge had pleaded with her to just help us out, but she refused. Satan's lawyer informed us that this was a simple misdemeanor with a seventy dollar fine, but there was no way we were going to drag our kid's name out into the public eye to MAYBE, reunite the family quicker.

No, I wasn't falling for that lie. I knew that lawyer was not allowing the reunification in a hurry. She would continue fighting for permanent removal to the end of her fight with us. She was next on my list to have removed from enjoying employment with the state, but that was tricky. I couldn't mess up our fight to get the twins back and that lawyer had a lot of lead way to bend the law her way. No, I'd have to go after a bigger fish to bring her down. I was trained to infiltrate organizations, find the weakness and strike the right way at the right time. It was only a matter of time before I would discover that weakness. It would have been better for them to just listen to that judge, give us the seventy dollar fine and the kids, then go away. You must be wondering how a strong willed father can face all that, win and then years later be driven to suicide. Like DCF, fathers are like an indestructible wall. Nothing can penetrate the wall to take it down. It is that tiny little pebble, hidden within the wall that pulls the whole thing down if that pebble is yanked out. I found DCF's pebble, my millennium baby found mine years later. The difference: my discovery was intentional, my millennium baby was just ignorant to my pain.

I didn't even realize I had a weak spot at that point in my life. I was getting pretty good sleep now and I was alert as heck. I was down to one job, and without the twins in the house, had way too much time on my hands. Forty something year half azzed fathers have a lot of spunk and are like a pit bull when it comes to their kids. I was no different. There is nothing worse than keeping us away from our kids. I already cherished every second I ever spent with the twins, but now, it had even more meaning than ever before. There was no doubt, my kids could be yanked from my life at any moment and there was nothing I could do about it. I already had a perfect understanding of my faults in this mess and I was determined that my answer to that: NEVER AGAIN! There was way too much time on my hands between now and Wednesday. It was already becoming evident that the state was making its play to stack the chips against me, and stick to their overwhelming blanket plan to always back up the mother of children. I had the gate keepers as informants and my lawyer. That was it. The system was backing Satan's play all the way. I figured that out within three minutes of our marriage counseling session.

He was nice enough, and very professional, but he had already established a very common bias against husbands. In his mind, we were all abusive towards our wives in one form or another. I never laid a hand on her and I very rarely talked to her unless I had to. She never listened to me anyways, but since we were court ordered to do this thing, I had one last chance to get her to listen to me. That idea was a bust within three minutes of our first marriage counseling meeting. He started the conversation out innocent enough, but that changed real quickly. "I will tell you both right away, just by showing up to comply with court orders will not be recorded that way from me. You have to actively participate in order for me to send your case worker a monthly report that you are in compliance. Let me start with you. Why are you here Mr. Stewart?" How on earth was I supposed to trust this guy to truly want to repair a broken marriage with that statement? I was about to lay everything on the table but my trump card to find out.

"I'm here because my cheating wife, who I was divorcing, pulled a stunt and put my whole family in jeopardy by driving away while I was asleep after working at my job. She refuses to work herself, but has absolutely no problem with spending all my hard earned bill money, that is not hers to spend. I've got the state playing hardball with me over a misdemeanor when they should be spending their time more wisely chasing child abusers and drug addicted parents. Since the courts are blackmailing me to either stay married or permanently be removed from having any parental rights or contact, I have no choice but try to fix this marriage. Maybe you can get her to understand where I'm coming from because she refuses to listen to me and purposefully does just the opposite of what we need to survive all this mess."

The shrink looked right at the non-responsiveness of Satan. She was spacing out again. Then he stared right at me like a cop and said the last words that I ever cared that came out of his mouth. "Thank you Mr. Stewart for your opinion. Now I am going to explain your reality. You talk too much. I can tell by the way your wife acts that you are an abusive husband. According to your court papers, you are the one who committed the child abandonment. It is my job to make her more comfortable with having a voice in your family or report that you refuse to comply with family counseling. So, if it's all right with you, I'm going to try and draw her out to see what she has to say." I was a bit shocked that this is how family counseling goes. I thought that the point of it was to create an environment where both parties feel comfortable speaking their minds. Apparently not. We glared at each other for some time, then I opened my palm facing up and stretched my arm his way. "Talk away!" That was the last time I ever spoke a word other than "Yes sir," or "no sir."

He switched his focus on her. It took a while to get her to say much, but the real Devil came out. She admitted that she was scared senseless about the breakup of the family by DCF. Who wouldn't be? She was in shock over the whole thing. I was too. If I had something to hide, maybe there would have been some justification with DCF using Gestapo tactics to abduct children. There was no abuse or true neglect going on. There were no drugs involved by either of us. The one truth that did come out of her mouth that day was the fact that there was a communication mix up. I made sure from there on out that there would be no mistake that I would take care of the kids. I would take full charge of the responsibility no matter what because there was no way I was going to have those Nazis point fingers at me again. Satan continued with telling the shrink about her feelings and all that good stuff. Fair enough, but then the lies came out. I was to be blamed for every bad thing in our lives by that woman. She played the victim real good. Too bad she didn't realize like I did that the children were the real victims here. Like the shrink, I made sure I took down notes in my book too.

When that weekly session was over, we booked the next appointment. I wouldn't ever have much more to say to Satan unless it had to do with family business. She had no problem opening her mouth with endless chatter about one silly topic to the next, merging separate stories into one but never quite reaching back to reality. I did manage to reach that mind of hers to think about where we needed to go next in my car. We had an appointment with the bankruptcy lawyer and I needed her to sign the papers. It took several attempts to get a straight answer from her whether or not she told her lawyer about the bankruptcy and if she was cool with it. Her lawyer, like mine was cool with it and saw no problem moving forward with getting the kids back home even if we had to relocate. If I learned anything on my own quickly, it was that I needed to make sure each step of my divorce lined up. This bankruptcy was very important to get out of the way.

We stepped out of my parked car and into the bankruptcy law office. We were lucky. Bankruptcy laws were changing and we were grandfathered into the old laws by filing them immediately. Satan got a reality check that day. We listed all the assets and debts, and we both signed the papers so the lawyer could file it before the deadline of our grandfather clause. Every debt would be cleared with the exception of Satan's school loans. Once I was divorced I was debt free again because she was responsible for that. Her truck had to be turned in. I used the next truck payment money I saved to pick her up a beater. All her credit cards had to be destroyed. We cut them up right there in the office. Since she had gone behind my back to leverage the house, I had to give that up, but at least I was free of all that debt. Otherwise, I still had about a hundred grand to pay back. The house wasn't worth it since I still had a lot of fix-ups to do and it gave Satan room to control my money. We walked away from the house. There were a few debts that she mustered up behind my back that I found out about that day since they ALL had to be listed. They were forgiven. There were still more that she forgot about that had to be amended in. The fee was only five hundred bucks and I had that reserved to pay on the spot. That court case was a walk in, make a sworn statement, sign final papers and walk out when we got the court date a month later. What a walk in the park compared to all the other dragged out court dates.

Meanwhile, back in the circus, there was a lot of time on my hands between that Monday morning and Wednesday when I would finally get to see the twins. We turned in Satan's truck and picked out her beater. I called the insurance company to remove the truck and get Satan's beater registered. I took Satan to a great rental community that I found in her home town. The three bedroom town house that we picked out to rent was secured with the money I had to pay the next round of Satan's debt for the month. First month and security was cheaper than her monthly debts and the rent was half what it would cost me to keep the house and pay off the debt. We had enough money left over to rent a truck to move anything of value to the town house and transfer the electric bill and gas account to the new home. We didn't have to give those two companies the shaft in bankruptcy. I still had credit on the oil contract and the electric bill was up to date.

It only took one trip with the truck to take everything of value and what we needed. Everything else got left behind. No more pack-ratting from Satan. The basement in the house was full of her junk that was never used. She had to give all that up too. The truck got filled up with our best furniture; three beds for each room, nice end tables and lamps to go with them, food and kitchen stuff, our living room furniture and descent TV, the computer we used for homeschooling, all the twins good toys and clothes and just enough of Satan's clothes to fill up the bedroom closet. Anything else Satan wanted, she had to stuff in her new beater. All my life's collection of belongings easily fit in the trunk of my car. Everything else got left behind. Whoever took over the house could deal with that junk. No more time would be put into that place making home improvements, just to have Satan tear it up because she didn't like how it looked. I scrubbed the townhouse from top to bottom, put all the contents of the rental truck in their places, returned the truck and made it to work in time Tuesday night. I did that all on my own. Satan took off somewhere, but never showed her face other than stuffing all her things into her closet and then reappear at DCF for our visit.

Everything was all set. Satan had her bedroom and each of the twins had one. None of my personals would ever wind up in that place. I kept everything in the trunk of my car so it wouldn't disappear mysteriously. Other than my briefcase full of paperwork, I stored everything else electronically. I had already set up a safety deposit box with my personal bank account to keep everything of value safe, especially documents. Other than my lap top, briefcase, a tool bag to take care of my car, and one suitcase full of clothes; I had nothing else. All my pictures were already scanned into the laptop and copied into the mass-storage unit I kept in the bank. Well, I did have my work boots and a nice pair of shoes back there too, next to a laundry bag that filled up with dirty clothes until I had enough to make a wash load; but that was it. That's all I needed. I did have my twelve string guitar and car seats for the twins in the back seat. I was highly mobile and finally capable of staying liquid with my money. I already had my own place to relocate with my twins when the time was right. I had to get my legal separation first and I wasn't going to leave Satan high and dry without a home for her to live in with the kids.

Everything was in order and looked all perfect for DCF's contentment. They would find out about my feet being firm about the divorce when the time was right. I would not send notes to the judge on my own anymore. I got a phone call from my lawyer and we agreed that I would let her handle that stuff from here on out. I just wanted everyone to get a warning shot that I wasn't taking anybody's bull without some consequence. I was satisfied for the moment that everyone got the message for now. Our lawyers had documentation of the bankruptcy and new home address and they sent the information to all involved parties. We handed the documentation to our case workers whom met us at the office for our visit on Wednesday. After we checked in with them and arranged their visit to the town house, they left us in the parent lobby to wait for our visit.

It was a horrible wait out in that lobby, watching other parents being led into a room, just to be followed in with another worker leading their kids into the room. Foster parents never showed up in the building. They got met out in the parking lot so an employee of DCF could lead the kids up into the room and keep the whereabouts of their living location a secret. All those precautions were understandable. There were many unruly parents that popped in and out of that place that couldn't figure out how to behave themselves even in the presence of the law. I was out of my element. I really didn't belong in that environment. Satan really didn't belong there either. She was an airhead, but didn't deserve the overkill treatment she got either. Neither one of us ever acted up once there. We didn't argue like other parents did. We didn't rush into the lobby ranting at the clerk about how unfair it was that they couldn't do what they wanted. We didn't do any of that even once, like many parents did. We just waited patiently until we were called.

A caseworker ducked out of one of the rooms with two kids. When the coast was clear, an elderly woman peeked out of the same room and called our names. "Mr. and Mrs. Stewart?" We both stood up and entered the room. Satan sat back down next to the woman in the room and chatted with her the whole time. I stayed standing and looked around. There were plenty of toys, crayons, coloring books and reading books. Other than that, there was only a baby changing station with a trash can with pop-up lid. I walked up to the tiny window looking out into the parking lot. It was a sealed window with thick glass that revealed only one thing: I was a caged animal. I didn't care about the circumstances. All I cared was that I finally got to see my twins. The central air vent blew in semi-cool air that smelled weird. It probably only took two minutes for the door to pop open, but it was a lifetime for me. The moment finally came.

When my twins saw me standing there, they ran up to me and gave me big hugs on my legs. I crouched down to their level to wrap my arms around them and return a very long hug. "Daddy!" they happily shouted as we gave each other kisses. "Go give mommy a hug" I told them, so they did, clinging to her legs. But she ignored them and kept talking to the woman sitting next to her. I stood back up to greet Satan's approaching case worker. She handed me the girls' brand new diaper bag they had conjured up from their vast financial resources. "I'll be back in an hour" she said in a businesslike tone. "See you then" I said happily. I was finally with my girls, and nothing else mattered. I didn't care that she would return in an hour to take them away again. I didn't care that they had me in a cage. My girls were safe, looked like they were being well cared for, and were with me for the moment. We colored, I read them books, we played and I changed my millennium baby's pull up since it got saggy. That fifty minutes went way too fast. Satan missed out, because she ignored the twins the whole time. Her case worker came back in the room to take the girls away five minutes before time was up. I would not see them for a whole week.

I did take the time to ask the elderly woman two questions before we got the signal to leave. "Can I bring some of their things so they can have them?" "Sure, you can do that. Just make it a couple of things." "Can I bring my guitar to play for them?" "Yes, but have the guard check it out before you bring it up. He will tell you if it is o.k." "I fully understand. Thanks." I could read between the lines. They wanted to make sure I wasn't taking a gun or something foolish like that up there. Funny how nobody seemed to be concerned with me bringing in something to the building that was "bug infested." SaddleBurr owned that one all on her own. As I left the building, I was filled with disappointment. I had completed everything that I needed to do for the day and it was early. I didn't have to go to work on a Wednesday night. I was disappointed because the highlight of the day, actually the whole week, was over. I had to wait for next Wednesday to see the twins again. No more work, work, work, sleep an hour, watch the kids and go back to work and start it all over again. I had time on my hands. Satan took off on her own in the beater I bought her. I wouldn't see her until later. What was a half azzed father to do with all that spare time? I didn't have that much spare time since my bachelor days. Having all the time in the world didn't make me feel free at all.

I was a caged animal, being watched with every move when I was with my kids. They questioned why I hugged my kids. They questioned why I was crawling around on the floor to play with them. They questioned what books I read them. They questioned why I was doing home schooling exercises. They questioned why I was changing a pull up. They questioned everything. I wanted to tell them where they could stick all of those questions, but I held my tongue. I wasn't going to make a bad situation worse. That's what half azzed fathers do. We pick our battles and fight them the right way. Only the guilty parties that get caught are hurt. No collateral damage handling it that way. I knew what to do with all that spare time. Complying with court orders was a breeze. They labeled me an incompetent father, well, I'll show them incompetence. Wait 'till I surprise them with all my extra-curricular activities I didn't have to do.

Act four: Circus Dogs

You must be familiar with circus dogs. The clowns bring them out on stage wearing those big, fluffy, colorful goofy rings around their necks. The clowns make them do all kinds of tricks, including jumping through hoops. They have a whole list of things to do in front of the audience. Parents caught in the DCF snare are just like circus dogs. It doesn't matter how or why they are there, they got to jump through the hoops or they get fired as a parent. Court orders set the stage for the act and if you were to closely look at how the circus act goes, the hoops for fathers are much more difficult to jump through than mothers. They are expected to do it on their own without help. Even the most difficult mother on the planet get a gentle nudge through the hoops from those clowns.

It was already very clear that the system was designed to cut every break they could for mothers and do everything they could to make a father fail so they had the right person to serve as a fall-guy. I was certain I would not let that happen to me. I was going to improve my life and make me even more knowledgeable as a parent. I had just re-certified with my advance first aider course before this mess, so I was going to add that paperwork as a surprise in court for August. My case worker had slipped me a paper showing all the "approved" parenting courses and where to go. There was a free "one, two, three magic" course on the list down at the community counseling office. What a joke that was, but I did the hour class, got my certificate and moved on. Why should I give the twins three chances to listen? I was raised by a dad that told you once, and you better not be told again. That's all right. The twins love games. I was going to have a little fun with that magic trick next visit.

Before I left the community counseling building, I did set up a four night course on parenting that the circus clowns approved. I played nice and signed Satan up with me and then paid for it. It only cost an extra ten bucks to sign up as a couple. It gave me a paper trail showing my effort to help her out. I would be there every night whether she showed up or not. She could show up or not. It made no difference to me. I'd be there and that course would be done before court in August and I would have the paperwork to prove it. Hmm, all this done before supper, what next? Oh yeah, there was an opening for a promotion at work. Got to get that application in. My store manager hates me to death, but he's on vacation. The assistant store manager is in charge and absolutely loves my hard work and the fact that I am one of the few workers in my crew that respect her. When I got there, the assistant store manager gladly signed it and sent my application in before the store manager got back. I was all done for the day. Not bad for one Wednesday. I was going to head back to the town house to get a bite to eat while I did a little legal research on my computer. That would occupy my time until the parent support group meeting later. It was on the list too.

Just as I walked out the main doors to my work; there she was walking in. She didn't see me approaching, so I greeted her. "Mrs. SaddleBurr! How's retirement?" She got a petrified look on her face when she saw who it was saying hi. She looked down at her feet as she hurried past me and into the store. I never saw her again. I'd imagine she found a new grocery store to shop at. I was pretty content with the payback I received. She got me in trouble. She went overboard. She got fired and lost her retirement. That was pretty good justice in my book. The matter was closed in my mind, but I doubted it was in her mind. She had enough experience to know it could get a whole lot worse. She was dumb enough to not realize that all those meetings in my house came with a little interrogation of my own. I got her real comfortable with opening up to me with that big trap of hers. I knew her daughter's name, where she went to school, where they lived and that the girls should all graduate from high school together. I knew everything about that idiot's life. The look of fear across her face told no lie. That moment in her life told her death could come at any time for her that I chose. She didn't know that I wasn't that type of lunatic, and that made it all the more joyous for me. Let the bitch sweat it out every time she misses out on that retirement check.

I went back to my temporary home at the town house to grab a bite to eat and do some research on line with the computer. Satan was not there. It was peaceful not to have her hounding me every step of the way in my life. I found a bunch of laws that confirmed why my lawyer was doing things the way she was. Get the kids home first, then battle Satan in a divorce. Found out a few things about our DCF court case too. It was civil court, not criminal. We'd have to go to Superior Court if it was criminal. DCF was just messing around with our heads. We still had to go to court at the end of August to clear things up. But I was pretty hopeful that the girls would have to come home then. I was wrong about that. DCF could drag its feet as long as they wanted up to a year. We had no control over that and would find out how they got away with doing that crap. As for now, all I could do was jump through hoops, land on my feet, not screw up and enjoy what little time they gave me with the girls. I had to start thinking beyond all this if I was to keep my sanity. I couldn't go back to college yet. Had to wait until the divorce for that.

It was time to go to the parent support group meeting. I locked up the town house and hopped in my car to get there. Still no Satan. It didn't surprise me that in spite of all the serious problems we face, she wasn't going to change her ways. I knew she was still chasing some dude, maybe the same one, maybe another. I didn't care. We were done. I just wanted her to comply with our hoops so we could move on. I was relieved to see her at the kid's club building where the meetings were held. At least she'd be in compliance with that. She still had to get a job before next court. I was worried about that court order. That would be a tough one for her. That was such a good place to have parent meetings. The kids could have lots of fun under supervision of staff while parents did their thing in a closed room. Satan was standing there chatting with a married couple that turned out to be the group facilitators. Yeah they ran the show.

The married couple running things was really cool. He was a shrink that dedicated his spare time helping parents cope with challenges. He wasn't like that other dope I was stuck with for marriage counseling. This guy was really there to try to help. He was a volunteer, not a paid employee. That's what I love about volunteers. There is no ulterior motive. Nobody ever tells them they have to be there. They are there with one sole purpose, to help. There was no bias with this guy. He was there to help me be a better parent. He was there to help Satan be a better parent. He was there for the whole group. I learned a lot from him until his funding ran out. The one thing that stuck with me good was our conversations about being a father for daughters. Sooner or later, they grow up to be women, and a father's best bet is to get them to think for themselves to avoid a lot of pitfalls. I liked his advice. All a dad can do is tell them the way things are and hope they will make good decisions. The toughest part of all that is being able to let them go at the right time. Kids always decide the right time, not half-azzed fathers.

The whole group was pretty cool. The shrink's wife was nice enough, other parents and even Satan knew how to behave herself there. Other parents that were in trouble with the law had sign in sheets like we did to hand in to their judge. Some parents were out of the hot seat with their judge and decided to keep going to the meeting just because they liked it. There was a couple in the group that were never in trouble with the law, and just joined because they wanted to. But there were three parents that were in deeper hot water than Satan and me. I wasn't obligated to talk about my situation and I learned my lesson from marriage counseling to keep my trap shut. I just sat and listened to that married couple try to cope with a very bad situation. Their judge had already decided to permanently remove all their parenting rights, including contact. I couldn't believe they were actually accepting that consequence without a fight. Who does that?

There was that one young girl who just got out of court and was in contempt of her court orders for not showing up at these meetings. She was belly aching of how unfair it was to her. What about those two kids of hers? How fair was it to them that she didn't take anything seriously in order to get them home? As she ranted on, I could tell that she wasn't very bright, but worse than that, she was high as a kite. It wouldn't be long before she lost her two kids and could party on to her hearts content until she dropped dead from it. What a nightmare being legally sized up to that. As other circus dogs described their hoops they jumped through, I knew I was up against tremendous odds. There is no innocents until proven guilty with parenting. The second you get on DCF radar, you are assumed to be on drugs, a drunk, a dead beat, a child abuser, a wife beater. Should I go on? I don't think so. You get the picture. I knew I was none of those, but I would have to prove it. All I could do was keep my cool until I did so.

It was pretty cool that all I had to do was show up and make sure my paper got signed. It was like showing up for detention for getting in a fight at school. I didn't have to say a thing. All I had to do was stay out of trouble. I let Satan do all the talking. It gave me a chance to see where her head was and eventually figure out what she was up to every time she disappeared. She didn't say much about our case which was good. She didn't admit a thing about any boyfriends at those meetings. That was part of her deniability in our up and coming court cases. I was happy to hear that she had been busy landing a part time job at the local taco stand. It was mid-day hours, perfect for mother's hours. It was just like her to do just enough to squeak through her court orders. She was being coached real good to set her life up to take over control of the kids. I'd figure that out later.

Those meeting would go by quick. I actually got to entertain the thought that there were actually some parents far worse than me. Everything for the most part was on the level there. I actually got to settle into a comfort zone there. I was able to carry on an adult conversation with Satan there that wouldn't be counter-productive. Nobody messed with me, or so I thought. There is such a thing known in the adult world called anger management. Now, there are plenty of classes a person can take if their out of control with that issue. However, it is understood with most adults that the best way to control any anger issues is to blow off some steam with sex. Gentlemen don't talk about it to keep their woman from being embarrassed, but women seem to chat about it among themselves all the time. That group of women were no different.

I would figure out soon enough that they all knew who was getting some, who was with who and who didn't have anybody. Yep, I was the center of attention. They all knew without me knowing they knew that I was refusing to sleep with my wife. Satan was getting some on the side, so they weren't worried about her. Sooner or later, they'd figure out I wasn't having any of that. As long as I was married, I wasn't going there. I'm a bit slow with picking up on female schemes. It took me a long time to wake up to the fact that those gals were trying to hook me up with someone. They had someone in mind who was in the group. This went on for weeks before I caught on. Satan took the lead with trying to get me to bite. She wanted an open marriage. I wanted out of the marriage. Either way, they all wanted me to get laid. I was oblivious to all this because nobody ever worried about my sex life before. I'm a twentieth century guy living in the twenty first century. Things are a lot different now.

Nobody really cares about who is sleeping with whom, not even the courts. Nobody cares about my old fashion marriage values, especially the courts. As long as nobody is doing it in front of the kids, nobody cares. That was a real eye opener for me. Cheating has no bearing on the outcome of a divorce or custody. The only fact that they care about is how bottled up you keep your frustrations. If you snap and the kids get hurt, you lose. Morality has nothing to do with it, only biology. Adults need sex, it reduces stress and as far as the courts go, it's pretty effective to manage anger. How adults go about that part of their lives is not their business as long as neither party raises the issue. The one that raises the issue will get burned. I'd figure that one out down the road. I was still totally in the dark to all that stuff on that first night at the parent meeting.

The girls went to work real fast on that first night. They went out of their way to introduce me to a woman that always showed up. She was always alone, other than her four kids. Those kids were rowdy as hell and she kept having to go out into the play room to break up some scuffle the boys had started. The fact that she had her hands full with a bunch of kids didn't scare me off, not even after I finally figured out how things worked. Kids will be kids and they just have to burn off some nervous energy in their own way. Everyone in the group, besides the three parents in deep with trouble, helped her out.

I even took my turn going out to help settle them down. It was pretty simple with those four kids, they were just starving for adult attention. It wasn't like she was ignoring them, she just had too many to handle at the same time. Those kids seemed to listen to me pretty good each time I would go out to settle them down. As time went on, I was encouraged by the group to handle the kids more and more. I was so blind. I was being set up to establish some kind of relationship with the kids.

I laugh at myself every time I look back at that whole deal as to how ignorant I was. All I was trying to do was keep the meetings going without so many disruptions. That's not what those gals were up to. They got their green light with me. The kids liked me, so that was the biggest obstacle gone. It was too bad nobody ever really gave me the chose in the matter. I really just wanted to get back with my own kids and didn't want to replace them. Not that I had any problem with adding more kids into my life, it's just that that was not where my head was. I wasn't looking to add anything new to my plate and I wasn't looking for a hookup. There are actually some men out there that can turn their sex lives off and on like a switch. That's me. I had already gone through all the withdrawals of a sex life when I shut off Satan. Why would I go through all that agony just for a hookup? Sex wasn't even entering my mind then, so that was a big part of me being blind to the building drama.

One obstacle with all that should have been whether or not she was attracted to me. She was apparently wide open to the prospect of getting with me the moment she set eyes on me. I'm no prize, but on the other hand, not some sweaty old beast that would turn off any woman. The more she looked at me, the more she smiled. There is only one explanation, she must have been really horny! I should have picked up on this emerging drama the first night when she and Satan spent a lot of time whispering together off in the corner and looking right at me. I just thought it was Satan talking junk about me. Even Satan was trying to hook me up. Who'd of thought that about their wife? My paranoia had me thinking she was setting me up for a fall in court, but I was wrong. She really wanted me to get laid, and with good reason. Something Satan should have told me the day we met, she was bi. Apparently, she was attracted to that mother and had a few ideas on how to jump start a new and improved spicy sex life with me. Maybe if she tried to wake me up to the twenty first century before all our trouble started, things could have turned out different. I was too hurt and there was no turning back with Satan. We were done, but that didn't stop her from trying.

Those two women were a real piece of work over that month. They gave me the full court press the whole time in their own ways. It was only wishful thinking that kept me from realizing that that was what was going on. "Were they really hitting on me? Naw, just my imagination" I kept telling myself. Oh, it was really happening whether I wanted to believe it or not. The worst part about it was that the whole parent group was trying to encourage it with those constant approvals, big grins and constant saying: "there's nothing wrong with that!" I guess Satan figured that if I jumped on board with her crazy idea of a sex life without boundaries, I'd get over my pain. She was wrong. There's nothing worse than betrayal in my book, but that didn't stop her from trying. Satan pulled a new trick to try and coax me along. She never fully admitted she was bisexual. She wanted me to figure it out for myself. "Take me to a strip club" she asked after the first parent meeting.

The mother with four kids worked her angles pretty hard from the beginning too. It was casual enough at first. Seemed innocent to me to just talk to her and get to know her. She was a really nice woman. She worked hard at work, got the kids home from daycare and school so she could slave away for their needs. She was happy to do it, but like anyone needed a break. The meetings gave her a break, but she needed more. She had no problem letting me know that she hadn't had sex in months. In her own words, "the throbbing between my legs is getting to be too much." Even my ignorance couldn't deny that she just gave me an open invitation. Like I was going to jump out of a boiling pot of water and straight into a burning flame. That wasn't going to happen unless I was absolutely sure I was with someone I wanted to be with. I had blocked out my sex drive and could take my time. I could have taken her into the closet in that room we were in that first night and everyone in the room would have approved but me. It was my decision, not theirs. However, that didn't stop everyone from trying over and over to make it happen.

If you think I was just being super picky about her looks, you got than one entirely wrong. She was very attractive with a smoking hot body. I am not exaggerating. I didn't think it was possible for a woman to have four kids and still have a body like that. She took great care of herself, and guys were always hitting on her. For some crazy reason, she wasn't interested in them, just me. She had a great personality and knew how to keep a friendly conversation going without being a drag. How does that happen and she still has a strong desire for me? There had to be something wrong with this picture beyond what I could see and until I figured it out, this wasn't happening

At first, I just shrugged it off that she was just super friendly.

Sooner or later, I was not able to fool myself. She wanted me

and she was going to do her best to get what she wanted.

Even the dumbest of men can't deny that she was

flirting with me from the get go. She just kept coming over to

me every time the meeting would take a break. She had no

problem brushing her body right up against mine in a subtle

way that looked innocent enough to eyes, but not to my groin.

She found every excuse to squeeze by me at the snack table

over and over rubbing her butt up against my groin. She

immediately turned her head to look at my response with a

girlish smirk across her face every time she did it. I didn't

respond with a facial expression or a change in groin size if you

follow my drift. I could see a frustrated look on her face every

time she went back to Satan, whispered something and then

tried again. No matter how hard she tried, I wasn't going to

respond that night. Maybe another time if she persisted to try.

Yes, she did keep trying every week, over and over again. That first meeting night was over.

I might have been kinda slow dealing with this new way of being an adult in the twenty first century, but everyone surrounding me was even slower at figuring me out. I had a one track mind; get my twins home and keep them that way. I really wasn't trying to take them away from Satan either. She needed a life with them too, but I had to be sure she wasn't taking away my life with them. Everything she suggested I needed to do, with or without her was a potential set up. She was in no position to act wild at this point either. One screw up from either of us could lose the twins forever. I knew it, she knew it, and everybody knew it. For everyone to suggest that it was o.k. to take Satan to a strip club kind of worried me. When the shrink spoke up and said "there's nothing illegal about it and damning to the case. Many women strippers have kids and it is an honest living by law." I figured what the heck. Everyone was trying to get me to relax a lot more so Satan and I could get back to talking. A strip club is a good place to try. Satan agreed

to my terms, I would drive so she could drink. There was no

way I was going to get stranded there.

Which club we were going to was an easy pick. There

were only two clubs nearby. The one in our town was a no go.

Our state only allows dancers to strip down to a G-string and

wear tape on the nipples of their bare chests. Satan didn't want

that. She wanted to check out fully naked women. The other

club was in the next town across the border of the state and

had all that. That's where she wanted to go and that is where

we went. There were a lot of man/woman couples going in on

that Wednesday night. Little did I know, it was amateur night.

Satan knew. She never admitted to it, but this was one of her

hangouts. We went right up to the center strip floor and got

two seats right next to the curtain that strippers came and went

from. A waitress approached us so I could order a cola for me

and a beer for Satan. I asked for the change in dollars. When

she returned with our drinks and my change, I gave her a couple of bucks for a tip and placed the stack of dollars in front of me with my drink.

Satan was pounding her drinks down pretty steady, so I kept the waitress busy with her beers. After Satan's third beer, she started to lighten up a bit and I was able to figure out some of what she was up to. Each dancer came out to three songs until all their clothes came off. They were all o.k., but one caught my eye and Satan knew it. I politely just gave up a dollar for each dance for each girl, including the one I was attracted to. Satan spoke up with her hand between my legs when that stripper finished up her routine. "I'm glad to see it still works. Maybe I should buy you a private dance?" "No, I'll pass." That girl finished her routine and the last professional dancer came out on stage. Satan really liked her and made sure I knew it. She loved her chest, she loved her long hair, and she loved everything about her. "Maybe I should buy you the private dance?" I said to Satan. "Maybe you should!" she quickly responded. I put a five dollar bill on the ledge to get the dancer's attention. She leaned in with her ear to hear what I had to say as she reached down to get the five. "My girl wants a private dance." "O.K. I'll be right out, but you need to meet me away from the stage." The naked woman's routine was over and she crawled around on the stage gathering up her money. She stopped in front of Satan long enough to give her a real close up look at what was between her naked legs. "I'll see you soon sweetie" she said with a wink to Satan.

The dancer came out quickly and met us by the doorway wearing nothing but a see-through gown and stilettos. Names were exchanged. "It's twenty per song, forty per song if you both go in." I declined the offer for both of us and handed over a twenty dollar bill. "Just one song for her, I'll wait for you up here at the bar." "We don't have to go right in, we can talk at the bar for a while first." The two women followed me to the bar so I could replace Satan's beer and get me a fresh cola. The dancer bought her own drink. After the dancer was sure I wouldn't change my mind, she took Satan by the hand into the private dance area. There was no door and everyone at the bar could watch the whole show. There was room for four private dances in the room at the same time. Satan sat along the edge where she knew I could watch the whole thing. The dancer slipped off her gown so her fully naked body could be seen as the new song began.

The rules in that club were pretty simple. No touching and the dancers had to stay on their feet. They could get their bodies up close and personal without touching, but that wasn't what was going on with Satan. I guess the rules were a little different for women. She brushed her nipples right up against Satan's face and sat squarely in Satan's lap as she squirmed around. I have good eye sight and wasn't imagining things. By the big smile on Satan's face, I could tell she was having a real good time. When the song was up, the dancer put back on the dress and the two of them talked in there for a few minutes. They soon came back out to me at the bar holding hands. By the excited look on Satan's face, I thought she had a hot date for the night, but that wasn't it at all. Amateur night was about to begin and most of the women in the club had disappeared and their men were sitting at the main stage.

The dancer left us alone to talk as she went up to another potential client to offer a dance. Satan looked at me with that wild girlish look that got me roped into that marriage in the first place. "I want to try this out! They're letting all the girls try out stripping tonight and I want to do it!" I knew Satan was a bit of an exhibitionist, but this was over the top, especially under the circumstances. "You sure it isn't just the booze telling you to do it?" "Nope! I've always wanted to try it out. C'mon, don't be a prude!" "With everything that's going on right now, I don't think it's a good idea." "I'm going to do it!" "I'm not your mamma so I won't stop you, but this better not go bad for us with the kids." "I won't tell if you don't. Go sit at the stage. I want you to watch!" I couldn't help but let a laugh slip out as I shook my head in disapproval. I got up to sit next to the stage as Satan whisked by me to get ready for her show. She

was so happy that I was going along with this.

It didn't really have anything to do with wanting to see

Satan strip down naked. I'd been to that show plenty of times.

It was more of a matter of wanting a front row seat to watch

her make a fool of herself. Most of the girlfriends or wives that

were getting ready to take it all off on that stage looked pretty

damn good. They either had awesome bodies or pretty faces or

both. That wasn't Satan. She still had some of her looks hiding

behind all that weight she gained. Not that I would have ever

been bothered by her weight gain, I was perfectly fine with all

that. It was just that deceitful personality she let come out at

the wrong place at the wrong time. If she wanted to be a

stripper, she should have said something before the kids. I

would have been fine with it. I went to plenty of strip clubs in

the army. I know how things are in that world. It just seemed

senseless for her to want to wait to do it after having kids and

not have a hot body like before. Besides, she couldn't dance to save her life. She was going to be the top clown act of the night!

Other than one bouncer and the bartender, I had to be the only sober person in the club. Every boyfriend and husband along the stage was having a great time when their woman came out on stage and took it all off for the crowd. Every drunk man in the house was egging them on to take it off. Nobody was ashamed and all the men surrounding each wife or girlfriend showed great approval by forking over lots of money to the stripping women as more and more clothes came off. The boyfriends and husbands made sure they bragged to the crowd who they were and got showered with compliments of what looked good on their woman. Even men without a partner got into the act. Female egos soared as they got showered with money. It didn't matter a thing about their looks or how badly they danced, they just had to take it all off. All the men around the strip floor knew I had a woman coming out because they constantly asked me. "You'll know when she comes out" I kept saying with a smirk on my face and my arms crossed.

In my opinion, most of those girls really belonged up there. They were much younger, good looking and in much better shape than Satan. Some of the girls had a little extra padding, but not like Satan's. The DJ saved her for the final act. When they announced Satan coming out for the final act, I just belted it out, "Here she comes!" There was an uproar of approval throughout the whole club. Even the women who had stripped for their men came out to watch her take it off. I could not have been more wrong about the crowd's reaction when she stepped out on stage. There was no laughter like I imagined would happen. Everyone just got even louder with clapping and hollering approval. Some of the men turned to me and gave me the thumbs up. All I could do was shake my head and laugh. This crowd was going even wilder when she came out. Apparently, thin was no longer in that night on the strip floor and everyone was in the mood to watch something a little chunkier. When I say chunky, I mean, really, really chunky. The crowd loved it and Satan fed off the energy.

She didn't come out in something sexy, she was still in those blue jeans and t-shirt she had on all day. She did have enough sense to already have her torn up sneakers and socks off before she came out. The crowd just kept getting louder and louder. I could tell that she was pretty buzzed with all that beer pounding, but at least she didn't fall down. Her attempt at a dance resembled something more like trying to shake a hornet out of her shirt, but everyone loved it. I was entertained too, just because she looked so silly. Her double D's bounced around creating shouts to take it off. She had no problem taking off the shirt. The bra was a different story. Not that she wasn't willing, that wasn't the problem. One of the hooks was tangled in the back and she couldn't get it unsnarled. She put her back up to me and asked me to unhook it. I looked right at the bouncer and he approved. "She's your woman, help her out!" The crowd chanted "help her out!" until I finally got the thing un-stuck and the bra went to the ground. They all cheered as her double D's bounced around the stage bare and showers of dollar bills found their way to the stage.

Her first song was up and the second one started. It finally dawned on me that she picked out her own selection. It was another song from Cher. Satan was having a great time bouncing her boobs around the stage as she unzipped her fly. When she finally got the jeans yanked down past her butt, she had to sit down to pull them off the rest of the way. Her jeans went flying my way and she crawled back up to her feet. Deep shouts of approval reached across the club as she sported a pair of my underwear on stage. As if it wasn't bad enough that she stole my boxers to wear, wash them, return them, just to make the newly stretched out underwear fall down past my ankles at work. Now she was sporting them in front of that crowd. Thank god they were my black boxers and not tidy whiteys or something like that. She could keep them now that I knew they would be all stretched out. She couldn't fit a third of her butt in them and it rode up her crack like a G-string. There was an airy bulge in the front where my package was supposed to go, but she had fun pulling it tight and creating a little camel toe for the crowd. They loved the show and rained down more doe her way.

Her third and final song came on and it was time for her to strip the shorts. She did it quickly and did all she could do to give each man surrounding her a close up view of everything she had. Every man she went up to showered her with all his bills that he had left. Men came up to the strip floor from other tables to shower her with their cash. She made more money in ten minutes than she could in two weeks with that taco job. I was really hoping she would realize that would only happen for her on amateur night because it was the last act and the place was closing down. Besides, everyone seemed to be drunk but me. As she created more cash for herself as the song finished up, some idiot decided that he wanted a little attention. He jumped up on his table and started stripping too. It didn't take the bouncers long to help him down from his table and escort him out. When the song was done, Satan rounded up all her money and collected her jeans from me. She disappeared out back to get dressed. I could have gone back there with her if I wanted. Men were allowed in the back with their woman, but I was all set with that. The night was over and I took her drunk azz home. I was really hoping this would be a one-time thing for her, but one can never tell with Satan.

That month went by so slow. In spite of keeping busy at work, complying with court orders, getting hit on by the woman with four kids, Satan's little stripping escapades (yes there were more than one); that month dragged on. My store manager was furious when he came back from vacation and found out the assistant store manager put me in for the promotion. "I would have ripped up your request if I was here" he told me. I really hated that man. I was excited that I was approved for the promotion and would be out from under his wing. I was going to finish training within two months at another store and then I would get a day shift. No more overnights. I could have my nights to myself. It didn't matter that good things were happening with work, I was still crushed. No matter what good was developing, how entertaining Satan had become, I could only think of one thing: my girls.

All I got for time with the twins was that short hour once a week in that stuffy little room. They would run right up to me and hug my legs and I would crouch down to hug them back. I didn't care anymore what was being said about my affection for the girls. I didn't care that Satan repeated herself to the room monitor that "she hated my guitar playing" as I played songs for the twins. I didn't care that Satan's case worker was giving me the third degree about her lack of interaction with children during our visits. Nothing mattered to me but to make the best of my time during that one hour a week to spend it with my twins. That's all the time they gave me with them and six days and twenty three hours in between visits. The waiting time was a killer. I was hoping that would all

change soon. I would find out in court tomorrow.

Act 5: King of the Jungle

Many people want to be the king of the jungle, but in family court, there is only one. Some lawyers work towards being a lion, but not all. The DCF lawyer for our case wanted that badly, and worked hard as a prosecutor to try to become a lion, king of her own court. She would have an obstacle getting there; me. We already had a judge, the king of our jungle, and the true lion of my circus. I already learned the laws of the jungle in the army. There's always a bigger lion in a higher court that has to be answered to. What people soon forget is that there is one animal even a lion won't mess with: a hyena. They are the most fearless animals out there. A hyena doesn't care about the odds, it doesn't care about the outcome and it only knows one thing. If cornered, it will fight. That would be me.

I don't know if you understand the true nature of a hyena. I've seen them in action in Africa. They are pack animals, and if you see one alone, it's usually a scout for food. Don't think there is anything cute about that crazy laughing noise they make. It can be used as a call to the pack to hunt. I watched a pack rip a bull elephant to shreds once. What a scary site that was. Once in a while, a hyena will wonder off alone. That makes them even more dangerous. I saw one cornered by a pack of wild dogs once. It gave off a very strange warning sound as it bumped one of the dogs to encourage the pack to just go away. They didn't listen and like lightning, the hyena had four of them dead on the ground and the rest of them running away. Nope, I guess a hyena fights hardest when scared. Nothing like the surge of adrenalin in a fight. Even a lion will back down from fighting a hyena. The king of the jungle will give off a warning growl to see what the hyena will do. If the hyena backs down, everything is cool. If it doesn't, the lion will simply move the cubs out of the area. I guess that's what the king of my jungle was trying to figure out. Did he need to return my kids to me or take them away?

Yeah I was scared! Who wouldn't be? They took my kids away and I had no clue what would happen. I suppose they wanted to rub it in a little bit to make sure I got that feeling of fear and confusion just like I'd imagine my twins were feeling. It was the moment of truth out in the court lobby to face the judge once again. It was the afternoon and regular court was over. We had the only closed family case of the day and everyone involved was waiting. Satan and I were there with our lawyers. Our two case workers were standing with their lawyer. The cop was in uniform and stood alone. I had my witnesses that gained court approval waiting there too. The twins' lawyer approached us with an elderly woman and introduced us. She was a very down to earth, but a friendly volunteer. She would be keeping an eye on things for her lawyer out of court. I would grow to respect her and trust her as things went along with our case. Without her truthful input to the court, I would never have survived that long grueling process.

It was time. Only the four lawyers were allowed in. They took their sweet time coming back out. In the meantime, Satan's case worker came up to us alone and asked her how the dancing was going. I was surprised that Satan was foolish enough to even mention it to her. I had talked to my lawyer about my concerns with Satan's stripping activities in regards to getting the twins back. My lawyer gave me that same surprised look that I had on my face when all those dudes liked seeing her naked. "Your wife, a stripper?" "Yes" I replied with my own version of a surprised look. She repeated herself in disbelief. "She's dancing for money?" "Yep!" "How's that going?" "She was making pretty good money at first, but she stopped dancing because the money got pretty short. I guess her novelty at the club wore thin." My lawyer laughed. She didn't seem surprised about that outcome. "Won't that be a problem with our case? What do I do?" "Don't say anything and don't worry about it. I'll handle it." So I tried not to worry about it. It wasn't as if it was me flashing my naked butt. Satan's case worker stared at my surprised look as they talked. She finally spoke to me directly in an effort to wipe that worried look off my face. "There's nothing wrong with her dancing in a club. Too bad the money ran out. It sure beats the amount of money she makes at the taco stand." I got that strange feeling that I was the only one out in the dark with our case when she said that.

The lawyers came back out. Our two lawyers joined Satan and me. The two case workers, volunteer and cop joined the other two lawyers as they just stood and watched my reactions as we talked to our lawyers. My witnesses were sitting patiently on the bench off to the side. It was comforting to know that I had three neighbors that were going to bat for me. One of them was a cop himself. His testimony would be rock solid against his co-worker. He was in uniform too. One thing that people don't realize, cops hate the gestapo tactics of DCF and my neighbor couldn't tolerate his co-worker's cowboy tactics. We were going to get to the bottom of this foolish case, or so I thought. My lawyer spoke up first. "The DCF attorney is complaining that you are in contempt of court." "What is she talking about? We've done everything on the list!" "She is upset that you didn't ask her permission to move from the house." "There's nothing in court papers that says anything about moving out of the house. We properly informed everyone about the move, nobody so much as raised an eyebrow about it. They all know about the bankruptcy and that we had to move into a new place." She nodded her head in approval to me and Satan's lawyer as they went back into the court room. The other two lawyers followed.

Nobody else was allowed in. We waited for a very long time before they came back out. Our lawyers came up to us with some papers as the other two lawyers went off to the corner with their case workers to watch us. My lawyer had a concerned look on her face. "We can't win this case." "Why not?" "The fact remains the same. No matter what the circumstances, this is a case of neglect because a child can never be unsupervised." "So what do we do, pay a seventy dollar fine and take 'm home?" "It's not that simple. This is not a criminal case." "So what are we, under CHINS?" My lawyer looked surprised that I knew that one. A child in need of supervision case is when a support system is put in place to help out parents. "Not exactly, that petition was never filed. The lawyer wants to be able to sink her teeth into you if there is another screw up. She just wants it on a closed court record that DCF tried to help you out. If you sign here admitting to neglect, they will help you out. There will be no public record of this." "What about coming home? When does that happen?" "I don't know, but at least it is in black and white. The purpose of this case is reunification, not removing parental rights. We have some teeth in this too!" She pointed to those words on the paperwork.

Even Satan didn't want to go along with it, but we both reluctantly signed the papers. I didn't see the harm in it. After all, there was some guilt in the matter and we needed to be able to move on and get this over with. They showed the signed papers to the other two lawyers and the cop was sent away. As the four lawyers went back into the court room, I sent my witnesses home. They wouldn't be needed. The two case workers, volunteer, Satan and I waited out in the lobby some more time until the lawyers came back out again. This time when they came back out, the case workers and volunteer were brought into the court room. Satan and I weren't invited yet. It took them a very long time to argue out the case plan among themselves without our presence. That's how things went for us for months. We'd anxiously wait to see when the reunification would happen as that DCF lawyer drew up some ridiculous new hoop for us to jump through. September was a simple one, keep the house clean and start supervised visits in the community.

Everyone came back out to us in the lobby with the parenting plan. We looked over it with our attorneys and signed them. That's when we were finally invited into the court room. The judge was sitting there waiting for us. The bailiff handed him the signed copies. He looked them over and approved the plan officially. He didn't have any snide remarks for me this time. I guess he was satisfied that I already got enough of that. Now he was just there to referee the circus.

The attorneys agreed on a new court date pretty quick this time, the judge approved that too and struck down his gavel before he left. Court was done until the next time, another month away. As we all waited for the clerk to make everyone their copies, the DCF lawyer got real cocky with me and gloated that "I won!" I couldn't resist putting her in her place. We were out of the court and what could she do? Take away my kids?

Everybody watch how I reacted to her comment without saying a word. They just wanted to enjoy the show and see what I would do next. It was obvious that the way things were shaping up that everyone considered me to be the loose cannon in this circus. They were very right about that, but had no idea that I knew how and when to shoot off my cannons. I gave her a very stern look as I spoke up. "You win, but kids lose! You are a real piece of work counselor. Let me make something very clear to you counselor. If you ever pull a stunt like that with my court case again, I will make sure you get disbarred. So, don't ever lie to the judge and say I am in contempt of court again. Do you understand me?" She grabbed her copies of the papers from the clerk and kept her smug look. She didn't get it. "I'm still going to permanently remove your parental rights. Watch me!" She walked away, but not before I got in the last word. "Good luck with the job hunting counselor!"

Everyone else was still gathered around me collecting their copies of paperwork. I could see the tense look on everyone's' faces. I needed to make sure they didn't think I was mad at them too. I eased everyone's concerns when I spoke up to Satan's case worker with a big grin on my face. "I can't believe that you are stuck working with that idiot!" "I know she's a bit odd, but it's the only lawyer we have. We are supposed to get another one someday, but who knows when that will happen. Until then, she has all the case load." "So what! Everyone's got to work. Maybe she should seek out employment somewhere else if she doesn't like it!" Nobody resisted a bit of a chuckle at that comment. Maybe I was a bit odd too, but I wasn't dangerous like they assumed. That became apparent to them on that day.

My case worker was all excited about something. "I love this! I can't wait to go to law school!" Evidently, he wasted no time going to law school because that was the last day I ever saw him. He quit the case and I wasn't given another case worker. Apparently, there was no need for one since Satan's case worker was content with handling our case and had a little rapport with me. It was odd that those folks could come and go as they pleased without proper notification to the courts, but god save Satan and me if we deviated one bit from the parenting plan, whether in writing or not. I got a dose of that bull crap every month on our court day. That lawyer was always complaining about something, just enough to write in a new condition on our parenting plan. She never complained about Satan, it was all about me. She knew all about Satan's stripping episodes and didn't even breathe a word about it. Talk about your double standards. That's o.k. I had something in mind for her shenanigans. Sooner or later, she'd get herself in hot water with me.

The other three lawyers finished up with us and said their goodbyes. The lawyer representing the twins shook my hand before he left. "I am very satisfied the way the case is going, so I won't be needed any further. I wouldn't pay any attention to her threats because this is a reunification case. I don't see this case going the other direction, so I will leave this in my volunteer's hands through the reunification. She will let me know if I'm needed. I hope you all have a nice day, and hang in there. You are doing just fine." I was surprised that he was doing his best to try and give me some encouragement. It really wasn't his job. I never saw the guy again. That's probably a good thing because if he had to show up in court, that meant we were losing the twins to the state. There was no need for that. The four of us were left standing alone to hash things out. Yeah, my case worker had taken off to catch up to his lawyer.

It would have been nice if it was just Satan and I left to work things out alone, but that would take some time and patience before everyone was satisfied that it would work out that way. In the meantime, we were stuck working as a team of four. It wasn't really a bad thing, one man and three women. Yeah, it was a bit lopsided to favor Satan, but it would work out. I would make it work. Satan's case worker wasn't a bad person per say. She was just a little thick headed some times. It was very clear that in her opinion, she was just there to keep me in line. Satan was a perfect mother in her eyes. She did have some concerns about why Satan was so disconnected to children. She did pull me to the side as the volunteer stood there listening to Satan's crazy story that swung from working at the taco stand to living in the town house and every other obscure subject but the kids. "Do you think she could have post-partum blues from the pregnancy?" the case worker asked me. "It's very possible. I can't think of anything else it could be. Her doctor and I talked about it once, but I don't know what to do about it." "I'll handle it, you just keep working on your end of things" she said back. It was a bit of a relief that I wasn't going to have to deal with that any more on my own.

The four of us got right down to business now. We finally were no longer stuck in that room with our visitations. We still just got one day a week out in the community, but the time limit was more reasonable. Everyone was in agreement. Wednesday worked perfect for everyone. We all could show up in a timely manner, including the foster mom. There was no more hiding her since the coast was clear and nobody was raising an alarm about any danger there. Satan got to choose the activity since our family counseling shrink insisted that she got to control everything. She loved bowling, so bowling it was. The foster mom met us in the DCF parking lot with the case worker. We got to meet and greet her as the twins were piled into the case workers car. The twins ran up to give me my usual hug before they would allow themselves to be buckled in. The foster mom left and would meet up with our case worker later for the pickup. We met up with the volunteer at the bowling alley. It turned out to be a fun time in spite of the circumstances.

Satan's parents and brother showed up to go bowling too. They hadn't been allowed to see the twins since the whole thing started. They were finally allowed to be back in their lives too and wouldn't miss it for the world. My family was always too busy. The three of us guys bowled away with the twins and had a great time. Satan and her mother just sat down and chatted with the case worker and volunteer the whole time. Satan started complaining when her brother and I started clowning around with the kindle pin balls to make it a little more fun for the twins. "I hate it when they don't take bowling serious" was all she could say. We didn't care.

The twins were having a good time and burst out laughing when their uncle released the ball late and sent it down the lane sailing without hitting the ground. The ball crashed into the head pin and knocked them all down. "Strike!" I declared as I gave him a high five. "That doesn't count!" Satan protested as she put a scratch mark in her brother's score. The twins clapped with joy. It was good to be back with family. Satan's father was a very serious bowler and ignored our antics. He sent his ball down the lane properly and left one pin standing. He got it down with the second ball. It was the twins' turns. They stood next to the line holding the ball between both legs and let it go. Six balls took their time wobbling back and forth in the lane until they eventually made it to the end. Some pins got knocked down and some of the balls just wound up in the gutter. I wanted the twins to know it was o.k. to throw a gutter ball. It was just a game, so I threw it a little too hard and the thing bounced right out of the gutter and soared down the lane next to it. To everyone's amazement, I gave the guy next to us a perfect strike. Satan's brother gave the guy a high five. "There's a strike for you man!"

Everyone was having a good time watching our antics. Other bowlers were starting to pay more attention to our game than their own. The guy next to us on the right was happy I gave him a strike. It's not like anybody was in an official league game on this side. That was happening on the other side of the bowling alley. We were all just having a little fun. Even Satan's dad could help himself. He had to laugh too. The owner was watching and smiling as we carried on with our usual antics. Everyone seemed to be happy. Even our case worker and volunteer found the humor with it. Everyone but Satan found it funny. "You can't do that!" she proclaimed as she put a scratch on my marks. As we all took turns bowling, we eventually finished up the one set and got ready to start a new one. We were in the far left corner lane and Satan's brother wasn't paying attention to the rack when he let his ball loose. The frame was still wrapped around the pins and the sweeper arm was down. We watched and hoped the sweeper arm would lift in time, but it didn't. He sent the ball down the lane so hard that it crashed into the sweeper arm and jammed it up into the frame arm. Every one made ooh and awe sounds with a few giggles in between. Even the owner who was standing near us watching had to laugh. "Broke my lane again!" he scoffed as he made his way down behind the lane to fix the jam up.

Everyone but Satan was having a good time. She took bowling way to seriously. "You guys never behave when we go bowling!" she protested. I just ignored it like usual. Our case worker and volunteer didn't seem to mind much. Everyone was having a good time. Who cares? I had something more important to worry about. My millennium baby got a blow out in her pull-up and it was sagging a bit and was definitely smelling ripe. I took her gently by the hand up to her mother. "She needs a change." "You can do it" Satan replied. I looked at my case worker to see what she would say. "Is there a changing station in the men's room?" "Yeah" I responded. "Go ahead. You're all set." I didn't have a problem changing her, but this was the first time I'd gotten stuck having to do it in public. If I was going to be a single dad, I'd better get used to it. That was the lesson to be learned here. I was very uncomfortable bringing her into the men's room, but it had to be done. I was going to have to sort out my mixed feelings about the matter in the parent support group. Our family counseling shrink was useless.

Our bowling time with the twins went bye way to quick and it was time to say goodbye. The twins gave me a big hug and tried to get one from Satan too. She just ignored their lingering hug and kept talking away to the volunteer worker without returning even a quick squeeze back to the twins. Our case worker just shrugged her shoulders and left with the twins. It was going to be a long month of waiting to go bowling with the twins once a week, but it was a lot better than being stuck in that room like a caged animal. I really didn't see what the holdup was getting the twins home, but DCF takes a long time to assess the situation and try to correct things. There wasn't really anything to fix other than try to get Satan a little more involved with the kids. Other than that, we could only jump through our hoops and not lose our minds. That's what they were really were waiting around to see happen. They would have a very long wait because that wasn't in our cards. Satan and I were very stressed over it, but would hang in there. Time was all in DCF's hands. They could drag their feet as long as they wanted. We had a time limit though. If the case reached a year before reunification, we'd lose the twins forever. That was our common stressor that loomed in our heads constantly.

Satan ducked out of the bowling alley to do her own thing until the parent support group meeting later that evening. We had already done our marriage counseling thing and I got an ear full from the shrink about how much of a bad husband I was for shutting Satan off from sex. He wanted to make sure I understood that his opinion about open marriages was going to be the law with our case and I had better straighten up or he was going to send a report to the judge that I was not in compliance with court orders with marriage counseling. I already had a conversation with my lawyer and she was definitely going to take care of that problem. I got a chance to talk to the volunteer about it as we walked out to our cars.

"That's just nasty!" she proclaimed "If he tries any of that nonsense, I will definitely recommend you get a new marriage counselor!" she added. I liked her a lot. I finally had someone involved with this mess that had a few old fashion values.

I was comfortable enough to talk honestly with her. "I've taken all those parenting classes down at the community center, even though I didn't have to. I want to learn something a little more in depth so I can improve on my parenting skills. Do you know any programs?" She hesitated a little bit before answering. "You do realize that you will never qualify to be a volunteer worker like me because of your court case. The training is great, but a little too close to home for you. Why don't you give the Parent Information Center a call? They are always looking for volunteers to become education advocates. I think you'll like that. The training is real good and you will learn a lot about the ins and outs of the education process." "Do you think I can handle it?" "You're a smart man. I could tell that from the moment I saw you talking to the DCF lawyer. You'll do just fine." "You don't think I'll be taking on too much?" "Nope! You need something in your life to help you put all this behind you. You're not a bad father, you just made a mistake. Try to remember that." "You've got to be the only person who's ever said that, thanks." "I just tell it the way I see it. Have a nice day." She climbed into her car and drove away.

I finally got someone to 'fess up that this whole case was a bunch of bull. They were just giving me the full court press to see how I would react. Fine! You want to see a half-azzed father, I'll show you one! Now I knew it was a big lie and I would wear my scarlet letter with pride. You dubbed me the half-azzed father of the year, now I'm going to work. There's nothing like putting a little fire under a father's butt to get him going. Maybe I was overcompensating, but it really irritated the hell out of me. I had a marriage counselor that was way out in left field. I was getting a divorce whether he liked it or not. My attorney advised me to keep waiting on that and just play along. You got to be kidding me! Like I ever wanted to sleep with her again. Not only did I have to face that foolishness, I was dealing with that DCF lawyer that kept shooting her mouth off in court causing trouble. All I wanted to do was get the twins home and get my divorce. I had to be real slick if I was going to get any payback on the lawyer, but even more sly with the marriage counselor.

I continued digging around with case law to find some screw up the DCF lawyer may have committed, but the whole process to get her disbarred was very complicated. She was much protected and there would have to be strong evidence of misconduct if I had a chance with filing a complaint. Her records were sealed tighter than a drum and there was no way of telling if she had a history of misconduct. Even if she did, I would never know. Everything was kept behind closed doors with the judges. I did find out one thing though; whatever the complaint, no matter what the outcome, if there was any truth to my complaint, it would stick to her record. That was good enough for me. Whether or not it helped my situation out, I was going to make sure the next sucker she messed with had something to fall back onto. I'd have to work on my complaint a lot more before it got into the hands of the circuit judge. I learned enough already from my lawyer about the tone and language of the complaint. She coached me along with that and would help me out when the time came to take a look at it and proof it.

The marriage counselor's threat was a whole different issue. The only person who saw something wrong with an open marriage besides myself was the volunteer. The DCF case worker was trying to encourage it. Even my lawyer just gave me that funny look she put on with one raised eyebrow to see what I would say without giving me her opinion on the matter. "You can't mean you want me to sleep with her too?" I protested. My attorney just raised her eyebrow even higher. "There's nothing illegal with it. I don't see the problem." I couldn't believe my own attorney was suggesting that I turn my marriage into a freak show. My attorney had slipped in a late afternoon meeting with me at her office before I went to the parent

support group meeting and she called it a day. She could tell

the subject at hand needed to end so she changed the subject

to give me time to think about it on my own. "How's the

visitation going?" "Real good! I had a great time bowling. I

can't wait until I get more time. When do you think that will

happen?" "If this month goes well, you will get more time out

in the community. After that, visits in your home. Eventually

reunification will happen, so just hang in there." I really had to

get to the meeting and we had said all we needed to for the

time being. My lawyer liked the fact that I had already taken

the initiative to get my education advocate certification going. I

didn't have a criminal record, so there wasn't any hang-ups with

that. "Make sure I get a copy of your certification, right?" "You

know I will." I headed out to my car and off to the meeting.

I was the last parent to show up and everyone was very

happy to see me. Maybe it was my suspicious nature, but I

knew something was up. I wasn't late, but most of them had

already gathered together to chit-chat with Satan. That married couple already lost their case and left the group. The nut-bag single mother who rarely showed up was no longer with us. She was in the process of losing her case and gave up trying too. All that was left of the group was all those responsible parents, Satan and me. The two of us were the only ones there on court orders. The single mother with four kids was definitely there. I broke up a fight between her two oldest boys on my way in. She didn't sit next to me as usual. I got encouraged to sit next to Satan for a change. I knew from the awkward silence in the room as I sat down that something was up.

Everyone else quickly checked in telling us briefly what was new with their week. When it became Satan's turn to speak up, it was abundantly clear what everyone was talking about before I got there. "I really want my husband to start having sex with me again." Everyone stopped looking at her and turned towards me as if I needed to say something. "You don't need me since you don't seem to be able to get rid of those boyfriends." Everyone turned back to watch her reaction. "You can have girlfriends if you want. I won't mind it." They all looked at me again. "I wasn't raised that way. I'm not your cabrone." The mother with four kids broke her silence. "I'll be your girlfriend!" Everyone else spoke up and admitted to having on form or another of an open relationship. Even the facilitator owned up to being a swinger with his wife. I couldn't believe that I was stuck in a room with a bunch of perverts!

The facilitator knew he needed to get to the root problem for me that nobody seemed to be willing to address. "She is your wife. Don't you think it would be appropriate for a married couple to have sex?" "Sure! If nobody is cheating!" "I know you feel betrayed. Infidelity is a very tough issue to overcome, but you need to try." "Why am I the bad guy here? I never cheated and never will. Don't my values count here?" "They would if it would work for your marriage, but she won't change. Maybe it would be easier if you did. You have a woman sitting right here that wants to be your girlfriend and a wife that is down with it. What are you really afraid of?" "I'm

afraid that my penis will fall off from disease if I ever sleep with

my wife again. She won't use protection!" Everyone kind of

giggled. "How do you know she won't use protection?" "She

told me herself the last time she cheated!" I was getting really

irritated at the conversation, but at least in here, I could vent.

Satan butted in. "I use protection! I just said that to piss you

off!" The facilitator looked at her sternly. "If you ever expect

for him to trust you again, don't you think you need to be more

honest about things?" "Yeah" she said sheepish as she hung

her head. She had been called out on the underlying problem;

honesty.

The facilitator looked back at me just like everyone else

with the exception of Satan. She kept her chin tucked in and

her eyes at the table. "If she can be honest about what she is

doing and be safe about it, will you try to work this out?" I

caught a glimpse at all the grinning faces looking my way. "I

can't believe that I'm even entertaining the idea of this. You're all a bunch of freaks, every one of you, even our case worker and my lawyer. What's the matter with you guys? Don't you think there's a problem with this idea? What kind of an explanation do you give your kids when they catch you?"

"Welcome to parenting!" the facilitator proclaimed as the room busted out with laughter. I didn't find anything funny about it so he clarified things a bit. "Children will eventually figure things out on their own. You just have to be discrete about things and answer children's questions openly and honestly when the subject comes up." "So basically what you're saying is to sneak around with your flings and answer for it when your kids catch you at it?" "Yup, what do you think play dates and sleep overs are all about? Parents need playtime too!" Everyone including Satan was smiling and laughing but me. "So how do I explain marriage values? Do I just toss that one out as a loss?" "No, you can explain as many options they have as you know about. They'll figure out their personal values on their own."

I couldn't believe this conversation had to go on throughout the whole meeting. Everyone kept reassuring me that I wasn't being set up, there was nothing illegal about it and open relationships were normal. I didn't see anything normal about it. I didn't fit in to this new freak act of my circus. I really should have been born at least a hundred years earlier. At least a hardworking man could find monogamy abundant back then and fit in to society nicely. Maybe I'd luck out tonight when I fell asleep and do an Ichabod Crane in reverse and wake up in the 1800's tomorrow. That would be nice. Unfortunately, that would never happen. The group kept harping on me to try it out. I was getting tired and just wanted to go home and sleep. I finally told them what they wanted to hear just to shut them up. "O.K. O.K! I'll think about it! Just don't hold your breath." That awkward meeting was finally over and I got to go home. Satan heard what she wanted to hear and headed straight for the shower. When she was done, she came out of the bathroom butt naked and hunted me down in the kitchen. "Go take a shower and get in my bedroom" she demanded before strolling off and plopping herself down on the bed.

I took my sweet time finishing my snack, taking a shower, brushing my teeth and thinking about this situation. I suppose I could wake up to the twenty first century. There were some benefits to it all. I could sleep with any woman I wanted, but the whole concept really bothered me. There really wasn't anything someone could do to me legally. It would be consensual even though I was going along with it reluctantly. The threat from our marriage counselor was the tipping scale with my decision. If I didn't do something, he was going to stir up trouble in court. I felt trapped. I really wanted a divorce, but I wanted my twins back home more than that. Half-azzed fathers make many sacrifices for their kids and I guess I needed to do this one for the twins. I cringed at the thought, but went into her bedroom. She was still lying there naked, patiently waiting with her pillow over her face and in a very familiar position. I rolled my eyes up and went for it.

Her back was against the mattress and her legs propped wide open. I was quite familiar with what she wanted to start with, even though it had been months. She wanted oral. She even shaved to make sure I didn't have an excuse. I went down on her. I knew exactly where to go, exactly how and for how long. She was my wife. I knew these things. Her moans got louder and longer as she got into it. She buried her face deeper in the pillow to muffle the sound, but the wrong noise slipped out. "Oh I wish Gary was doing this to me!" What a way to interrogate a woman to get the truth out of her. Now I knew his name and that she had a new boyfriend. If there was a glimmer of hope that I would go along with an open marriage, it got killed off right there. As if I wanted to be some sex toy she used to think about another man. I was done! I got up to leave the bedroom. "Don't stop! I thought you were good with this?" She tossed the pillow at me in frustration as I left the room, never to enter it again.

The rest of the month went by slow as usual since I only got to spend three more days with the twins and the rest of the time waiting to see when they would come home. My training at work was going well. I was with a different store manager and he was very cool. I just had to make it through September and October with training to get my full promotion to assistant grocery manager and get my permanent assignment at one of the two new stores getting opened up. My old one was getting shut down and replaced with a new and improved store that was almost built. I was training at a store that was getting shut down due to landslides and would be replaced with a remodeled building at a different location. I didn't know which one I would get, but it didn't matter to me. I was supposed to get back on the day shift. What a plus that would be. I was doing some over-night training, but also some day shifts, depending on the required training.

My training as a certified education advocate went well. I only needed one full day to receive the certificate. I needed a

Saturday off and my new boss arranged my work schedule so I could do it. He was very understanding. He was getting ready to retire and everybody was going to miss him, including me. It would be a great loss to the company, but he earned his time off. Talking to him was like night and day compared to my last boss. The parent information center presented me with my certificate that Saturday, but they needed more. They had a great need for volunteers that would do much more than hold parents hands through the process of initiate testing for their children that may have a learning disability. They needed surrogate parents that would look out for the educational needs for children in permanent custody of the state. I took the information, but wanted to run it by my lawyer first. It would take for individual nights over the span of a month to complete that training. I needed to make sure it wouldn't interfere with anything including work.

I had to deal with that nightmare of a marriage counselor. Each session brought on more insults to me from him for failing to reconcile my marriage. He was insistent that there would be severe consequences for refusing to have sex with Satan. I informed my attorney what was going on with him and she nipped it in the bud. Apparently, she filed a complaint to the medical board about his antics and that shut him up about the sex thing. He never threatened me again and he didn't file any complaints to the judge. He just simply wrote we were in compliance. My attorney did say to wait until our case closed before I started up my new certification course. She thought it would be awkward if I ran into a DCF worker I knew with my volunteer work while my case was still open. It was good to start out just by helping parents for now and getting to know some of the teachers and administrators at the different schools as a volunteer.

The parent support group meeting were going o.k. People finally got the hint that I wasn't down with an open marriage. They just focused on helping us move on. The mother with four kids turned up the heat on me though. She tried everything she could do to try to get me to slip over to her home after the kids went to bed. I wasn't biting. There was something not quite right about the situation. I couldn't put my finger on it, but that inner voice told me to hold off. There was something about her that everyone in the room knew about her but me. Sooner or later, somebody would slip up and I would know. September was already almost over and the leaves were starting to turn colors. I really hated missing out on sharing these kind of moments with the twins. Another court date was at hand, along with another disappointment.

We went through our usual routine of waiting out in the lobby as the lawyers hashed things out. Satan and I were handed a copy of the case worker's report to the judge before they went in with the lawyers. Things were a little different now. Three lawyers, the DCF case worker and volunteer all went in to court without Satan and me. I read through the case worker's report. Everything was in compliance, all conditions met, including a clean home and, oh, this is cute, Mr. Stewart is proud of his new certification as an education advocate and uses his spare time volunteering to help parents. What the heck does pride have anything to do with it? I just do it. "Oh this is real great!" I said to Satan as I read her next statement from the report out loud. "Mr. Steward wants to have an open marriage. Why am I getting blamed for this? That was your idea not mine!" Satan just shrugged her shoulders. I just stood there and waited for them all to come out of the courtroom.

As soon as they came out, I went straight to our case worker. "Why would you put something like this in your report? That's your idea, not mine!" "Oh, don't worry about it. It's just a typo. It didn't even come up in conversation." Everyone was gathered together in one group. I looked right at the DCF lawyer. "So what new issue did you bring up this time counselor?" "Don't worry stud! What you do in your bed is no concern of mine. I just don't like you lying that you served in the army." "I told you, my DD214 got ruined when the water pipes burst in that house. I put in the paperwork for a new one several months ago. I don't know when I will get the new one."

"I don't care. The only new condition you need to meet is get me the records before next court. You have a month!" She flung the new parent plan in my hands. I was pleased to see that no additional conditions were there with that ridiculous demand over the DD214. It was encouraging that we got unlimited supervised community visits for the month too, but this demand about the military record was an impossibility to control. I didn't know when I would get the thing. I let my lawyer know how I felt before we all went into the court room. I was finally going to get to see her in action.

After formalities, the judge spoke up first. "Are we all in agreement with the new parent plan?" My attorney spoke up first. "Yes we are your honor with only one exception. The request for Mr. Stewart to produce his military records is irrelevant to the case and we wish to have that portion removed." The DCF lawyer shot her mouth off next. "It goes to the credibility issues we have with Mr. Stewart and we request that the condition remains in the parenting plan." My lawyer went to bat again. "Mr. Stewart has put in the request for new copies from the military since his were lost. He is perfectly willing to share that information with the courts, but has no control of when the documents will arrive. We would like to have the wording on the parenting plan modified to state "as soon as the documents are available," not by the end of the month of October." Before the DCF lawyer could shoot her mouth off again, the judge held up his finger to keep her quiet. "Mr. Stewart, how long ago did you send in the request?" "I have that documentation right here your honor." The judge waited patiently as I leafed through my briefcase and pulled out a certified mail receipt from the post office and a copy of the request form. "It has been over four months your honor. It can take up to six."

The judge gave the bailiff a nod and he came up to me to hand over the documents I had for the judge to see. The judge smiled as he looked over my proof. I wondered if he was surprised that I was prepared for this stunt. I had a hunch that I needed to be prepared with documentation of any kind of complaint I heard through the grape vine. I was correct about this one. "I must agree that the condition is unreasonable and will be modified to satisfy Mr. Stewart's request. Is everyone in agreement to everything else?" Everyone nodded yes. "O.K. This matter is settled for another month. Let's set an agreeable date for October and I will see you then." The date was set, formalities followed and another court date was done. What a drag it was to have to keep going there each month. I jockeyed for position right behind the DCF Lawyer as we all filed out of the court house. As soon as I was out of the Lion's sacred ground, I gave her one of my own comments. "Keep it up counselor, and you will be enjoying early retirement."

Act six: The Hyena is Loose!

I briefly mentioned how hyenas act. From what I have observed, they are also intelligent and much focused animals. Yes, they are predators, but they hunt big game, not little animals unless forced to. I have never seen one caged up in a circus, but imagine if some dummy decided to do so. What would happen if someone shouted "the hyena is loose?" Panic would well up in the minds of every parent in the room and they would head for shelter. Utter chaos would be happening all around the tent and only a selected few would actually be trying to re-capture the beast. Anyone slick enough to find it will probably get hurt because the hyena knows only one thing: escape and go back to big game hunting. The chaos will help the hyena figure out who is in the way of his escape. Those individuals will have a serious problem if they get in the hyena's way. So don't try to capture and cage one up and think it will be tamed like a lion. It won't happen.

Like a hyena, military veterans are highly skilled in the art of hunting big game. Many veterans with disabilities go on to have families and children. They don't care that you may label them half-azzed fathers. They are focused on one thing: raising their kids. They have hunted down dangerous groups of people such as terrorists and enemy armies. Do you honestly think they care about some jackass in the court system giving them a hard time? All they are going to do is remove them from the problem so the children are not at risk any more. If some out of control lawyer insists on being a problem without just cause, they will be removed from the situation. Like a hyena, it is extremely rare for a veteran with a disability to go so out of control that innocent people get hurt. They are more of a risk at harming themselves than others. The last time I checked, the rate of completed suicides is at 15%. So we all need to ask ourselves, what has any veteran done to deserve harassment that goes above and beyond the scope of what the law is supposed to do? How disrespectful is that to have lawyers arrogantly harass a veteran to a breaking point?

Let's look at this from the veteran's perspective who is put in this cage. What has he really done? He was getting badly needed sleep to take care of his kids, there was bad blood between him and his wife to cause a miscommunication, the community over-reacted, a judge played hardball that only drug addicts and child abusers are supposed to face, the children should have been sent home already because the point was well taken by the parents and the lawyers insisted on rubbing it in. In the eyes of a veteran that put his life on the line to protect the laws, this situation was a case of lawyers grossly abusing their authority. Veterans lived by the rules of deadly force during their service. Those rules are drilled into their heads. Use the least amount of force necessary to repel the enemy. What that means to you civilians is: we don't shoot at protesters that wandered into a restricted area, we just make them leave. We don't put civilians' needlessly in harm's way and only true threats with guns and explosives get shot at. Most of us, when we go home to enjoy family life for ourselves, still live by those laws. We just want to live in peace and illegal behavior of lawyers will be dealt with accordingly.

So what was that arrogant lawyer thinking when she cornered me with my military background? What did she honestly think she could gain by questioning my loyalty to the federal government by poking her head around into classified information? Did she really think there was anything in there that had any relevance to our court case? There wasn't anything available in the civilian world to even give a hint that she needed to go there. I had absolutely no criminal record what so ever, not even a moving violation. I did have one parking ticket that was paid up at the time. No history of domestic violence, their drug tests came back clean on me because I never used that crap. I rarely drank alcohol and never picked up car keys if I did. She had no evidence that she needed documents of my military record and the courts somewhat supported that perspective. Now she woke up the hyena in me and I was on the loose. Where else would I run to but back to the pack of hyenas?

I have an obligation to the military for life as a protector of classified information to let them know when there is a breach in security. I finally had court documentation pointing a finger at the DCF lawyer for creating a breach in military security. I knew she didn't have the need to know, the department of defense knew she didn't have the need to know, let alone open up classified information in a public court. That was a big no-no. She didn't know yet, but would soon find out. This was post 911 and suspicious behavior against the military was taken very seriously. Did she honestly think I was going to let this one slide? I immediately typed up my complaint to the department of defense on my computer. I used a few buzz words that would get the military's attention, one phrase; "I suspect," was language my lawyer taught me to accuse someone without directly accusing them. The rest was on me. I explained who I was, my job in the military, that my children were in the lawyer's custody and I was under duress. I gave her name and contact information, with the explanation that she was using my children to force me to disclose classified information. I finished up the complaint explaining that "I suspect this act of treason being committed by her is due to terrorist connections." She was now on their radar.

I didn't stop there. I provided copies of court orders to support my complaint and explained that two bits of information was needed from the department of defense to potentially stop this breach of security. I needed my DD214 expedited and some form of communication to the courts that they didn't have the need to know anything not within my DD214. The judges name and contact information was provided and his boss, the circuit judge, was named and contact information provided. I made my phone call to the department of defense, they put me in contact with the appropriate field office, I sent them all the information in a fax and then waited. If I was still active duty, they would have sent me a JAG officer immediately. However, they had other methods of dealing with this. Their instructions to me: "soldier, you've done the right thing. Stick to your story next court. They don't have the need to know." "What if they hold me in contempt of court?" "That's not going to happen. The judge should know better, but if it does, call us again. You have my phone number and extension. I will be handling the case." My part was done other than waiting, but I made sure the circuit judge got a copy of my complaint too.

It was a miracle how soon after all that crap that a copy of my DD214 and military medical records wound up in my mail box. Of course my lawyer got her copy and she forwarded copies to the interested parties to keep me out of contempt of court. October came to an end slowly. My job was going well. The marriage counselor was still giving me crap, but stopped making threats. I was still the bad guy in his mind. I was helping parents weave their way through the red tape of getting their children tested for any special needs in school. I was following my court orders to the letter of the law and I was getting more time with my twins out in public.

Our DCF case worker had dropped down to seeing us one day a week to do just enough work with our case to stay out of trouble. She let the volunteer handle supervision of visits. The foster mother was pretty cool and had no problem meeting us anywhere, any time as long as schedules didn't conflict. She even invited us over to her house. Her husband seemed a bit standoffish, but who could really tell. Everything was going better with the visitations other than not being allowed a supervised visitation in our home. I had a lot more time with the twins until somebody screwed up. It would seem that nobody informed the DCF caseworker about one of the visits until I mentioned it after the fact. She was really pissed and switched the twins' foster home. The foster mother insisted that we had no contact with her, and we only got the one day a week at the bowling alley. I was getting punished so the DCF caseworker could cover her azz, but there was a lot more to it.

I found out years later from my Millennium baby that the foster father was stabbing at her hand during dinner time to teach her not to rest her arms on the table. She told the volunteer about it and she told the DCF caseworker. That was the real reason the twins were pulled from the foster home. I don't blame the system for keeping the kids safe and it was only a coincidence that the new foster mother handled things the way she did. She was just covering her butt too. But why did they find it necessary to blame us for the move? The answer is pretty clear. It is much easier to blame everything on parents to cover up the flaws in the system that is designed to protect children. We just got caught up in all that. It is perfectly fine for a government worker to lie in order to protect the system that abducts children and fails to keep them safe. However, it is not fine for a military veteran- half azzed father to make even one simple mistake. Where is the justice if you don't seize it for yourself? I was going to get some of mine sooner than I

realized.

October was a dreary month for me. The weather was

fine and the autumn colors were beautiful. I just lost out on

sharing that with my twins. There wasn't much I could show

them in the bowling alley parking lot. There were only a couple

of trees, nothing like taking a ride in the car to go see a rainbow

of colors with the trees in the White Mountains. It was like

being in a cage again with the twins; one day a week, just at the

bowling alley and nothing else. Satan and I didn't even get to

take them trick-or-treating. We were getting the full Gestapo

tactic as if we were guilty of serious crimes. I often kid around

about Satan, but even she didn't deserve this bull. Another

drug addicted mother was in the news for killing her kid. I

wonder what happened to the Gestapo tactics with her? I just

kept up my faith in myself that sooner or later, the courts would

have no choice but release the twins.

If you think there is justice in this world, dream on. There is no such thing as real justice. Criminals get away with a slap on the hand and people who just get caught up in bad circumstances are made poster children of the law and how far the law will go to punish someone. I don't think that is what honest citizens had in mind when they trusted lawyers to create a justice system. I know what I experienced with the practice of law that I certainly didn't serve in the army to protect this way of life. As far as I am concerned, a case like mine is just an excuse to justify the existence of our justice system. The system is far too complicated and it creates an easy way out for anyone who has the cash to do it. Keep in mind what I just said about money because wherever there is loads of money, there is always some type of corruption.

I did have one exceptionally positive thing happen to me in October; I was finally able to file my claim with the VA system to get medical help. That would take some time as I waited for their response, but at least the ball was rolling along with that. It was a slow process, kind of like watching my twins' bowling balls roll down the alley, but moving along none the less. No excitement to speak of with work, marriage therapy, DCF meetings, my volunteer work, parent group meetings or even Satan. Same old story, just a different month waiting to see what would happen in court. Satan was her usual sneaky self. That single mother was still hitting on me in the parent group meetings. I kept filling my vacant time with helping other parents. My marriage counselor was still a prick and work is work. What else can I say?

Meetings with the DCF case worker were a different story. No matter how much we both tried, there was no budging on the amount of time we had with the twins. It was supposedly up to the foster mom how that went down, but I knew there was more to it than that. I knew our case worker was ticked off about not being told about that visit until after the fact. She had some major control issues. She didn't care. She was in the driver's seat and had all the control at this point.

All I could do was to suck it up until court on the end of

October. I did tell my lawyer about it and that the state needed

to move forward with reunification, not back tracking. Other

than that, there was nothing else I could do. I was powerless.

The case worker did try to stir up some crap with Satan

though. Every Wednesday that we went bowling with the

twins, Satan would just sit there and talk to either the DCF case

worker, our volunteer or somebody else. She never interacted

with the twins even once. She was the one that loved to go

bowling and insisted that bowling was going to be the activity

each week. However she never even bowled once. She just sat

there like a lump on a log, ignoring our children. Of course we

were all concerned about that behavior. Who wouldn't be? I

thought we had established the likelihood of post-partum

depression. I was under the impression that DCF was trying to

help her with that, but obviously, they aren't truly in the

business to help out families. There is a lot of finger pointing and punishments, but not much on the help side of families. The whole system is a joke as I found out that October.

It started making a lot of sense why her depression never came up in our family counseling meetings. The shrink was on the payroll and had no intentions of helping us with real problems. Satan wouldn't spend time with the girls and I wanted to see that happen. Any time I tried to speak up on the matter, he shut me down. "You need to worry about what you are doing, not what she is doing." It was bad enough that he shut me down on issues I had with infidelity, but be serious. No matter the outcome of our marriage, she needed to be a mother and I wanted to see that happen. The shrink wouldn't put anything in official reports other than "counseling was being conducted as ordered in court," nothing more, nothing less. However, it was very suspicious that anything said only within those marriage counseling meetings always got back to our DCF case worker, just to have her twist things around a bit.

She pulled me to the side one bowling Wednesday like she often did just to stir things up. I got only an hour with my twins a week since anything more was too inconvenient to the foster mother. I couldn't believe the DCF case worker had the stones to waste my precious time with the twins to chit-chat about some nonsense. She didn't even ask a question, the DCF caseworker insinuated a very strong accusation that really pissed me off. "When are you going to tell me about your wife's drug and alcohol problems?" After about a half second of shock from that statement, I let her get an ear full of what I thought about those words. "Just because you know I still plan on divorcing her doesn't mean I am going to say lies about her. My wife may be many things, but a drug addict or alcoholic isn't it! I'm not going to lie to you or the courts about that caucomamy story. There is no proof of her being a drug addict or alcoholic because it doesn't exist. If you so much as imply this accusation in court, I am going to make sure you pay the price to the extent of the law. Do you understand me?"

The DCF case worker didn't even nod a yes or a no answer. She just gave me that scared look because she knew I meant business. She eventually went about that fishing expedition in a different way. As for Satan, well, you won't hear this story come from her lips. I let her know what was said about her afterward, so it isn't as if she didn't know what was going on. I might have harbored a lot of resentment towards Satan for her infidelity, but not that much. Even she deserved a heads up that she was in the cross-hairs of the courts. Satan will never admit that I always had her back. It doesn't fit her plan to smear me as a half-azzed father. It never mattered to me. I knew the twins would eventually grow up and figure things out for themselves. I just wanted them home, or at least for the time being, get more time with them. The court date in October would at least give me that, but not for apparent reasons.

I had grown very tired of being told one thing to my face and everyone's behavior behind my back told me something else. It was time to discover who my true enemies were with this case. Was my wife and lawyer truly working for co-parenting rights, or was that a lie. What was the judge really up to and was my lawyer speaking truthful about his reactions to the case? Was the volunteer a true neutral party and speaking honestly in court? Was I the only target of DCF or had Satan gotten in their cross hairs? Most importantly, was my use of the chain of command effective? It was a long shot to see what the department of defense would do. Did they do anything about my complaint or did it get ignored? I was going to find out first hand and not from the words of my attorney.

Satan and I weren't allowed to hear everything being said about our case, just what everyone wanted us to hear. I was going to change the game that October. I'm a veteran, and there are many things I learned about gathering information. I'm not a law breaker, but there were two times in my life that I had to bend the law just a bit. Even if someone could argue in a court of law that I had broken them, it's too late! There is such a thing as statute of limitations, so you can hear all about it now. I am a strong believer in military law called: need to know. That DCF lawyer didn't need to know what my job was during military service, but every citizen in this country needs to know what really goes on behind closed doors in a courtroom.

Hobby shops are a great thing to find all kinds of the newest technology in electronic gadgets. Yep, I bought myself a bug. I was going to find out what kind of junk was being said about me for sure. It's neat how you can stick a bug to the underneath side of a wooden bench right up close to a judge. I stuck it in the front row seat, right in front of the judge that October morning. They always held general court in the morning. It was easy to sit right up there, plant it and leave without anyone being suspicious. I always showed up in the morning, just to let the judge know I was there. It worked real well too. I tested it as I listened to the courtroom from my car out in the parking lot. Fresh batteries, everything was a go. I just had to wait for the afternoon when everyone but Satan and

I went into the courtroom to talk about our case. I just used the excuse that I needed to go outside to smoke. The bailiffs were used to me doing this.

It was the best time I ever had waiting for something or someone out in my car. You talk about a circus hidden behind closed doors! That was definitely our court case. As I listened over my radio, I heard the bailiff clearly announce the judge and the room got dead silent. I heard the judge's gavel hit the bench and the judge speak in more than his usual stern tone. "Before we begin this hearing, let me tell you about how my month went. It would seem that the circuit judge got a phone call from the department of defense. Somebody is very unhappy that this court would violate classified military information just to lean on a parent. She called me and informed me that there would be some delays with my superior court appointment. Quit-pro-quo, because we all know who is behind all this, I guarantee you counselor, any hopes and dreams of a judgeship for you will not happen."

I heard his gavel slam down very hard. "I warned you not to mess with my veterans, and you did anyways. In my courtroom! You have his DD214 and that better be the end of it! If I so much as hear a peep out of any of you about Mr. Stewart's military background, I will hold you in contempt of court! Do I make myself understood?" There was a lot of murmuring and then silence again. "Now then, since we are putting that all behind us, and I do mean, we will put that issue aside, let's talk about a couple of complaints coming from Mr. Stewart. Since he seems to be the only one telling me the truth around here, I'm inclined to listen to his complaints. Does anyone have a problem with that?" There was total silence. I had finally scored a victory, it was a bit unorthodox how I did it, but that seemed to be the only way to deal with these sneaky devils. As I happily listened on, I knew there was a long way to go. I managed to clear the air of some irrelevant nonsense, but the real issues with getting the twins home were still at hand.

"Why has there been delays with visitations? It's my understanding that this has been going very well. The parents were given more than one day a week with visits and then it was taken away abruptly. You are the case worker, so why don't you explain to me what happened." "The original foster parents had a family emergency and could no longer provide care. The new foster parents are exercising their right to have no contact with the parents. Scheduling extra visitations has been difficult your honor." "This is a very simple reunification case and I am becoming very suspicious over these delays. I better not hear any more excuses that create delays with visitations. I expect YOU to make the time so the parents get an increase in visitation time for November. Is that understood?" "Yes your honor" our case worker answered. "I will expect to see home visitations within the report too."

"Objection your honor" came the voice of the DCF lawyer. "We have a protocol and until an increase of public visitations is established within this court, we cannot allow home visits." "If I overrule your position on this matter, what is your response?" "I will have to object and bring the case to a higher court." "The proper answer is *I will have to object and bring the case to a higher court your honor!* Make sure you remember that from here on out counselor." "Yes your honor." "What is the position of my CASA volunteer on this matter?" Our volunteer spoke up. "I have seen absolutely no bad behavior on either parents' part that should delay reunification any further. I would imagine that allowing DCF to raise an objection to a higher court would complicate reunification even further. I think the easiest way around this is to just increase visitation in November and move on with the case." "What is the position of counsel for the respondents?" Both my lawyer and Satan's lawyer spoke up. "We agree your honor with CASA. DCF is just making excuses to delay the case. The simplest way to reunify the family is to increase visits for November so home visits and reunification will happen in December."

"I must object again your honor. I will agree to an increase of public visitation for November and IF that goes well, we may agree to home visits in December. That is as far as I can agree to. We don't know how the public visits will go and certainly have no idea how well they can establish their parenting abilities within the home. That will take much more time to evaluate than a month. I cannot agree to anything more than increasing public visitations at this time. Anything else is based on speculation. The parents have not been able to properly supervise a minor in their own home and that is well established as the issue." "Yes, yes counselor. We certainly know how you personally feel about this case, but I will remind you that YOU presented me this case purely based on Circumstantial evidence. I have seen absolutely NO further evidence supporting YOUR opinion. Therefore, I am going to inform you of the court's position on the matter. The public visitations will be increased in November and without any SERIOS evidence of parental neglect, the reunification process will begin in December. Is that clear enough for you counselor?" "Yes your honor." "Is everyone here in agreement

on how we will proceed with Mr. Stewart's first complaint?"

The words "Yes your honor" rang out in my listening device.

"Now, let's talk about Mr. Stewart's second complaint.

As his case worker, why would you even imply that his wife is on

drugs? There has been no mention of this issue to the court

and why is it coming up now?" "I was simply trying to talk to

him about why his wife wasn't interacting during visits. I

apologize for any misunderstanding your honor." "I thought we

all agreed that she suffers from post-partum depression. What

is being done about that?" The DCF lawyer butted in. "I must

object your honor. We all agreed that is the most likely cause.

We never agreed that there was not a possibility of drug or

alcohol use." The judge spoke to the volunteer. "What are your

observations so far?" "There is absolutely no evidence

indicating any drug or alcohol abuse by either parent your

honor." "Well, this looks like another unnecessary distraction

from the case and unless there is evidence, I don't want to hear another complaint from Mr. Stewart on the matter. I don't blame him one bit for being offended by the accusation. So, no more insults like that, Understood?" "Yes your honor" rang out across my speaker again.

The judge got pretty harsh with the group in his courtroom. "I am growing very tired with all these delay tactics I am seeing with this case. If I get any more SURPRISES I WILL end the case immediately and reunification will happen within an hour of my judgement. So, this is your last chance to add any new conditions to the case. What are they? You usually get court orders for psychological evaluations by now counselor. What are you waiting for?" "There is no need to establish that point so far your honor." "I don't see how that can be the truth unless you are up to something. You openly accuse Mr. Stewart of being dangerous and the only danger he has presented so far is to hold everyone accountable for breaking the law. Everyone seems to be in agreement on the limitations of Mrs. Stewart's parenting skills, but nothing is being established on how to help her with that. It is my opinion at this time that DCF is getting in the way of services for this family at this point in time. I will make it an official court opinion on the matter next month if this or any other issue creates any further delays, understood?" Most people present in that courtroom murmured "yes your honor."

The DCF lawyer complained again. "I cannot agree to how we proceed with psychologic evaluations based on speculation. It is not our position at this time that they are not required. Furthermore, I cannot agree that they won't need to become a requirement of conditions in the future." "Since you are tying my hands on this, what is CASA's view on the matter?" The volunteer spoke up. "I think it is a complete waste of time seeking psychological evaluations. There is no monkey business going on; speaking for the parents. I can't say that for other interested parties. Mr. Stewart has shown exceptional parenting skills in my presence and I want to see him given even more time. Mrs. Stewart is getting better with her skills. Both the DCF case worker and I have been able to get her more interactive with parenting. She informs me that her doctor is helping her with her depression and she has shared the documentation with me. More child interaction is needed so the transitional period can go smoother. If I see any more delays with this transition, I will have to bring my lawyer into this case and end this foolishness. We will switch sides where we stand; with the respondents and not on the side of DCF." The judge laughed and now I could see that I had a true ally.

The judge spoke to Satan's and my lawyers next. "Perhaps you could suggest your clients have evaluations done just in case DCF decides to pull that rabbit out of her hat next month." "We agree your honor." "It won't be entered into this month's conditions, but do you have any objections to this counselor?" The DCF lawyer spoke up in a very cheerful voice as if she had scored a win. "No objections your honor." I would have to act surprised when my lawyer brought the subject up. "Any other issues before we write this thing up?" "None your honor" everyone said. "Well, unfortunately I do have an issue involving the holidays coming up. The Stewarts missed out on Halloween because of some very unorthodox circumstances that I am not convinced were unplanned. Thanksgiving is up this month and the parents will not be punished on that holiday or I will end the case." The DCF lawyer got real flip over the subject. "The circumstances over Halloween could not be foreseen. The Stewarts will be allowed to have Thanksgiving dinner at a public restaurant, but that is all we will allow. If they can't do that, it's on the parents, not us --- YOUR HONOR."

"It has become very clear to me counselor that you have taken too much personal interest in this case. How many more holidays do you think I will allow you to rub in the parents' faces?" "DCF isn't using holidays as a punishment your honor." "I didn't tell you to speak. I am giving you something to think about. I am going to be real nice how I put a suggestion into your head this time, but not next month. I think you are overworked handling all the cases for your department and it has clouded your judgement on this particular case. Maybe I shouldn't see you handling this case any further. Now you may speak." "We just acquired a new attorney and he will not be able to take on a case load until December. I will have to be present in court for this case at the end of November and then I will make sure this case gets handed over to him your honor." "You better make sure it does. Now let's write this thing up."

I knew I had plenty of time to finish my sandwich out in my car. They probably would argue about the paperwork and when we would have to show back up for November. I shut off my listening device, put in in a paper bag and hid it in the trunk of my car. As I ate my sandwich, I thought about how I was going to remove my bug from the courtroom. That would be easy enough. I could see how this case was going. They just wanted to make excuses to delay getting my twins home, but why? We were doing everything by the book and I was doing everything within my power to help out Satan with any of her issues. Everyone involved with the case knew I was divorcing

Satan, but why didn't that issue come up? We were running out of time to get the kids home. July may be nine months away, but these idiots had every trick in the book to delay things and keep the kids in their custody so we would lose them. I had to step up my efforts to help out Satan over the long haul so we wouldn't get any more problems. I finished eating and locked up my car. I wasn't surprised to see that Satan was still alone with the outer chamber bailiff in the lobby. I was surprised to see the other bailiff come out within two minutes to motion for Satan and me to come into the courtroom.

Satan and I took our places next to our lawyers. Our volunteer was still standing with our case worker and her lawyer on the prosecuting side, but that would change next month if there were any more shenanigans. It would be six of us against those two. I was beginning to see how the unwritten and unspoken language worked in a courtroom. The tables were starting to turn in favor of this half-azzed father and I knew it. I just had to pretend I didn't know as much as I did.

Everything rested on me, and I knew it. I was the key to everything whether or not things fell apart. I couldn't let Satan fail. Nothing was said, no objections, no arguing over the next court date. They had already done all that. Everyone had their copies of our new monthly conditions in their hands. Our lawyers handed Satan and me our copies. The judge struck down his gavel right away. "Court adjourned" was all he said as he stood up and left the room. The bailiff shouted "All rise" even though we were all standing already. Once the judge left, I sat down on the front row bench to pretend I was looking over the new papers. I was able to easily remove the bug from the bottom of the bench without raising an eyebrow.

Everyone left the courtroom but me to give me my space to read the papers alone. Even the bailiff left me alone. As I sat there reading, I looked up at individuals lingering too long in the courtroom. The DCF Lawyer boogied out first and very fast. She already got a taste of my wrath and didn't want any more. My lawyer put her hand on my shoulder as she left.

"I'll meet you outside." Everyone saw the look on my face and left quickly. I was becoming a pretty good actor in a courtroom. I kept looking at the section about public visitations as I looked up with an angry face. They probably figured that I was upset about it, but they would have been wrong. I just needed them out of that room to pull the bug. The bailiff was the last one to leave before me. "Take your time Mr. Stewart. I can lock up after you are ready." The door shut behind the bailiff and I was alone. I pulled the bug and waited for a couple of minutes. Then I left so the bailiff could lock up. Satan and our two attorneys were the only ones left out in the lobby.

My lawyer spoke up first. I guess she figured it was her job to keep me calm. "I know you are disappointed, but you will get a lot more visit time. Try to be patient, you will be reunited soon. Your case worker assured me that she will call you this afternoon and get more visitations started right away." Satan's lawyer added her encouraging words. "If the two of you keep working together, this will happen. I assure you." Satan managed to get a weak smile on her face. "Try not to be angry!" I put a smirk on my face. "I'm not angry. What would give you that idea?" They all managed to smile back at me, but were not convinced that I wasn't angry. I guess I put on a better act than I expected. "Just because I put my foot down doesn't mean I'm angry. So, what's the plan and what surprises should we expect?" I had that psychological evaluation in mind, but couldn't tell them I knew. I needed them to bring it up. The three of them had already been talking about it and had to fill me in. At least our lawyers weren't being sneaky about it.

Satan's lawyer filled me in about being prepared with psychological evaluations for the end of November. "I have a copy of mine from military medical records. Will that work?" Her lawyer asked if she could see them and my lawyer nodded. I pulled them out and she read them as my attorney had already done as soon as I got them. "Any concerns? Will this work?" "I don't see anything in this to worry about. You will be fine with this." My lawyer agreed with her. "What about my wife? My insurance will pay for hers and she has a copy of the insurance card. Can she have it ready before we show back up in court?" "Yes, we have that handled and will give your attorney a copy of it within two weeks. Keep in mind, this is just in case it comes up next court date, we don't need to raise the issue unless DCF does." "I have no problem with that, but what about this drug accusation? Shouldn't we both be prepared for that? I just had a physical and made them test for drugs, I'm clean. It would go a long way in our favor if my wife is prepared like that too." "She just got her physical with a drug test too. We are ready." "Any other surprises?" "Nope. Just keep doing what's best in the interest of the family." My lawyer agreed.

"What about our next visitation. My wife and I agreed that we want family pictures taken. You think there will be any issue with giving the judge a copy of that? I bet it would go well for us if he can put a face to this case." Both attorneys got big smiles over their faces as if they were a bit happily surprised. It should have been very apparent that I was always thinking a step ahead of things. My attorney spoke sarcastically. "I don't see why he wouldn't be delighted with getting a picture!" "What about that DCF layer? You think she will complain about it?" "I don't think you need to worry about any more of her objections." Satan and her lawyer went their separate way from us. I had a couple of things I wanted to talk about to my lawyer in private. I really needed to know what was going on with my divorce.

"What are we doing about my divorce?" "You need to be patient and let me handle that. It's a timing thing. I'm worried that if you move too soon, it won't go well for you. Just keep jumping through your hoops for now." "Everyone knows about the divorce and I would imagine the judge does too." "He does, but it can't come up as an issue in court. I don't want you to even say a word in court about it." "That's fine, but if it is on my mind, I'll give you this look." I raised my eyebrows at her and she chuckled. "I'll nod yes if you can talk about it and nod no if you need to leave it alone. Remember, it's a timing thing."

"O.K. I follow you. Maybe we should practice some of our sign language so we know we have it down to a science." She laughed cheerfully. "No, I think we have it right."

"What about that shrink of ours that calls himself a marriage counselor. He's a total pain in the butt and isn't doing anything to deal with our real issues. I really don't care about her cheating as long as we eventually get a divorce. It's not my problem anymore. I just want to deal with how we will co-parent in the future and he is too busy playing the blaming game on me. I want a new counselor." "We can't rock the boat. Just hang in there until this case is over and you no longer have court orders to see him. Get rid of him then." "Fine, I'll deal with it until then, but I really think he needs to lose his license. He is useless as a marriage counselor." "It sure sounds like it, but you need to keep in mind that the chips are stacked against you more than your wife's. We can't rock the boat until it is time to rock the boat."

I got a devilish grin on my face that couldn't be hidden. "Do you think I rocked the boat too much with the department of defense?" She couldn't help but let a girlish laugh slip out. It was the first time she laughed near me that didn't seem staged or calculated. "Uh, yeah! Just a little bit!" "Am I in any trouble with the case over it?" She was still snickering. "No, not yet, but I wouldn't draw from that well too often if I was you." "I only show my teeth when I have to, I guarantee you that. I just wanted to make sure they knew I wasn't a chump." "Oh, I think you made it perfectly clear that you are no chump. But you showed a high level of intelligence to the judge without any question. Be careful how you use it." "I have no problem with that. He may be the king of his jungle, but I am a hyena. Lions know not to mess with hyenas and he should have me figured out by now. Everyone has a boss, including him. If I get played again, I will make him pay the legal consequences. He's the king of his jungle and he better act that way." My lawyer knew where I was going with this and knew I was justified. If I was ultimately responsible for my family, he was responsible for his

circus act.

Act 7: The Ring Leaders are freed!

Every circus act is a little bit different, but the clowns always try to play some kind of a joke on the ring leader or in this case, ring leaders. Clowns are always pulling stunts on the ring leader and he or she tries to shoo them away without success. It always gets a rise out of the audience, but this audience didn't find it the least bit funny. My twins were the ring leaders of this circus act, and this was no laughing matter. They already had missed out on trick or treating because I found out that the foster mother they were stuck with didn't believe in holidays because of some messed up religion she was mixed up with. Like a bunch of clowns, DCF kept coming back with some new antic that delayed reunification. They had made their punishment very clear to Satan and me and the point was well taken. Nobody would find this abuse funny anymore. It had become a damaging punishment to the twins being stuck in a foreign home away from their parents, not being allowed to celebrate holidays and being alienated from their real home. I saw a circus act once where the ring leaders noticed the jokes no longer were funny to the audience. The ring leader unlocked the tamed lion cage and sent it after the clowns. They didn't prank him anymore that night. What I did to our judge was justified. I unleashed the lion on the DCF clowns to make them behave. That's how a hyena works. This was all about my kids and they were powerless. Their hyena knew how to open up the lion's cage. What else was a half-azzed father to do?

We had a lot to do that month. I knew where my lawyer was going with that timing thing and went along with it. I had already gotten a taste of how stacked things were against fathers and knew without anyone telling me to make sure Satan had my full support. I would have to do everything within my power to not get blamed for any excuse of her failures after we got separated. One of the issues was about a car. The bankruptcy had long sense been over and Satan had been stuck without a vehicle. The money I had since saved from not having a truck payment or high insurance premium was enough to get her a cheap car to get her back on the road again. She was waiting alone next to my car talking on her phone. "The case worker is on the phone and we can do a visit on Monday from ten a.m. to two in the afternoon. Isn't that great!" It was nice to see a little enthusiasm over the twins for once. "Yeah, that's perfect. I usually get Monday and Wednesday off from work." I could hear the DCF case worker speaking loud over the phone. "Where should I meet the two of you at ten?" Satan looked at me and I responded. "See if you can call her right back after WE decide what we want to do." "Can I call you right back on that?" "Yes, that's fine." Satan hung up.

Satan was smiling at me and waiting for a suggestion to come out of my mouth. That was a first. "Why don't you set up an appointment for ten with that photography studio so we can get those pictures taken?" Satan called the place and made the appointment. "That won't take more than an hour. What else should we do?" "What do you want to do" I asked? "I don't know!" That girl could never make up her mind. It was getting a bit tiresome having to suggest things. "Why don't we keep this simple? I can pack a lunch in the cooler. We can go to the park and see if they are prepared for the cool weather. If not, we can go to the store and pick up the clothes needed. Let's see how well prepared they are all the time!" Satan giggled and dialed the phone again. She told the case worker the plan and hung up. "All set." It was rare that Satan and I were on the same page. "Thanks for not letting the cat out of the bag" I said to her. "What are you talking about?" "You didn't say anything about clothes shopping. That's a good thing. Let's see how irresponsible they are." Satan just smiled. She knew me well. They had set us up and now it was my turn.

As I drove off, I asked "did you eat yet? I did." "Not yet. I'll get something at work." "When you going in to work?" "Not until five." "It's not even three yet. I'll buy your lunch. What do you want?" She just shrugged her shoulders. "You want a burger?" She shrugged her shoulders again. "What are you in the mood for?" "An Italian would be nice." I was two blocks away from her favorite sub shop so I pulled in and handed her a ten spot. "Here, get what you want and get me a receipt please." She came back out with a paper bag with her food in one hand and a drink in the other. She hopped in to the passenger side, put her drink in the holder, dropped the change into the ashtray and handed over the receipt with one swift motion of her hand. Nine and change was a pretty expensive sandwich and drink. I stuffed the receipt in my pocket and continued driving as she ate. I learned about creating a paper trail the hard way. Wife or not, I was accounting for every dime I spent, especially what I had to spend on her.

When we got back in town, I pulled into my mechanic's parking lot. Satan had finished up her sub and threw her paper trash in the back seat. She gave me a puzzled look. "What?" You know Mike has a trash barrel here. Throw you trash in that!" "You stopped here just to make me throw away my trash?" "No, you need a car. Mike has one ready for you." "How am I supposed to pay for it?" "I've got that covered.

C'mon, let's see if the sticker is on it and ready to go." "What about insurance?" "I already called it in and it's all set with my policy." She just gave me that clueless look she always shot at me on a constant basis. She did actually reach back into the back seat and remove her trash. I did have to lock and shut her passenger door because she left it wide open as she went into the office of the garage. All the paperwork was all set with the car. I already had the title tucked away in my safety deposit box. I had picked up the registration the day before and Mike got the inspection sticker on the car. Satan was good to go. Mike handed her one key and me the other and Satan drove off and I didn't see her again that night. She got out at nine, way before I had to be to work that night, but I still didn't see her. I was on my last week of overnight training. I would be on the day shift next week.

It was Friday night and it was my second to last night shift. I liked my new boss and he was so understanding about my court problems. He was also sincere about my promotion.

If he wasn't, he would have buried me on the night shift so I couldn't advance my training on the day shift so I would eventually qualify for a department supervisor. Friday night came and went quickly at work so I went home; still no Satan. Now that she had her car, she was pulling her disappearing acts again. I showered and ate breakfast before I went to bed.

When I woke back up at four p.m., still no Satan. I chilled out and watched TV while eating some supper. When I had to leave for work, still no Satan; and everyone wondered why I insisted on a divorce. It was Saturday night, last evening shift. I was so grateful. Saturday night came and went quickly at work again. It was so easy to stay busy and make the time go by quick. I went home to find it still empty of Satan's presence. That made it easy for me to shower, eat and sleep without any of her distractions. Last night counted as my Sunday, so I wouldn't go back to work until Tuesday. That was like getting two days off in a row.

I woke up without an alarm clock at four p.m. My body had gotten use to the routine and would have to get in tune with the day shift quickly. I couldn't risk losing the twins again if anyone believed my sleep pattern was messed up. I ate some supper and watched a little TV alone until eight. Still no Satan, but it didn't matter. I went to bed to try and establish a sleeping pattern between eight p.m. and four a.m. I would be expected to be at work by five in the morning some days. I wanted to be ready for that change. It took some time before I dozed off on the couch, my established bedroom. I figured out that it was too quiet for me with the TV off, so I put it back on. I dozed off into a peaceful sleep until I felt a body slip under the covers next to me. I sat up wide awake on the couch to see Satan trying to be slick and sleep next to me. I mean mugged her. "Are you kidding me?" I shouted! Satan got the message and removed her naked body from the couch and scooped up her clothes from the floor next to it. She strolled up the stairs and into her own bedroom. It took me some time to fall back to sleep after seeing that horror show.

"Are you kidding me?" came the words out of my mouth again. It was Monday morning and we were supposed to be heading out soon to do the family pictures with the twins. Satan was dressed very casual in a ripped up pair of jeans and a t-shirt. "I don't have anything else unless you want me to wear my taco stand uniform." "What about that dress you always wear to church?" "What about after? I want to be comfortable at the park. It's a little cold for a dress!" "Bring the jeans with you. I'm sure they'll let you change in the bathroom." Satan went back upstairs to her room and changed. When she came back down, I had to remind her that it would be better if we showed up together in my car. She was a bit reluctant about it, but she angrily climbed into the passenger seat of my car. When we got there, it took a while before the DCF case worker showed up with the twins. Fortunately, the studio photographer reserved the whole hour for us. "Sorry I'm late. The foster mother was running late." The twins looked real nice in their new dresses and winter coats.

The twins ran right up to me and hugged my legs. I bent down to scoop them up and hold them. It felt good to hold my girls in my arms and have them hug me back. My situation had gotten very surreal and without the twins' physical presence, everything seemed like a bad nightmare. What was real and what wasn't. Crazy ideas swarmed my thoughts on a continuous basis. Was I really in trouble with the law? I was never in trouble a day of my life, well not like this. Was I stuck being married to Satan herself, forced by the law, or was it something I would wake up from and find a loving wife sleeping next to me? Was I really a parent or just a lonely bachelor with no family to speak of that missed out on that part of life? Things got really clouded in my mind until the moment my twins gave me hugs. They were my reality and always made those swarming thoughts go away. They were worth the hell I was being put in. I had nobody to talk to about how I truly felt about things. I was surrounded by enemies that would waste no time keeping my girls away from me forever for the smallest hint that I was not doing and thinking perfect. I had to hold it together.

I put them back down and reminded them to give mommy a hug too. They did and she still didn't hug them back. It was so sad to see her that way. Imagine that; me, actually having sympathy for Satan? What choice did I have? She was the mother of my kids and they needed her. No matter how lost her mind got with all this crap, she needed them too. I guess everyone reacts a little different to trauma. Her mind was blanking everything out. I understood where she was because we were in the same boat. We needed this problem to go away to move on. I was only one step away from having a mind drawing a blank just like her. I knew exactly how she felt and it sucked. We had to get these people out of our lives.

The picture taking went smoothly. They had pretty good gear, so we got to see the proofs on a computer screen. There was only two snap shots that didn't make Satan look like she was high on something. Satan liked a couple of them and I had to remind her that everyone was part of the picture, including her. The kids looked good in them, but when I discretely pointed out her mug shot, she agreed that it would be best to pick between the two I was recommending. My millennium baby was looking the wrong way for one of them. The choice was made and we looked like a happy family. How ridiculously ironic it is that a family picture can hide the true pain everyone is feeling at that moment.

Nobody can truly know what is going on in the minds of two year olds, well, almost three. I would have to rely on what they recollected about things when they got older. For the most part, it was all a blur and they admitted to me that they didn't know much about it other than what we told them. I always thought it was best to be honest with them. It was better to admit that I was just a half-azzed father that made mistakes than pretend I was perfect. I think it worked out better for them because they always moved on quickly from any of their mistakes or challenges. I was glad for them, but I was damaged for life. I didn't realize it at the time, but this ordeal would shape my life forever. Without it, my disability may have never surfaced. I was so glad the twins didn't remember much, just that fork that the foster father stabbed at their tiny hands to keep their elbows off the dinner table. The wonderful mind of a two year old can block out crap so much better than someone cruising on to fifty years old. By the time they were six, I never brought up the subject to them unless they asked. That rarely happened.

I didn't have to do hardly anything to mend a two year old's mind, but somebody needed a pull-up changed. The DCF caseworker handed me the diaper bag and I took the twins into the men's room with me. Satan was changing in the ladies' room. When I opened up the bag, there were plenty of spare clothes, but only two pull-ups and few wipes. I quickly took care of the twins and came back out with them and the bag. Satan was still changing. "I need to get more pull-ups and wipes on the way to the park. We can meet you there" I told the DCF case worker. "That's fine" she casually replied. I knew she wasn't that ignorant to show up unprepared for a longer visit than usual. She was obviously testing to see how ignorant I was. Fat chance of that happening. I never screwed that one up even before this circus began. Satan came out so we were able to leave and get the stuff for the twins. They were already happily playing in the park when we pulled up twenty minutes later. Our volunteer was chit-chatting with the DCF caseworker on a bench with the twins playing with some toys in front of them.

Satan plopped herself between the volunteer and case worker so they could gab away as I spread out a blanket, used wipes on the twins' hands and fed them a picnic lunch. It was a wonderful afternoon for me to spend with the twins. I didn't care that Satan, DCF and the volunteer sat there watching me. It was no different than the strangers coming and going in the park to me. I just had a great time of uninterrupted memories of being happy. I got to gently push them on the swings, we chased the few leaves that were still hanging on to the trees, I read to them on the blanket and played with them. This was the first time in a very long time that I actually felt like things were getting better. I got time with my twins the way I wanted; not in a cage, not at the bowling alley. It was my choice. I promised the twins that next fall, we would get to see more pretty leaves.

November came and went by so fast. Work was work, the marriage counselor was still a jerk, I was still getting hit on at the parenting meetings and Satan was her usual self. However, the extra time with the twins was great. I got the usual time with them at the bowling alley, but also got time in the park several times and we actually were allowed to take them for dinner in restaurants a few times. Yes, thanksgiving was a meal in a restaurant too. I wasn't use to that, but we made the best of it and invited Satan's folks and brother along. Of course they were there, not just for the bazar Thanksgiving meal, but bowling and play time in the park. We even started having them be present for each parent support group meetings. They got to play with the other kids during the meeting as I kept a watchful eye on them. At least the volunteer and DCF caseworker didn't embarrass us by being there for that. One or the other would meet us there afterwards. By the end of the month, we were allowed to take them with us in the car on Wednesdays. We'd pick them up at the DCF office just before bowling time and the DCF case worker would show up at the meeting to pick them back up. Everything was moving at a fast pace. It seemed at the time that the twins would be home for December.

We had only one rule during our time with the twins by the end of November; do not bring them to the home. That was an easy enough rule to follow. I knew how much that DCF case worker over-reacted the last time a rule was broken. Why would I want to be punished again? I was having too much fun with the twins. The case worker was given a lot of latitude with our case that month and it was even put in the paperwork that way. She began giving us unsupervised visitation time in the last week. It really seemed like she was sincere about my rights as a parent and wanted me to have equal time with the girls. I was wrong and was being set up like all fathers face. I was just a pawn to help them help Satan get custody of my children. She was being allowed unsupervised visitation time with the twins when I wasn't around. It wasn't fair. I asked for some one-on-one time too, but the DCF case worker refused.

I went straight to my lawyer with the problem. She listened to my complaint, was sympathetic, but not surprised. "If you want any chance at having any custody rights, you have to let this one go. You can't control everything and we need to know what she can do on her own. Let's see what she brings to the table. You have to trust me on this one." I reluctantly agreed with her. I was learning how to let things go and pick my battles. This was one that could not be won. They did have a point about the whole thing. What was Satan capable of doing on her own? I played it off and showed support to her on the issue and just asked how much fun she had those three times she got alone with them. I didn't get much of an answer from her, but I found out later. She was maneuvering things with all the medical, school and benefits for the children through her name. She couldn't get things done officially until the kids were back home with us, but she could block me from doing the same. The biggest part of her success was how well everyone knew about it but me. Keeping me in the dark was crucial to her tactics. I fell for it like most fathers do. We are nothing but pawns and have no rights as a parent no matter how the laws are sugar coated. Those words are put in the laws just to pretend they give fathers' equal parental rights. The way law makers go about pre-arranging things shows without any doubt that fathers are still just a backup plan.

I played my role well, right up to the court date, at way beyond it. I didn't get a clear picture of the whole thing until it was too late. I didn't really care then, and I don't care to this day. I got as much quality time with the twins as was physically possible, and that is all that mattered. I was there for them in a cage, I was there in the park and I was everywhere that I promised THEM that I would be. That's all that mattered. It didn't matter that it was the whole world against this half-azzed father, trying to end the time I got with my girls. They lost that battle because they had no grounds to stop me. I did everything including showing a cheerful attitude about Satan's free time alone with the girls. In my mind, there was no way they could keep the twins from coming home by Christmas. Boy, was I so wrong about that one.

We showed up for court as usual at the end of November, but things got a lot different for that little date. Everyone was there waiting ahead of time and DCF already had the December court proposal waiting for us to look at before we faced the judge. Our lawyers already had their copies and our DCF case worker handed us our two copies. Her lawyer just hung back to see how we would react. I went over it with Satan as everyone eagerly watched us work together. Fine, the usual conditions were there that were no surprise, but there were two things in there that needed attention. That DCF lawyer finally slipped in psychological evaluations to delay things further. Yes, we were being allowed home visits for December, but not reunification. Even Satan agreed with me that we needed to fix this.

"Why isn't there even any mention about reunification yet" I asked the DCF lawyer with a glaring look? She switched her mean tactics to acting like a civilized human being. With a smile, she just said "we need to take our time with a gradual reunification. These things take time so we can be sure that reunification is the proper thing to do." In her own slick way, she still threw that vail threat in my face. I let it go. Satan and I agreed to go along with it. "What about our evaluations? We both have them ready for you with current drug testing that are obviously clean." "I don't need drug testing that isn't a concern at this point in time and I can't even look at those psychological evaluations. They aren't ones conducted by approved facilities.

You'll have to do them again." "Our insurance already paid for this, and won't pay for another one. How do you expect me to pay for this?" "Our department will cover the costs." It seemed like a big waste of time and money to me, but Satan and I agreed. I was tired of all the delay tactics and would get to the bottom of it whether my lawyer liked it or not.

It was time to face the judge, but not in the courtroom. He was busy with another case and his boss pulled us into chambers. He was a lot nicer than the other judge. I guess they liked to play good cop-bad cop like everyone else. I was even being treated like a human being for once. It wasn't a formal court appearance. It was just a sit down in chambers, but I was the only one really talking to the judge. Even Satan kept her mouth shut. It became very apparent that I was the center of the whole case from the start. It was all about me and how I was going to react. I could play along with that. I needed answers to why the full court press over such a silly case. Neither one of us was doing anything to justify this crap; no drugs, no alcohol abuse, no child abuse and just one isolated incident involving a miscommunication between Satan and me. They had made their point to us to never let that happen again. Why did they need to delay reunification for no less than one more month? Community visits went from supervised to unsupervised visits within a month. What was so important about slowing things down now?

There wasn't even a bailiff in there with us, nothing formal and the judge even invited us to sit down. I sat right next to him with my lawyer next to me. Satan hung back with her lawyer facing the judge directly and the other three (DCF lawyer & caseworker and volunteer) sat across from me. "Mr. Stewart, how are you doing today?" the judge asked me in a cheerful voice. "Real good your honor. I have a family picture for you." I slipped a 5 by 8 across the table of the picture Satan and I took that month with the twins. He looked at it and tried to hand it back to me. "That's a very nice picture of your family." "I want you to keep it your honor if that is o.k."

Nobody dared object. "Thank you Mr. Stewart. That is very kind of you." He tucked it away to keep it. Everyone remained completely silent except the judge and me. "Do you have any questions for me Mr. Stewart?" I looked right at Satan and knew the burning question in her mind. It was the same as mine. "When are we going to be reunited?" "I don't know that Mr. Stewart" he said with sincerity. He really was powerless over this. He was just an observer like the rest of them except Satan and me. I looked at her and Satan had the same sad look on her face that spread over mine. I hung my head down in shame and couldn't look at him anymore. It would have just made me break out bawling.

I broke the silence in the room. "We've all agreed to the December orders, but I don't understand why we have to do another Psychologic evaluation. We already paid for these and they really should have been more honest about this a long time ago. It would have been done way before we were at the point of reuniting. We don't mind taking them again, DCF said the costs are covered, but this is just one more unnecessary delay." I was very teary eyed at this point. I couldn't hold it back any more. "I need to be with my family" was what slipped out of my mouth as I looked right at the judge. I took a quick glimpse at Satan and could see that she was crying quietly too. I kept my head down in shame but still caught the look on the judge's face from the corner of my eye. His demeanor changed from that consoling look to anger as he spoke very few words directed to the DCF lawyer. "This better not be about the money counselor!" he said to her with a very stern voice. I had just made it very clear that money wasn't an issue with re-taking a psyche evaluation. Now I knew exactly what DCF was up to and it was pure evil.

I knew what the judge was talking about. I had a business degree and it was ALL about the money with our case, nothing more. The judge just confirmed it and without breaking the law himself, threw a very large clue my way. I asked the question and he answered it very directly. I was a quick learner about reading faces, body language and the timing of words being spoken in a courtroom. Everyone present in that pow-wow was pretty convinced that I was a horrible father, but none of them could believe I was stupid after the last stunt I pulled with the department of defense. Everyone in that room but Satan knew the conversation that just happened. She was still clueless. Judging from the scared looks from two faces (DCF case worker and lawyer) from my cold stare and the worried looks on the volunteer and other two lawyers' faces, they all knew I knew what the judge just told me. He just handed me all the power to end things quickly and they all knew it.

I looked at the judge again as I wiped my tears. "Thank you for spending your time to help us out your honor. Do we have anything else we need to do today?" "Not unless you think so." "No I'm o.k. with the orders your honor." "Fine, we are all set until January. We won't meet back until after the holidays. Did you have a nice Thanksgiving Mr. Stewart?" "It was a bit strange eating Thanksgiving dinner at a restaurant, but it was nice." The judge obviously had a plan with the way the conversation was going. He looked right at the case worker. "Holidays are a time for family tradition. I noticed that Christmas and a birthday will happen before we meet again. Kids look forward to waiting for Santa in their own beds at home." I knew what the judge was up to. The DCF case worker was being told to get the twins home for Christmas Eve and New Year's Eve by the Judge. She was smart enough to cover her own butt. "We strive to get children home for the holidays as long as there is no danger and unforeseen circumstances don't come up." "Let's hope they don't" he told her back. That was the end of that court hearing. I never realized that it could become a casual meeting as long as everyone was behaving themselves.

There was nothing casual with what I was up to next. I was in no way going to behave myself either. I knew now, without any doubt, that my family had got caught in the system all over a very dirty thing called money. DCF has a very bad reputation to start with. Children slip through the cracks because of a grossly understaffed system and wind up hurt or dead. People remember those stories when they hit the media. We don't hear about any success stories because of several reasons. Mostly, child protection laws keep the information confidential for good reason, protect the innocent. But there really aren't any success stories here. It's just an attempt to keep a bad situation from going worse. There are no happy ending stories in this world and it would seem that DCF needs to fool itself into believing they have some success stories. The only way to do that is numbers. They need to justify their existence and the only way to do that is to fudge the numbers a bit. That's where my family came in.

You already get a pretty good picture that DCF really went overboard with our case. Yes, we as parents were ultimately responsible for the safety and wellbeing of the twins. Even Satan understood that concept within a month of losing the right to be close enough to even see our children. At this point, even the judge was not subtle about expressing that point. For the agency to want to risk being in contempt of court, there had to be a bigger reason behind the surface of our case to motivate them to incarcerate the twins further. When the judge said "this better not be about the money," I knew that was exactly what it was all about. I was still pretty naïve about how things ran in the court system, but I was learning quick. I didn't have a law degree, but I did have a business degree. The judge was speaking my language. Follow the trail of money; simple enough. It was a state agency; state agencies get federal funding and now I had something to work with. Greed was the motive to insist on treating Satan and me like a bunch of criminals that needed to be tortured even further. It was unnecessary and a waste of tax dollars to punish us any further. I had the motive and found the weakness in their levels and levels of laws that protected the agency from their crimes.

If it was just a simple matter of a band of bad case workers taking out their personal vendettas on Satan and me just because they could, our case would have ended months ago. The problem went much further up the chain of command than that and the true criminals that dragged this case out over three calendar years were the money handlers. Lawyers and executives control the pace of a case within the state. The longer they drag things out, the more federal money they get. If you think they need to provide services for three years to receive federal funding for three years, you are wrong. All they have to do is keep a case open for one day past the New Year and they rake in federal cash to pay for a whole year of services for that certain case. They don't even have to provide a home, or any other financial resource for the child in question, just keep the case open and show up in court. Each child is a number to them, a number to bring in more cash. The more numbers they can create, the more money they rake in. How sad is that, to use children like that and the taxpayers.

I've been told so many times "so what, you got caught up in something bad, forget about it and move on!" I can't forget about it because, well, you created me. I was a throw away child and had no options. I volunteered at the age of seventeen to serve my country because that is the best option for throw away pieces of trash like me. I figured at the time that at least I could do something of value there, and I was valued there for four years. Part of the problem for you is that we swear an oath, not just for four years, but for the rest of our lives. Veterans, whether they get paid to do so or not, are the nation's protectors for life because we promised to do so. I made that promise and will live up to it until the day that I die. When 911 hit, did I run off to fight on the front line with my brothers and sisters? No, I couldn't abandon my children and my true brothers and sisters wouldn't expect that of me. Instead, I stayed home to take care of my children and used my spare time to locate terrorist message boards for the feds. Did I get paid or even thanked for my help with these foreign enemies? No, I did it just because I promised you I would do so.

Protect against foreign enemies is only half of my promise to you. I also made a promise to you to provide protection from domestic enemies. This is far more complicated since we are talking about DCF. They are your enemy, not because they use unorthodox methods to make sure a child is safe first, then find out how bad things really are back at home. They are your domestic enemy because they misuse your hard earned tax dollar to create more revenue with cases like mine. If you decide that there are too few casualties like me to give a hoot, then so be it, but it is my responsibility to let you know what's going on here. Perhaps if DCF starts telling you the truth that there are no success stories here, if they let you see the true numbers and not some doctored up spread sheet to make it look good, then maybe the next veteran like me won't become a casualty.

There is no service connected disability with what happened to me. That is all on you. DCF opened up Pandora's Box for me. They saw my psychological profile and it scared them for the wrong reasons. Yes it scared them that I have the most dangerous predator profile known to man, but they forgot to read the fine print. The danger becomes internalized and not externalized. I was no threat to the twins, Satan or any person working the case, only a danger to myself. That's what the army knew about me since I was sixteen years old. Why do you think they recruited me for a high security job? If I was ever captured as a POW, I had to off myself to protect millions of people. Only rare cases like me have the profile to train and complete a mission like that. I know my value is far less than yours, especially if being dead protects you. Not many of us are comfortable with that fact. Don't you think I know that if I have become the enemy, I am a danger to you, my kids, don't you think I would gladly put a bullet in my head and end the problem? DCF was the bullet to pierce through my brains, and I thank them for it, very much.

PTSD is like an alarm clock that goes off in a veteran's head. Wake up! It's time to die! Now, the first time it goes off, many of us just hit the snooze button and put our suicide back to sleep. We don't even know that's what is happening, but there it is. My alarm clock hadn't quite gone off yet for the first time, I'll tell you about it later, but DCF was the trigger. It wasn't my military experience. It wasn't some trauma from my childhood. It was them. They just had to insist on reminding me how little I really mattered even to my kids. I was expendable and they wanted me to know it beyond any shadow of a doubt. They did a good job with that, dragging things out for another year and a half or so. They spent little to no money over that time reminding me that I was a half-azzed father. I had to get my twins home and do everything within my power to do so. The judge gave me a clue to the answer. DCF was misusing federal funding to harass me, and I needed to find a loophole.

I knew they were misusing federal funding, but I didn't know what to call the crime. It took some digging, research and a little dumb luck. I was listening to the news when I heard the words "misappropriation of federal funding" on the TV. The crime did have a name and a punishment. Now I knew how to dig into the laws since I had a name for the crime. I found the punishment a state faces if the federal government finds it guilty of the crime. I found who to report the crime to. I had a glimmer of hope. Half-azzed fathers do have a way to fight back. If I filed a complaint to the US treasury department for suspicion of the state of New Hampshire misappropriating federal funding, I had a chance to get the kids home in a hurry. No bean counter up at the state capital would suggest DCF keep the twins in custody if 104 million dollars would be lost in federal aid. I just had to tell them my side of the story and how inappropriate it was to keep my kids in custody any longer. That would trigger a state wide audit and if it was found to be true, the state of New Hampshire would be sanctioned from receiving federal aid for no less than two years. At the time, no less than 104 million dollars.

DCF put a bullet in my head and I put one back in theirs'. I made a complaint, but had to be patient and wait. I couldn't send it out until after the New Year, not until they started the next physical period. I had it prepared, but made sure the certified letter got mailed out during the busy holiday season so it would not get to the US treasury department in time to save DCF's butt. I wasn't the only one busy with an agenda during that December. The twins' foster mother knew the routine and would lose them soon. She wasn't all about the money. She was a soldier for her god. Her god hated holidays and she was going to do everything in her power to keep the twins from being home for Christmas. She knew from the fast pace of our case that the twins wouldn't be with her for long, but she didn't care. She got them in her most important month of December to fight her god's war against Christmas. She had her loophole. The judge didn't put it in writing to make sure the twins were home for Christmas to spend time with Satan and me.

Home visits started immediately after that November court date. It started out with simple drop ins with the DCF case worker. Everything was cool, so unsupervised drop-ins happened right after. They only lasted for a few hours, but it gave the case worker enough evidence that we were ready to have them come home over night. The most important clue was the twins. They didn't freak out like I would imagine abused kids react to when they have to show up in abusive parents' home. No, the twins went right into play mode the moment they hit the door just as if nothing ever happened. It made me very happy to see them happy. Nothing else mattered, not even the fact that I had found it fishy that Satan was given time alone with the twins but I wasn't yet. Having them home made it possible for that. I would deal with divorce problems later. Right now I had a holiday to prepare for.

The Christmas tree and decorations went up. Gifts were stuffed under the tree. Most of them for the twins, but some for Satan and her family. They were always a big part of our lives no matter what was going on between Satan and me. The twins were fully involved with it all, putting up the tree and decorations, wrapping presents and seeing family come and go to drop off presents. Satan's whole family set aside their Christmas day to be there with the twins. It was a happy time for all of us, preparing for the home coming of the twins. We knew it would only be for a sleep over for two nights, but it didn't matter. Even our DCF case worker was excited about it. The girl actually had a heart. The whole month went by, right up to December 24th without a hiccup. We thought our DCF had the power to make it happen, but apparently not all the power. No one ever really knew for sure if DCF just set us up for disappointment. Was it an act or did the excuse with the foster mother hold any truth. Did she really have the power to just say no to letting the twins come home for Christmas? I suppose only her god truly knows.

It happened with just a phone call from the DCF case worker. She left a message that the foster mother couldn't deliver the twins for those days and we would have to wait until

New Year's Eve day for DCF to drop off the twins. The whole

family was crushed. We had all pitched in to make Christmas a

big event for the twins, but we made the best of the situation.

Look on the bright side! New Years was right around the corner

and we just had to wait a little while longer. It was a quadruple

celebration! It was a delayed Christmas, New Years, and

birthday party for the twins and kind of a home coming for

them too. Since nobody but me flipped out about it, we got our

reward. They knew I would retaliate for that one, but how?

They'd find out soon enough when that letter got to the US

treasury department. Merry Christmas and Happy New Year to

myself! All my revenge wrapped up in one pretty little package.

We never found out for sure how my little letter hit the fan, but

it did. We didn't have the need to know, but somebody did.

Pages and pages of my little letter must have scattered

everywhere when it hit the fan. How do I know? Just from the

look on everyone's face when they looked at me for the

remainder of time with the case. Even my lawyer became

especially cautious with what she said to me. It went beyond

DCF, our lawyers and judges with that look they gave me and

their behavior. Judges talk and after I finally got my divorce and

certification to be a surrogate parent, every judge greeted me

warmly and made sure they knew they knew about me. The

second I used the word "appropriation" in their courtroom, they

got scared. They knew I was angry. It always worked because I

never cried wolf.   It worked on that sad

December of 2002. Wouldn't you know? The twins were

permanently home with court orders by an emergency court

appearance that first week in January. I wonder why they did

that. We already had a date set for the end of January. Nobody

knows for sure, but my money says the US treasury department

had something to say about it. The twins were home! The ring

leaders of my circus were free at last! What would the ring

leaders say on the microphone to the circus audience now that

they were freed from a circus clown stunt? Would they say to

you, "Welcome to my circus from hell?"

Act 8: Now enters the Strong Man

Many circuses bring out a strong man to show off his ability to do marvelous feats of strength. You would think that the ring leaders would bring him out, but not in my circus. Satan brought our strong man into the script. It was inevitable that she would need a new man in her life, she couldn't do without one. I knew it would happen and had no problem with her moving on. If she could find one that treated my twins with respect, I was all for it. If he had the ability to work with me with our untraditional family arrangement, I could do it. If he had the strength to pull Satan out of that dangerous sexual activity she was caught in, he was the right strong man. She found one just like that, a man that valued the same three rules I had with his involvement with my kids. I would eventually figure out he was the perfect step dad to make this work over the long haul. Unfortunately, it was the way Satan introduced him to me that spun things out of control.

I guess somewhere in that mind of Satan's, she felt the need of protection from me. She hooked up with an ex-gang banger and made sure I knew it. I was even introduced to his friends. I knew it was a setup from the start when everyone was especially friendly to me and Satan's man had three friends giving me an interrogation. Even thugs have respect for a father that only cares about his kids. I didn't know it for sure at the time, but it was worth the gamble. Gang bangers don't give a father a beat down just because mommy don't like her baby daddy. I wouldn't get confirmation of my suspicions about that night until years later, but Satan's plans to rough me up a bit backfired on her. Yeah, her new man was a bit rough around the edges, he liked to punch the mailbox or break a window if I came by for the twins, but that didn't last long. We both figured out quickly that we had a lot more in common than not. I'll get to that part soon enough, but I need to backpedal a bit.

I left you behind on a different scene of my circus. We still needed to get the DCF circus clowns out of our lives, I still needed my divorce and I only knew there was some man in Satan's life. I hadn't met him just yet, but when I did meet him it was who he was introduced as that set me off. I don't know what demons Satan is stuck with, but for some crazy reason, she said he was her cousin. I don't know if it was out of fear that I would be upset over her having a boyfriend or if she was just insane. What on earth did she think would happen the moment I found out she was sleeping with her cousin? Of course I would flip out! What father wouldn't be creeped out over the mother of his children having sex with her cousin while the kids were stuck living with her? I told you I owned the circus from hell! Come to find out, he wasn't even her cousin! Her uncle married her boyfriend's mother and he wasn't blood. They didn't even know each other growing up! Whether she did it on purpose or not, she was the one who pulled the trigger on the gun that DCF put the bullet into.

Yeah, that's right, the gun, the bullet, the trigger and the alarm clock; all put together nicely to shoot me in the head.

DCF provided the trauma to create my PTSD, the bullet. Their relentless harassment over and over put the bullet in the chamber of the gun and cocked back the handle. The moment I found out that Satan was sleeping with her strong man was the exact moment that alarm clock went off. Would I be able to hit the snooze button to stop the bullet from piercing my brain? For the moment, yes I did, but there was far more strange circumstances that led up to that momentous occasion. Satan and I still had to get rid of DCF for good. That took us another whole year, just after the new year of 2004. Amazing how DCF can squeeze another whole year's worth of cash out of the federal piggy bank over something as trivial as our case. The circumstances over that year were just too strange to believe actually happened.

Satan was well prepared by her attorney and DCF to manipulate paperwork quickly for the twins in order to block me from my custody. The second the judge signed off to release custody to both of us under the supervision of DCF, she went to work. I didn't understand how that works at the time,

but my lawyer sure did. She really should have given me a

heads up to make sure I didn't allow Satan to create a paper

trail that showed her doing all the work. She got day care for

the twins set up right away at a reduced cost. That was great!

Where was this information before they kidnapped the twins. I

was happy to drop them off and pick them back up every day.

Unfortunately for me, Satan signed all the paperwork in her

name and only listed me as an alternate pickup for the kids. No

mention that I was just as involved with everything here. All the

paperwork testing the twins for special needs in the school was

in her name. I was the one that brought them to the school and

sat down to review the results. She got all the credit for that.

She made sure that all medical records at the twin's hospital

listed her as soul custodian and I was just an alternate. She

even got supplemental insurance for the twins through the

state. It didn't matter that I was the one that physically got

them to and from doctor appointment on time. She made sure

it looked like she was doing everything on paper. I would figure this one out too late and after the fact. One very important trip to the emergency room with my millennium baby is proof of the truth.

My Millennium baby was running a very high temperature one day when Satan and I were still stuck living together. I came home from work and Satan was in a very big hurry to duck out. "Just give her aspirin to kill the fever" Satan said as she rushed out. Aspirin my foot! Those were my thoughts as I gathered the twins' things, watching Satan drive off and got ready to do the right thing. I took them both to the emergency room. All I had in mind was what my mom use to say before she died. "Children get high temperatures all the time, but aspirin only masks the symptom. A high temperature means the body is fighting something. If a child's temperature breaks 100, get the doctor involved." That was exactly what I was doing. My Millennium baby's temperature was almost 102 and that wasn't even questionable to me. Getting her to her doctor was exactly what I was going to do. It was too late to take her to the pediatrician office, so off to the emergency room I went.

My double miracle and I sat in the waiting room all night alone. She didn't complain and just sat next to me with her head on my chest as I read to her until she fell asleep. I didn't sleep a wink. I text Satan several times without getting a response. It was strange that we weren't allowed to stay in my Millennium baby's room at first. They just kept telling me that she had to be ran in and out of the room several times for different tests and we would be disruptive. "I'm her father" I protested over and over without any success. For some reason they didn't want me in there. If this was just a simple fever, we'd have been sent home within an hour or two. Something was going on more than that. I knew my daughter's whole medical network had all the confidential information about our case. A cop showed up in the lobby and briefly talked to the doctor on call and left. If it had anything to do with us, they found nothing as usual. I asked the doctor what was going on and he gave the same explanations and that I would know when he knew. I was getting tired of this foolishness. I had the pediatrician's emergency paging number and gave that a shot. She showed up within the hour. Much better results from her than that first pediatrician Satan and I had to fire.

I knew her from all the checkups I took the twins too and she recognized me right away. I explained what happened and why I brought her in. I told her what was going on with me and how the hospital was keeping me in the dark and wouldn't even let me sit with her in the room. "I'll take care of that. You just keep trying to get your wife and get her here too." So that's what I did as my double miracle baby continued to rest her head on me peacefully. It didn't take my daughters' pediatrician long to get results. She came right back out within two minutes and instructed the desk to make sure I was allowed in, and to let Satan in too the minute she showed up. She motioned for me to follow her into an intensive care unit where

my Millennium baby was wide awake and sitting up. The
pediatrician wanted to talk to me in private.

"I'm sorry about the delay with letting you in her room.
It was a good thing you didn't waste any time getting her here.
I know you must be annoyed about being kept out of the room
so long, but look on the bright side. It is dumb luck that the
doctor on call is our new intern specialist that detected what is
happening with your daughter. He didn't want to scare you
unless he was sure, and he felt it was best the information came
from me. He was trying to get ahold of me too. I was out of
town when we spoke and it took me a couple of hours to get
here. I rushed right over because this is very important."
"Thank you for taking time out of your personal life to help us,
but what is going on?" "Have you reached your wife? I really
need to talk to her too since she is the primary custodian and
you are only the alternate." What a fine time to find out that
Satan was sneaking behind my back to officially steal my
children from me. "No we are joint custodians. We aren't

divorced yet and she will not take my custody from me." "Oh, I see, but we do need to get her here right away. This is a true emergency." "I told her that, maybe if you call her, she will answer." The pediatrician called Satan's phone from her cell phone and just left a message. She also sent a text.

I spoke up as soon as she finish sending the text. "I have paperwork proving I have parental rights to make these decisions alone if you need me to show you!" "No, my medical decision kind of trumps any parental decision anyways. I need to act fast. Please sign this consent form so we can run the biopsy right away. It's a very simple procedure and we can move her upstairs to a private room where you can wait for her." I knew they suspected something and signed the paper right away. I also knew they would kick me out the second she needed to be prepped for surgery. "Can you give me a copy of this paper I just signed?" "I'll have the desk make you a copy right away. Please say goodnight to your daughter and wait for me out in the waiting room. I need to scrub down and suit up to assist the surgeon. Don't worry, the biopsy is a needle incision; just to get a sample of her liver. When it is done, you will be sent up to her private room." "So you think she has liver disease?" "Only the biopsy can tell for sure, but yes, the symptoms are there. This is very early detection and if she does have Pediatric Liver Disease, this could be a highly successful fix." "O.K. Let's do this." I went out into the waiting room again with my double miracle baby.

The desk nurse wasted no time handing me a copy of my signed papers. It had the date and time right on it. I finally was building a paper trail of my own that would eventually battle Satan and win my parental rights that really shouldn't have been in question. Fathers should be with their kids and mothers too, that's how I looked at it. That's not how courts looked at it, but I really didn't think about it at this point in time. All I wanted to do was take care of my babies. That's all that mattered. Getting paperwork was an automatic reflex, that's all. Where in the world was Satan! I took the girls to the emergency room at nine p.m. and it was already three in the morning and still no Satan. Within an hour of sitting out in the waiting room in the ER, the pediatrician came out to greet me. "Your daughter is fine and the biopsy went well. She is in recovery and will be moved up to her room on the third floor. You can wait for her there if you like. Any sign of her mother?" "Not yet. How soon will we know the lab results?" "It's a Wednesday, so the results will be back sometime today. We are sending the results down to specialists in Boston just to be sure." "What about organ donation? I know there must be some kind of test you need to run for that! If she needs it and I am a match, I don't want to waste any time." "Let's wait for the results first. We do need to involve your wife with this."

My double miracle baby and I went up into her room to wait for my Millennium baby. She was wheeled in before five a.m. She was still groggy and when she kind of saw my smiling face and felt my hand touch hers, she went right back to sleep. Time crept by and still no Satan. My double miracle baby curled up her tiny little body on a chair and was fast asleep. I placed a pillow under her head and blanket over her body and then sat in my chair next to my Millennium baby so I could hold her hand. Both twins stayed sleeping, but I didn't get a wink. It was my night off from work and I wouldn't have to go back until overnight tonight. Yeah, I had finished my training and got stuck with the new store that had my old manager. He hid me back on overnights to keep me out of sight and out of mind. It would only be a matter of time before time ran out on my training and I would be demoted again for not completing it. He was making sure I failed. An attendant was kind enough to bring me a coffee and a couple pieces of toast. Satan finally ambled in past nine a.m.

"Who's this?" I asked as she entered the room with some stranger. "He's my cousin" she simply replied. It was Satan's strong man and it was the first time I ever saw him. The dude gave her a funny look and then reluctantly shook my hand. He had a very strong grip, but released it fast because he was very uncomfortable. Satan could have erased any drama before it began if she would have either introduced the man as her boyfriend or just kept him the hell out of there. It wasn't the time or place for any of that. He even knew it. "I'm going to leave so the two of you can be alone" he said and then left. He heard it with his own ears what she said to me. Down the road, it was the strong man that had to explain things to me when it wasn't so awkward. When he figured out that I was no threat to his life with Satan, we were able to talk like men. "I really don't know what possessed her to tell you I am her cousin" were the words he opened up with. We had a lot of fun poking fun of her creepy incestuous comment for many years after that. She could be really stupid some times and deserved to be reminded from the two of us that her comment was way out of line.

We waited and waited together. The pediatrician came in immediately the moment she found out Satan had arrived. She was brought up to speed. We both agreed that we both wanted to be tested for being an organ donor. We still needed

to wait for the results to come back from Boston. It's amazing

how two bitter enemies can work together when there is a

common foe. We both loved our daughter dearly and it didn't

matter how she would be healed, that's all either of us wanted

to happen. Noon time came and went. Finally, about two in

the afternoon, the pediatrician came in with the intern. The

results were positive and we would need to be tested for organ

donation. The intern spoke up. "We caught this very early and

the chances of success are overwhelmingly high. By the time

she is fully grown, the scar will be as small as a pin prick and she

probably won't even remember all this. We will take her down

to Boston to have the best surgeons in the area do the

procedure. We can assist as long as you allow us."

We both agreed to that. "You obviously will have a

great future as a surgeon yourself and I think you deserve to be

there since you are the one that figured this out so fast. Thank

you" I said. "We aren't out of the woods yet and we need your bloodwork right away to see how fast we can begin and you are most welcome" he responded. Satan and I went down to the lab to get bloodwork done and have it shipped out ASAP. We wouldn't hear about the results until tomorrow. I really didn't want to go anywhere. I just wanted to stay there holding my Millennium baby's hand until she was all better. Reality was reality and by supper time, Satan had to say something. "We can't afford to have you stay out of work. We aren't going to find out anything until tomorrow, so go to work. I'll be here all night." That was the first time I ever saw her act like a mother, so I didn't argue. "I'll get a little nap before work. I'll let them know what's going on just in case I need to take some leave. I do have those benefits since I've worked there for so long. I'm coming right back after work." "Do what you have to do" Satan said smugly.

I went to work and my store manager finally had the excuse he needed to demote me. I let him know what was going with a phone call and he agreed to have me still run the overnight shift. I had to break down the load for my crew and it was an especially large one. The warehouse forgot to label the pallets and I was too consumed with grief to notice that we had three extra ones. He was breaking me down by keeping me tired, working overnights and this was a breaking point. When the next morning came, he didn't let me leave. A call came in from another store indicating that the other store with a drop off after us was missing three pallets. He made me hunt through everything and find all the missing cases. I was stuck there for over twelve hours. We knew the cases had already been stocked on our shelves and there was a simple procedure; transfer the cases from that store to ours with the computer. However, my store manager finally had an excuse to demote me. He brought in loss prevention to examine the evidence.

What was a simple mistake done under duress could have been overlooked, but he wanted to turn it into a theft case and have me fired. Fortunately for me, loss prevention was there and it was labeled as a mistake, not theft. I had a copy of their report which they gave to me in the presence of the store manager behind closed doors in his office. He showed me no mercy. He gave me no choice but two. I am calling this incompetence and that you do not qualify as a manager. He didn't care about my extenuating circumstances and used it to demote me. "You can either take a demotion with pay cut or have a full time job overnights, or you can be fired." I had no choice but take the demotion. He had my pay-cut scale already written in the paperwork and I had to sign it, or find a new job. I needed my health insurance for the family. I signed it and was finally allowed to leave. He couldn't take away any of my benefits as long as I kept working. I was ashamed, but showed it to Satan back in my Millennium baby's hospital room. She was just as pissed about it as I was and I won't repeat the words she called him. She didn't give a hoot about me, but certainly cared about the money I was making. The more I made, the more she could keep in child support.

Our daughters' pediatrician was already in the room when I told Satan the news. "I'm sorry this happened to you. Under different circumstances, a lawyer could have fought this for you, but you have a more important decision to make. You did keep your medical benefits, and that is greatly needed right now. Your wife is not a candidate for donation for your daughter, but you are. It's a good match to give a 90% chance of long term success. Your wife's results give less than 50% chance." There was no argument here. I would have to give up a piece of my liver to cure my daughter. As if I would say no! Satan spoke up. "There is another problem. There is a delay of a month before the extra health insurance will cover costs that your insurance won't. They are using that one day transfer delay between the state and me to deny coverages for the whole month." I looked at the pediatrician and the intern surgeon (who slipped in the room shortly after me). "Can we delay this a month?" He answered me back. "I would not recommend it." I looked at Satan. "How much do we have to come up with?" "We need fifteen hundred dollars." "I don't have that. I'll either have to put a loan on my car or sell it."

The pediatrician butted in. "You can worry about that later. I have the paperwork ready for you to sign. We can fax copies over to your work. Do you have any leave time available? My paperwork will at the very least give you emergency parental leave so you won't get fired." "I have long term and short term disability insurance. I know it will cover this. I have read the fine print" I said as I signed the papers. "Perfect! We will get this straight to your work. We will start transporting you with your daughter immediately to Boston. I will give directions to your wife. She can drive down there." That was a switch. Usually Satan got the red carpet treatment, but I suddenly became a little more important than her under the circumstances. I called my human resources agent at work on my cell phone on the way down to Boston. Ambulance crews don't usually allow that, but when I explained the problem, they understood. Neither of us was on any machines that could be disrupted by a phone call anyways. My HR agent hated what my boss was doing to me because I was a very hard worker. She had a few tricks up her own sleeve that he had no power over. She had the fax and found a loophole that gave me my short-term benefits for a whole month and assured me they would kick in today without delay. My boss was stuck dealing with my responsibilities for no less than a month and I would get paid two thirds of my pay without working.

My Millennium baby got a kick out of taking an ambulance ride with her dad. It wasn't a dire emergency that required the sirens, but the lights did get put on to warn any idiot drivers to be cautious because there were patients inside. I would have had as much fun on that ride as she did, but I knew there was serious business behind that ride. I didn't care how "simple of a procedure" everyone kept telling me it was. I had already been to that circus with Satan and almost lost three people in my life over a "simple procedure." I was worried, but had to keep it to myself and make sure my Millennium baby stayed cheerful." I got an idea on how I could force my boss to keep me on the day shift. I called my primary physician and told him what was going on and included the fact that working overnights was making it impossible for me to function, even without this surgery. "Just get yourself through this, and when you get back home, make an appointment. I will give you medical paperwork so you are permanently disabled from working overnights. You won't be going back to work for at least a month as far as I'm concerned. Just concentrate on getting well."

I didn't know why he was worried about me getting well until after the surgery. Boy was I sore and stiff as a board for a long time. I was kept under observation for three days down in Boston. My Millennium baby stayed longer. Our DCF case worker didn't make the trip, but out volunteer went out of her way to come down to see my Millennium baby; and I was shocked! She even spent a lot of time visiting me too! She actually cared what happened to me. I guess she figured that even a half-azzed dad needed to stay alive and be there for a child that is growing up. She even slipped in the word "hero" with our conversation. Hero my butt. That's just what half-azzed fathers do for their kids. It was just a piece of my liver, and I would give more if I had to. Both of my twins already owned my whole heart. I loved them more than anything else. If I literally had to give it up to save either one of them, I would have made it happen. My death for their life; it was more than a fair trade. I was no hero and I wanted to keep it that way. This little incident liver needed to be forgotten, and I knew Satan would make sure that happened. My Millennium baby wouldn't remember a thing about it and as she grew older, than pin prick of a scar on her body was only seen by people who knew what really went down.

Our volunteer spent a brief visit with my Millennium baby, but spent a couple hours with me. We talked about many things, especially how happy I was that the surgery was a complete success. The results would prove to be a success over the years too. Mission accomplished. I had to explain the financial problem that came out of the surgery. Fifteen hundred bucks was a lot of money for me, and the volunteer

knew it. Nobody had ever explained about debt forgiveness

from a hospital until that day when my volunteer told me about

it. A piece of paper could be filled out at the hospital and they

had the power to forgive the whole thing if our finances were

too small. She put Satan on that job, but showed me more

interesting information that was kept from me. She handed me

a sheet of paper that showed nearly two dozen area agencies

that could help me with so many resources. "Here is a copy of

the resources available to you that DCF should have given you a

long time ago." She circled one of them with a pen. "When you

get back in town, call me. I will go with you to this one and see

if they will help you out with this co-pay."

"What about the VFW? You are a veteran. Will they

help out?" She asked. "I'm not a member since I wasn't a

formal combat veteran. I don't know if they will help out." "Ask

them anyways. All they can do is say no." She stayed with me

beyond the time we spent talking about business. She knew all about my volunteer work with the schools and was encouraging me to become a surrogate parent for children without parents as soon as the time was right. "You are a good man Mr. Stewart. I really hope everything that has happened with the courts won't make you forget that." I really had forgotten that there was an ounce of good left in me because of all that court crap. I knew she meant well, but it was too late for me to believe a word she said. I was a half-azzed father and that was all I knew. I was also a veteran and had a mission, which was all I could stay focused on. My mission was to take care of my kids, no matter what the cost. The volunteer was the only visitor I got in Boston; not even my own family visited. Satan spent time with our Millennium baby, but not me. She took it on the hospital staff's word that I was fine.

I did run into Satan's strong man out in the hall as I took my walks to show the doctors that I was physically fit to go back home by the third day. I looked like a tool walking around the hallway in that Johnny, but he didn't pay any attention to that.

He came right up to me and talked a bit to make sure I was o.k. That was a lot more respectful than the ignoring routine Satan gave me. Her parents didn't come down to visit since their car broke down, but at least they called my room to check up on me. My family was too busy to even return my calls. Since I left a message that both of us were recovering just fine with the surgery, they didn't find it necessary to call. I was always the black sheep of the family anyhow. I didn't care.   My Millennium baby and I were ready for transport by the end of the third day. She was kept in my local hospital for a couple more days and I was sent home. I had to take a cab. Are you surprised? I sure wasn't. The hospital didn't care who picked me up, just as long as I wasn't driving myself home.

This was the first time since I was sixteen years old that I took any break from going to work. Yeah I took the occasional week off for vacation, but never a whole month. All I had to do was get my rest and spend time with the twins. It was a great vacation! A very sore vacation filled with doctor appointments, parent meetings with a single mother still hitting on me and those dreaded court order marriage counseling meetings. I had to get rid of that jerk. He was very "matter of fact" about my recovery and laid back into insults about my horrible husbandry. Nobody cared about my misery over being stuck in a marriage that everyone with any power over me gave Satan all the power to continue cheating and continue pretending she was the primary parent. I was home for a month, so I rarely saw her and I took care of the twins in spite of my physical pain. I took them everywhere I went, to my doctor appointments, my Millennium baby's doctor since she was taken home two days later and to our newly acquired day care. Satan popped her head into the home just for a few brief moments to get clean clothes and leave her dirty ones for me to wash. She did show up every time the DCF case worker needed to show up but that was it. Her strong man was always with her.

Our volunteer was so helpful. She came by not to see if this half-azzed, surgery recovering father was screwing up. She came by to help me out. Satan was never there during her visits and knew it. She didn't use it as ammunition against Satan, but did use it to back my play. Under extenuating circumstances, I was still able to completely take care of the twins without any help. She made sure that went into her report. She didn't include the fact that she helped me with the heavy laundry baskets I was forced to lift and stuff like that. We were both shocked to find out that the VFW had enough funds to donate a thousand dollars for my medical debt. They sent a check to me as beneficiary but to the hospital. That was very kind of them. The area agency that my volunteer took me to kicked in two hundred dollars too. I only had to cough up three hundred dollars. If the hospital would have gotten the paperwork from Satan ahead of the surgery, the three hundred dollars would have been forgiven. I didn't care since they pledged total forgiveness for anything not covered from insurance for the next six months. I could handle three hundred dollars from the emergency fund I had already scraped up.

That did make money even tighter since I was down to two-thirds pay and Satan refused to pay anything towards the household. I was refused food stamps, not because I didn't qualify under the emergency conditions, but because Satan already had filed a claim for the children and I was blocked from that benefit. It didn't matter. The list of area agencies had a ton of churches and non-profit agencies that helped out with food. I had plenty of time to stand in line and get some food for the kids. It was so embarrassing standing there; having young men drive by in expensive cars yelling at me "get a job you bum!" I had a job. What did they know? After the first time I had to humble myself to this shame, I was able to block it out. My children were more important than my shame. I was learning how to survive on my own and take advantage of help that was there for me. Feeling guilty about taking charity would never go away. I was ashamed that I wasn't good enough to do it without help like so many perfect fathers were able to do.

Satan never showed up even to sleep at the home. She only came back once a day to check up on the twins or put on a good show for the DCF caseworker. I had to get out of this marriage that was obviously over. I called my lawyer and explained things. She was glad to see that I was recovering well and made me assure her that I would have a day job. "It is imperative that you make that happen. Let me handle the rest of it. You need to face the judge one more time before I make the request for divorce in a higher court. Just hang in there a little longer." I knew she had the right plan to keep me from losing the twins. At least I finally saw the plan starting to fall into place. We went through the motions to pretend all was well with the marriage one more time. It was a pleasant meeting for me in court since I could limp my way into the courtroom and show them what I had just done for my daughter. The judge was pretty pissed that the state dropped the ball with the insurance, but was very pleased to hear that alternate options made it happen right away. There was no real need to leave any conditions on our case other than DCF visits to the home and keep up with marriage counseling. Everything else was given back to Satan and me as parents.

I knew my lawyer had filed the divorce papers and was concerned about the marriage counseling condition still left on our court orders. We didn't even have to go to parent meetings any more even though we both elected to meet up there every Wednesday night. I think Satan got a kick out of watching that single mom hitting on me. My lawyer had a simple solution. "You can let your wife know you filed the papers if you want to, but she will find out soon enough from the sheriff. Just keep going to the meetings whether or not she shows up. You will be out of that situation by the next court hearing in February if I have anything to say about it. Just be patient." I liked having a choice in the matter on how I would handle it. I preferred to tell Satan myself and not have her hear it from somebody else, because I knew exactly where I wanted to tell it to her, right in front of that jerk of a marriage counselor.

Wednesdays always started out with dread having to go to marriage counseling, and then ending with parent meetings. This was one I would never forget because it was great for me and a complete shock to more than just Satan. There were a lot of people in our lives that thought I was content with being a Carbone. People were about to find out how slick I could be too. It was more exhilarating than I ever imagined. I was nervous and excited at the same time when we sat ourselves down in front of that so-called marriage counselor. He and Satan tried to start their routine of bad mouthing me and reminding me of how bad a person I was, but I shut them down. "Before we start, the two of you need to know something. I filed divorce papers against my wife and she will be served with the papers soon. I am highly disappointed with your failure to make any real effort to help us with our marriage. We have court orders, so you are stuck with us until the judge changes things!" They were both in shock. All Satan could do was be in denial. "Why are you doing this to me!" she kept repeating. The counselor excused himself and left the room. I put him in a very precarious ethical dilemma and he knew it. That was his problem.

He came back in after he consulted with one of the other partners. He looked like death when he came back in the room. "I can no longer be your counselor. It would be inappropriate" he said. "That's not what court orders say, and I will hold you in contempt and file an ethical complaint to the medical board if you do that" I responded. "No there is a way around that. I will send papers to the judge showing that marriage counseling is no longer appropriate for you. You can see one of our partners as a personal counselor separately under my recommendation. That will cover you so you won't be in contempt." He basically begged me for this, and didn't tell me that's what had to happen. I liked the idea and made him give me copies of those statement immediately. He agreed to my conditions because an alternate would bring a law suit on the company. Satan and I left the counseling room. She ranted "why are you doing this to me?" all the way out to her car without waiting around for any paperwork for herself. I waited in the lobby until I got those papers. I also waited for him to give me the meet and greet with the woman who would become my personal counselor. He looked like a death in the family just hit him. He was a failure with our case, and he knew it.

I was finally rid of that jerk and good riddance. There was no need to show up at the parent meetings anymore, but I went. I couldn't wait to announce my news. Satan was already there, sobbing and started up on me again. "Why are you doing this to me?" "You did this to yourself" I said straight up. She had brought the twins there, but abruptly left without them. I was there alone with the twins and with the whole group looking at me with shock. Even the single mom who relentlessly hit on me was in shock. Someone had already slipped up to me that her baby daddy was locked up in jail. She had no clue that I wasn't dumb enough to get caught up in that drama, but it didn't matter anymore. The whole group was waiting for me to break the news. "Since you are not court ordered to be here, and it wouldn't be fair to have both you and your wife in the meetings, we need to ask you to leave. Here is a card with the leader of another group meeting. You can join them." There it was. I was the unwelcome guest all along and this confirmed it. I was glad to leave, and I did so with the twins forever. I did tuck the card in my wallet to check it out later. I wanted to get the twins home. Satan's strong man was there waiting with her, lurking about in the dark kitchen. When he was sure everything would be fine, he left just for the night. He would remain in the twins' lives for good, but so long to that fraud of a marriage counselor. I had gotten rid of one circus clown and now it was time to get rid of some more of them.

Act 9: Say goodnight and farewell to the clowns

When a circus act is done and it is time to go home, the clowns always come out to greet the crowds to say goodnight and farewell. Once you've entered into the DCF circus, their clowns never really go away. You could jump through all their hoops, perform admirably and justifiably make them go away, but they never do. It's not just a simple case of paranoia, it is a real fear that they put into your head. You are already on their radar, so all it takes is a phone call from some hater to set off all their alarms to send their clowns out to investigate what you are up to. Anyone can do this evil prank call on anyone at any time and the clowns will come out. If there is no real danger to your child, they will go away quickly. You can't find out who pranked you because they are protected. Most people aren't in real danger from DCF clowns even if haters make accusations against them. DCF clowns don't have time to waste creating a case on parents that they can't win in court. They prey on the weak, the unfortunate and yes, once in a while a truly negligent or abusive parent.

That's not how it goes for someone who's been to their show. The DCF clowns feel obligated to start up their clown act again for those who've been to the show. They won't care if you are not really doing anything wrong and they won't care if the person making accusations is notorious for ratting on people without just cause. DCF clowns know how to keep people in line who have been to the show. These parents have already been severely traumatized by their Gestapo tactics. They don't need the courts, the isolation room, none of that; those things are already buried in the parents' heads. They don't even need to knock on your door and hand over their business card. It won't even take that. All they have to do is make sure you know they are around. A quick drive by, a random passing where they just say hello, sometimes even stranger ways. Does this sound like paranoia? Perhaps, but I am a hyena. It's always been my job to scout for the truth.

If it was just my word against theirs, you would chalk up my rants as paranoia. The cars that would park close to my home and I would get them on film, catching their license plates before they took off, the random behavior towards me from their vast network of snitches; all that could be just my wild imagination. However, I belong to a much larger circus long before all that, and had been trained by the best talent on earth. They know how to use hyenas, slipping us in and out of borders, keeping us undetected until it is time to strike. I have slipped in and out of borders across continents without anyone even knowing I exist. What makes DCF think they have a better circus than I have already been involved with? Yes, I became a volunteer surrogate parent for the pure joy of helping out; but the benefits of it all was so worth becoming a fly on the wall. I know firsthand how messed up DCF can make some innocent parent's life when they want to. There are many workers in the system with vendettas and they will use their power to strike.

Being a hyena, I know the best way to strike back; not with a gun, not with the law, but with my diary. Maybe someday, some other half-azzed father will read this and keep himself out of trouble. Maybe some baby mama will get her hands on this diary and decide to treat the father of her kids with a little more respect. Maybe somebody who actually cares will make the world a better place for veterans after hearing about this. Maybe some congressman will be forced to make changes to the system because of angry parents that ask how children are dying from the hands of abusive parents, but innocent parents keep getting harassed. Maybe DCF will be forced to be honest about their situation so good changes will be made for our children. Maybe the US treasury department will wise up and enforce the laws better to stop wasting tax payers' money over foolishness. Probably, nothing will change. Most probably, my beloved daughter, you will read this and throw it away, but at least I will know you are ready for what you must face out there.

Like every other fool, I jumped through all my hoops to get those DCF clowns out of my life forever. I didn't know it at the time, but like a grey cloud hanging overhead, they never really go away. We all got through it though; you are starting your second year in college and well, here I am, one month away from 65 years old. Just one month to freedom, but I'm not as strong as I was back then, turning the corner to 50. I could handle it when I was younger, but I am just used up now, nothing left to give, no value to anyone. The VA hospital system tries so hard to keep us alive and they have done such a good job; far better than any civilian medical organization. They always ask the standard questions; do you feel safe, do you feel like hurting yourself, things like that. Nobody ever figured out how to ask the right questions though. Suicide is a very private thing for a hyena. We just go off on our own without a scene and fade away. You hear about the veterans that off themselves with guns and stuff like that, but you don't hear about the ones that use other weapons like drugs. Most of us know we don't even need anything at all but nature. Those are the ones you find dead out in an alleyway somewhere. So what is the question everyone should be asking us? "Have you done enough?"

Yeah, I hadn't done enough back then. Now, well I'm all used up and have nothing left to give you. You have everything I ever had and I am so disappointed in myself that there is no more that I can do for you. You deserved a better father than you got stuck with. We did have a few good years together, at least I enjoyed them. I am sorry that all you got out of the deal was misery. You deserved better, but I did fight hard back then. I did the best I knew how for you. That's what half-azzed fathers do. We battle on and on until the problem goes away, just to fight the next bad thing that crosses your path. No matter what it does to us, we always try our best to protect you. It doesn't always work because we are not perfect fathers, but at least we try and we were there. I was there to get rid of those DCF clowns; not just in my world, but your mother's world too. You won't hear that side of the story from her as you well know.

You and I recovered from our little surgery. It didn't take you long to start playing with your sister, just as if nothing had happened. If you think it's my imagination, just look hard for that tiny little scar on your side. It's there. It took me a bit longer to recover from that, but what do you expect from an old man cruising on a half century? It was all worth it though, especially all that crap from DCF. With all the support from both DCF and divorce courts, Satan's two lawyers, child support laws that favor mothers, welfare that she got, DCF, marriage counselors and every other weapon she had against me; Satan failed to take you away from me. All I had was a talented lawyer and I was wise enough to listen to her and be patient. I thank whatever god truly exists that he didn't make me snap before I did. Were those years you spent with me really that bad? Didn't you have even one good memory of it all? I guess you never really wanted me to know. Maybe we will talk in another world about it. If that world is filled with DCF, I'm going to kick god's butt.

I know Satan's new man was in your life behind my back during those dark days. Try to understand that she truly didn't know how I'd react to her moving on with that part of her life. The two of you really got a good opportunity to have another father figure in your life that did things a lot differently than me. I'm glad you got to see things from a wider view than just having me. He turned out to be a pretty good step dad. If you would have been stuck with one of those other goons Satan was sleeping around with, I really don't think they would have respected you like he did. A lot of little girls get abused by their step dads and you didn't have to face that, so try to keep that in mind with him. He's all you got left now. Your mother was facing a lot of pressure from DCF clowns just as much as I was back then, so I think he helped keep her sane through it all. I didn't have anyone but the two of you and that's all I needed.

Somebody should have told me he wasn't her cousin. That one really blew up in my face.

I had to wait to see how things would play out in district court with DCF. I was bringing in the big dogs with superior court. I already knew how things worked by now. If you don't like the way things go, take it to a higher court. You have to be patient though, keeping the lower court involved with your case just long enough to block any tactics your soon to be ex-wife will use to gain physical custody ahead of court orders. My lawyer was the best at using timing and the right words on paper. January court orders got sped up because I ratted them out to the treasury department, but they still got their federal funding for the twins for the next whole year just because official court papers listed the state as custodians of them into the next year. Talk about being slick, keeping children locked up away from kids just so the feds get financially gouged for money that was not truly spent on the children. Now it was my lawyer's turn to be slick. February came and went keeping things in place with the district court, but creating a paper trail that showed the children living with both Satan and me. If I would have broken away from her sooner, the district court would have given the twins to Satan and I would have no chance at all. That's how fathers truly get treated by the law. Mothers can do whatever they want and go where ever they want with children without being at risk of losing them. They have to be real dangerous to lose their children. Talk about prejudice.

I had the sympathy vote going for me in February because of the surgery. That sympathy vote never lasts long for half-azzed fathers. We have to shake it off and step up to the plate without delays or we lose our kids. One month; that is it and back to business. We did get an adjustment on our orders to see personal therapists instead of a marriage counselor. No harm, no foul. I don't know if it was the sympathy vote or not, but everything I could use to sway the courts had to be used. I had just given up a piece of my liver to save your life, I had their forced marriage counselor on the ropes for a law suit, I had the US treasury department snooping around; I shoved a lot in their faces. I think they got the message that they needed to play nice with me. Nothing like keeping a bunch of circus clowns at bay.

I was keeping the judge pretty jumpy too. Word got to our judge from another judge from a case with my volunteer work. Our judge let me know that he know what I pulled in the other court without anyone there knowing what we were talking about. "I heard from judge so and so that you are a real good advocate. Did you ever consider becoming a lawyer?" "Yes your honor, but I can't do the residency with my current obligations. I will have to go back to school for something else when I settle into my life as a single father." "Oh! So you're going back to school?" "Yes your honor. I want to get my MBA in finance. I'm thinking about becoming an auditor for the treasury department." All the lawyers knew that I just made a vail threat because they put their heads down in shame for ever opening up Pandora's Box with me. The judge knew what I was saying too and he made me pay for making that crack in his court. He was pretty slick too with making vail threats and he had the teeth to do it, but he was probably the only one that knew how confident I had become.

Judges can't officially talk to anyone about what they think about the court cases they have to babysit, but they most definitely talk to each other on the phone. I was using my advocacy certification to help more than just parents. I was able to use it to help juvenile delinquents too. More and more prosecutors and psychiatrists were getting jacked up by me in the county. There was a little game they liked to play with juvenile delinquents over simple cases of getting into fights at school or underage drinking and simple stuff like that. Delinquents were falling into the trap of not knowing how the game is played. They complete all their court ordered tasks such as anger management, writing letters of apology and stuff like that. Those poor kids didn't realize that not having the right paper trail would get them in trouble whether or not they did what they were supposed to. Psychiatrists were accidently on purpose forgetting to report that the kids completed their anger management. Prosecutors dragged their feet just enough to trap the juveniles into contempt just after they turned eighteen so those kids would get adult charges.

It was my job to put an end to that nonsense. I armed these kids with the truth and taught them how to create a paper trail. When psychiatrists forgot to send out paperwork, my documentation got their practice in jeopardy with the medical board. More and more prosecutors were getting their butts chewed out in open court because they just got outsmarted by a grocery clerk. The funniest part of all that was the cops involved with the cases found it hilarious even if it meant they lost their case. They hated lawyers worse than civilians do. They would leave the court laughing and joking among themselves, usually to pay me a cheerful visit to joke about it with me. It was entertaining for them to see a nobody come out of the blue, just to make jerks of a bunch of lawyers.

Most cops hate DCF workers even more. I was going to be real

dangerous once I got my surrogate parent certification for those

clowns. I would learn even more about their world while doing

some good for a bunch of kids that nobody cares about. That

would have to wait until I cleared things up in my own world.

The more my case dragged on, the more control I had

over my destiny. I was confident that my lawyer knew what she

was doing, even though it was annoying as hell. I wanted to just

pack up and leave Satan behind, but I had no chance if I did

that. The girls already had all their services in place in that town

and I couldn't afford any place in that town on my own. Satan

had no choice but help out with the bills. My sister was willing

to let me move into the second side of her duplex in the next

town over, but my lawyer needed time to get the legal wheels

rolling in my direction to make that move. I needed to prove

that I could still live in the same house with her despite a

divorce. I had to prove that beyond any shadow of any doubt, I would be supportive to her. I had to prove that I wasn't going to just snap and go off on somebody. I would have to support two homes if I had any chance at all with having my twins live with me. If I could do that, I could win.

First things first and I needed to get back to work to get my full paycheck back in swing. I did that before we met in court in March. The soreness went away and the doctors gave me the green light to go back to work full time with light duty. The insurance company was so happy about that and my jerk of a boss had no choice but comply. He had a permanent problem with me though. I came back to work with temporary doctor's order for light duty, but permanently disabled from working overnights. How do you like that? Doctors can be a wonderful tool to straighten things out some times. Publicly traded corporations are scared stiff of disability laws and my jerk of a boss had his hands tied. He had no choice but keep me working full time on the day shift. No more overnights, and no second shifts either! My doctors made sure the words were clear:

starting time at work no earlier than six a.m. and no later than five p.m. They tied my boss's hands even tighter.

When I say doctors, I'm talking about my primary physician and the psychiatrist that I now started seeing under court orders. She was awesome. She helped me out with real problems like this and used her power to help me. She didn't take anybody's crap about keeping my sessions confidential either. Satan's and my DCF case worker tried to call her once in order to pry into my business. My shrink shut her down and that never happened again. Besides that, she let me know DCF was prying. I let my lawyer know and she let DCF's lawyer know as a warning shot that we would go to the judge if it happened again. It was going to take some time to get those clowns gone for good. My lawyer was trying to speed me up with getting back to full duty as soon as possible. I didn't understand at first, but she knew what she was doing. We both knew that I would have to take another pay cut and it was better to face a judge in divorce court with the lower of the two incomes. It didn't matter if I had shared custody or not, I was going to have to pony up the dough.

Court in March came and went. Everything was smooth sailing. I was back to work full time on the day shift with a pay cut. Superior court was scheduled for June for the preliminary court hearing. Everything looked perfect for everyone in March at the district hearing. Everyone played nice, everyone was optimistic about the future of our family. Nothing appeared to be sneaky on the surface. The judge was openly discussing the divorce with us in court and what the plans were. I let everyone know when I would be able to move into my new home with the kids. Everyone, and I mean everyone including my lawyer belly ached about the horrible school system in my new town. When I said I had no intention of changing schools and I simply refused to give up my custody; we would share custody and I would drive to the school each day, they settled down a bit. This was the first time the court system heard my words "It will cost me more in day care than to just pay child support, but I will never give up my custody." The courts heard that many times after, but I still had to prove myself. I had to prove this was more than talk.

Courts are all about timing tactics. I needed to keep DCF in our lives long enough so Satan didn't have a clear shot at primary custody. She held all the trump cards but one. She was staying in the same town where all the services were; day care, good schools, doctors were there, she was the mother, welfare services were in her name and child support would eventually be mandatory since she was dipping into the system. If I could have afforded to stay put in the same town, I could have fought for primary myself, but that wasn't what I was after. I knew the minute Satan had any leverage against me, she would abuse it and keep the twins out of my life for good. That's just the kind of person she is. She always says the right words, pretending to want me in your life, but her actions say something much different. There was no way I was going to be turned into a weekend dad during a time of your life when you needed a dad.

Court in April coming soon. Everyone was giving me the full court press but the judge. His hands were tied. All he could do was sit back and babysit. Everyone was putting pressure on me and my lawyer knew it. Every time I called her or showed up at her office, she just kept telling me the same thing, "get your rest and keep doing the things that are helping your family." Her tactics were dead on right and I am glad that I listened. Satan started a new full time job for a marketing agency that payed her thirty bucks short of my paycheck. I made sure it was easy as slicing pie for her to want to go to work every day. The longer she held down that job, the better it was for me. I took care of most of the bills too so she had the opportunity to have enough saved up to take over the condo rent when I left for my new home just before April court. I kept it quiet, but had all the financial documentation ready. Money was my trump card that she never mastered.

With two court systems involved with our case officially, my lawyer had sabotaged any power either of them had to make any permanent decisions. Time was on my side and the slightest shift in opinion with the courts that favored me made it easy to adjust things for my advantage. Everyone hated the fact that my lawyer and I were using the DCF case to tie everyone's hands behind their backs. They did it to me, so now it was their turn. I picked my lawyer with good reason, the streets talk and she is very well known to many divorcees that faced her. She never loses. Every divorced parent I cross in our area always ask "who's your lawyer?" Most answers I get back: "oh, I got burned by her!" There's a funny thing about her living up to her name "Burner." She just lets people burn themselves. She doesn't really have to do anything to set them up, they do it for her. You don't even need a fancy lawyer like her to face this stuff. She prepared me to face courts all on my own afterwards and I thank her for the one solid thing that is universal across the globe. Just do what's best for your kids. When you do that, nobody with a sane mind in the court system will take away the time you spend with your kids. It's not in the best interest of the child to do that.

I was so busy fixing up the duplex for my new home with the two of you. I came back to the town house that I was still stuck living in with Satan after re-painting the ceiling. I was excited because I finally finished all the painting and prep work. "You can't imagine what a mess it makes to paint over stucco" I shouted to Satan as I burst into the door. Our volunteer worker from the case was sitting on the couch in the living room chatting with Satan. "Oh, I'm sorry. Did I interrupt something" I asked as the two of them looked up at me a little bit annoyed. "No, we are finishing up here" our volunteer answered abruptly. It was amazing how hush hush those two were about everything they were up to, but the moment it had anything to do with me, it was an open book to Satan. "Let me know when you move in so I can check it out" she said as she got up from the couch and left. Everyone's hands were tied. I would have all my time with the twins at my new home before the April court date. They couldn't take it away from me.

Satan's new job was far away and my job was so close

to the day care. She had to leave too early in the morning so I

had to drop the twins off at day care every day. I had the

registration as a paper trail to prove it. I always got out of work

early enough to pick them back up. Satan never got home

before seven or eight at night. I had the day care registration to

prove that too. Satan didn't realize it until too late. I was

keeping the twins overnight in my home more nights in the

week than she kept them at her place. According to federal

law, that made me the primary custodian. I kept proof of that

too. Our volunteer tried to encourage me to let Satan have you

girls more nights than she was doing, but I refused to listen.

She knew what I was up to and didn't like it. "Children belong

with their mother" she said. Her true bias finally came out. She

also threw in her two cents about ending the DCF case so she

could "volunteer her time where it was needed more." She

wasn't stupid and knew I could have had my lawyer close the

case anytime I wanted. I wasn't stupid either and it wasn't time

for that yet. "I don't have any say about that" I told her which, was obviously a lie. So what! Nobody was taking my kids! The chips were grossly stacked against me and I wasn't going down without a fight.

The volunteer wasn't the only one paying me a visit at my new home with you girls. The DCF case worker was obligated to do so. How ironic it had become that unwanted guests in my life were now stuck as eye witnesses that I was a highly successful single dad; juggling work, picking up kids, getting them exactly where they needed to be on time, keeping an immaculate home, spending quality time with the twins and being supportive to Satan without violating any laws. Satan was struggling just to keep the town house clean. I was over at Satan's home, helping her clean up one day when the DCF case worker arrived. You won't see anything in her reports about me helping Satan out. You won't hear that story coming from Satan's mouth, but it was true.

I did everything in my power to keep her from failure. DCF knew it, but made excuses for her. "There is nothing wrong with a little clutter" the DCF case worker made for an excuse. I showed that case worker the real evidence. "Dirty dishes that I had to clean up. Trash blown in with the wind from the deck. Tampons still stuck in underwear that were thrown on the floor. Here is my time stamped video of the mess and ME cleaning it up for her. I know you visited yesterday and saw the mess, Satan told me. All I have to do is subpoena your visitation records and catch you in your lie. All I want you to do is help her straighten out her own home and stop sending reports to the judge that she is the better parent." The DCF case worker got the message loud and clear. Her report was a stale mate; both parents have adequate homes. As for her attitude about my lawyer and me dragging things out even longer, I didn't care. You take my kids away from me, I'm going to get them back and you will pay consequences for messing with me. Her lawyer must have coached her from there on out because the only words coming out of her mouth from there on were "I can't get involved with your divorce case."

We tied up the DCF lawyer's hand pretty tight. He was a softy compared to that other jerk and the moment he opened up his mouth in the lobby just before the April hearing, we let him see all the evidence stacked against Satan and his department. He had no choice but reluctantly be forced to swing his vote our way. Some of it couldn't be used as evidence in a courtroom such as the tapes I made, but they sure could be used to give DCF a black eye in the media. Another clown was shut down. There was one more to run over before the hearing got started in district court on that sunny April day, but where did my lawyer disappear to? I didn't know where she was. Satan was standing in the lobby with the volunteer and DCF case worker, but her lawyer went missing too. I knew where they were.

I pretended to need to use the john down stairs. Just as I suspected, the two lawyers were hashing things out over dropping the DCF case. Satan's lawyer kept pleading "I don't know why we can't just end the case today!" and my lawyer just kept telling her "no." My lawyer must have known I would figure out where she had gone because she was facing the stairs and Satan's back was to me. She didn't know I was there listening, so I just watched the show. My lawyer was looking right at me. She knew I was there. "We should end this case before the divorce hearing" Satan's lawyer went on but my lawyer held her ground as she looked for my response. This went on and on until I heard the words I wanted to hear. "The DCF case will be kept open until the final divorce hearing is completed." My attorney looked at me and I nodded yes. Like a master, she held her ground a little longer for me to disappear without being detected back up the stairs. I heard it happen. One more set of hand got tied up. My lawyer and I had become a pretty good team working together.

We tied the district judges hands pretty good too. They all know what my lawyer and I were up to but had no choice but go along with it. Since nobody in that courtroom dared raise an objection to keeping the case open, the judge had to make the orders stand. The case would officially stay open until the district judge received the official report from superior court that a divorce settlement had been reached. There would be no more district court hearings. That was a thing of the past. There were no more visits from the volunteer or DCF. That was a thing of the past. There were no more court orders to receive psychological counseling. That was a thing of the past and now my choice. I kept my shrink on board and it was a good thing for me. I was officially free from the district court, but it was hung up in my lawyer's snare. Without being cleared from DCF supervision officially, Satan's lawyer couldn't even take a stab at taking over custody. It didn't matter what paper trail she had because it meant nothing in the eyes of the courts when it came to procedures. Time was finally on my hands.

The judge verbally agreed to all the conditions I demanded including keeping shared custody. He had no power over child support. That was above his pay grade. He let us all know that his official papers would be sent to us when he had time to have the clerk type them up later today, put his seal on it and send everyone's copy in the mail. He adjourned the court and I never had to show up in front of him again. Officially, I got to say goodnight and farewell to all those circus clowns. Unofficially, they just couldn't learn to leave me alone. I told you that judge didn't like my vail threat from the month before. He showed his teeth with what he sent my attorney in the mail. I guess he was too afraid to face me in person that he was bias towards fathers too. He could have typed up those papers and signed them right there just like every other court appearance we faced him with. No, he was a coward and couldn't look me in the eye and say he didn't like fathers either.

My lawyer wasted no time calling me within a week to let me know the judge's orders got received at meet up with her at her office. We sat down and she handed me my copy. As I read it, everything was exactly as we demanded except the custody thing. The judge had twisted things a bit and granted

Satan primary custody. I showed it to my lawyer and she said "yes, I saw that." I knew he didn't really have the power to do so, but his recommendation to a fellow judge would be a serious hurdle to get around. "Can we beat this?" I asked my lawyer. "It won't be easy with judge Hamster, but it can be done" she replied. I got stuck with the worst judge in the history of divorce court. Judge Hamster looked like one, a tiny man, but he was brutal to fathers. He never awarded so much as shared custody to fathers unless the mother was downright negligent or dangerous to the kids. I was facing the one judge that was so old school, fathers were lucky to see their kids on weekends and holidays. I was well informed by my lawyer and she said the best strategy was to reach a settlement with Satan. Every judge on the planet has their hands tied to rubber stamp an agreement to the exact wording of the agreement. Judge Hamster could only make a ruling if we didn't agree on something. It was my best shot.

We had a little bit of time to maneuver things before the May hearing. I could bring in five witnesses if we listed them soon. I had five ready to go that I knew would scare Satan and her lawyer. It was simple enough to squash the district judge's recommendation for Satan to take primary custody. We requested a guardian ad litem to be appointed to the case which is an unbiased lawyer that reports directly to the judge on the progress of our negotiations and what was currently going on in the two households. Current information trumped anything in the past and gave me more time. That could be dragged out for months or even years if I wanted. I knew that it would only be a matter of time before Satan screwed up again. It didn't take her long. It was just a simple thing at first before the temporary custody hearing in May, but it was enough.

Satan used her welfare case to switch over the town house home to an apartment within the complex that she received state funding for to live in. It created a low income home for her and the twins to be able to afford to live in with state help. She got her food stamps based on her part time income and lack of child support, but she was now working a job that squashed all those benefits and she wasn't quick to report it. She got all that state money, I was paying for the daycare, the insurances, I let her keep all the security deposit and she had a functional car to get to that high paying job. She had already filed her financial affidavit, we got a copy. She had to report her current income to superior court and now that the car I bought her broke down, she was in a pinch. She was caught in a legal mess that I could have easily reported to the state welfare department and made her face divorce court from a jail cell in Valley Street. No, that would have been short sighted of me and I just kept stacking the chips against her. I picked up Satan and the twins every day in my car, brought the twins to day care, dropped Satan off at work, went to work myself, picked the twins back up, picked up Satan and got them all home each day.

I could play dumb and just be supportive with the shared custody thing until she hung herself. Her lawyer already knew she was beat and quit her case. It is illegal for a lawyer to quit a client unless the client commits some form of felony during the fact. Without saying a word, your lawyer is telling the judge you committed a crime. Satan's lawyer paid me a visit at work one day to say goodbye and "think about what's best for the child." She used the excuse that she was moving out of state, but Satan would have been appointed a new attorney because the DCF case was still open. If she would have understood how this works, the state was still obligated to give her representation. Maybe not in divorce court, but some court appointed attorney on the district level could have thrown a monkey wrench in things for me. They nailed her instead and she was stuck finding a lawyer that was going to get paid. Not a single lawyer on the planet would take her case pro-bono. I guess they chat among themselves too.

So I kept helping Satan stack the felony chips against herself, making sure she earned that high paying check each week. I kept paying the daycare, my own bills and spending the extra gas money to get her to work. I didn't pay to fix her car and I didn't help with her bills. She'd have to figure that one out on her own. She'd have to pony up the doe for a lawyer pretty soon because our May hearing was right around the corner. I just chewed up time, taking care of minimal things for Satan, but taking advantage of that very tired look on her face every day during the week, keeping the twins home with me five nights and switching off weekends with Satan. By the time we had our temporary custody hearing in May, Satan only had the twins stay overnight in her home eight times, I had them each and every night other than that. Satan did manage to scrape up enough money to get a lawyer to show up on that court date, but not enough to fix the car. She still needed me for that.

When that day finally came, I got a chance to meet her new lawyer. She wasn't going to play nice, but she had no choice that day. Satan didn't have a single witness sitting in that courtroom, not even her parents. Her mother just kept saying "why do they have to get divorced?" and Satan's dad knew why. I had to hedge my bet and make sure we both had custody just in case those idiots from DCF ever gave us trouble again. He kept Satan's mom out of court because she would have been a disruption for everyone. I had my five witnesses sitting there, and not just any witnesses. I had a cop, state financial auditor and three fellow volunteers that I frequently invited over to my home to give an unbiased opinion to the judge about my living conditions. The cop was just there to be a witness to all the good things he saw me doing with my kids over that month. Try to argue with that witness in a court room. However, the auditor was there just in case we needed to present financial evidence to the judge with an expert that would have forced him to arrest her on the spot. Satan's lawyer knew she was screwed and had no choice but dance with us.

As we waited for our case to start, I listened to some idiot that was dragged into court for falling behind on his child support. He owed about five grand and was explaining how the ten thousand dollar loan he received for his new business venture was all used up and he was hoping to start making some money from the business soon. I whispered in my lawyer's ear as she and I both shared a puzzled look on our faces, "why didn't he just use half the money to get caught up on child support?" My lawyer shrugged her shoulders and shook her head that she didn't know. How dumb was that? Did he really think Judge Hamster would have a sympathetic ear for that nonsense? Not a chance! He got hauled away to Valley Street jail for that one. It was our turn. I was very shocked that Judge Hamster was much kinder to me. What happened to that ruthless destroyer of fathers? His hands were tied too! With two courts having an open case over custody issues for a child, and the state still being officially involved, neither parent could gain any custody advantage. It was a stale mate!

Judge Hamster moved on to more important things once he declared that the wording for temporary custody was joint custody, but the words physical custody could not be applied to our case. What a loophole my lawyer found! Furthermore, I requested a guardian ad litem that blocked it too. "Mr. Stewart, you do realize you will have to pay for the guardian?" "Yes your honor." "I see by the affidavits that your incomes are comparable and Mr. Stewart is paying for most of the shared expenses. I can't award any child support for this temporary hearing. Do you understand this Mrs. Stewart?" Satan nodded her head yes. "I didn't quite hear that Mrs. Stewart. Do you agree?" "Yes your honor" she reluctantly replied. "You both agree that the reason for divorce is irreconcilable differences?" "Yes your honor" we both chimed in. "I am granting a legal separation until the final hearing. I am declaring that no child support orders will be granted at this time and shared custody is awarded until the final hearing. Is that in agreement?" "Yes your honor" we repeated. He checked with the clerk to set a date. "The next hearing will be

January 4th, 2004. I will see you then." "Thank you for your help your honor" I said cheerfully. He returned my smile. "Any time Mr. Stewart." The bailiff motioned for us that we were all set to go.

Satan was rather disappointed. Both the judge and I could see it on her face as she left without a word. Her new attorney had a matter of fact look on her face. Apparently she had no clue how much damage I could have caused with that auditor. All I had to do was disagree and start handing over evidence to the judge. That silly lawyer thought it was a bluff. I had scored major points with Judge Hamster. I was facing the judge from hell and found his weakness right away. All I had to do was play nice and do what's right for the twins. That's all he wanted. He wasn't the ten headed monster everyone proclaimed he was. He just had no tolerance for deadbeat fathers. I didn't blame him. They gave all of us fathers a bad name. I wasn't sure if the judge knew I had facts lined up or not at that point in time, but he knew. I had to wait for our next hearing for the words that would come out of his mouth. When I heard them, I knew somehow, he already knew I could have shut down Satan at any time. I'm glad I never did, because it turned out for the best for you.

So you think it was over with the DCF clowns? Not a chance! They didn't have any official obligations to keep an eye on things, but that didn't stop them from spying anyways. You remember that cop I told you that showed up in court? Well, he was one of my local cops that kind of filled me in on things one day I took the two of you to the station to get fingerprinted. Yeah I wanted to make sure the cops had my girls fingerprints on file, pictures, DNA; all that good stuff. I wanted to be prepared just in case anyone took off with you. You hear all about strangers taking off with kids, but the biggest danger comes from somebody close. Yeah, Satan was threatening to take you down to Florida, just as soon as she beat me in court. She let me know it, I told my lawyer and my lawyer told Satan's lawyer we knew in hopes of straightening out your mother's mind. You won't hear that story from her. That cop helped me be prepared and he helped me out with another problem.

DCF was still following me around. I saw their cars parked out across the street from our home. They would follow me to the store. They followed me everywhere, just to remind me they were watching. Cameras are a wonderful thing to have when somebody is stocking you, especially when you catch the license plates and get a good fix on the faces. Everything digital can be time stamped. I had all that and brought it into the police station to have the cop take a look. What would you know! It was such a big coincidence that every plate he ran from my film had DCF written all over it. He really didn't like DCF to start with and when he saw they were harassing me, that cop hated them even more. He made a couple of phone calls while I sat down and listened. It was amazing how the harassment stopped all of a sudden. Now I had truly said goodnight and farewell to the DCF clowns for the time being.

They never really go away though. They just have to wait for a

half-azzed father to pop back on their grid.

Act 10: How Hyenas Die

I can't think of a better way to describe a veteran's death than to compare it to a hyena. Hyenas really don't like being trapped and will fight if the captor isn't smart enough to let it go. It really isn't a good idea for the civilian world to push a veteran around in a court room. We are all different and you don't know how that kind of a mess will blow up in your face. Some rare cases will get a lot of people hurt or tragically killed, but most of us can act civilized. Many of my brothers and sisters never make it to become veterans. They sacrificed their lives in combat or during service to our country. It really isn't the timing or the method of our deaths that I'm talking about. It is why we die. Everyone has to die sooner or later and we have no control over that. We do have control over speeding the process up a bit if we get to the point that we have no other options and we just don't fit into society anymore. For veterans the completed suicide rate was at fifteen percent the last I heard. That is way too many of my brothers and sisters getting to a point that they need to join our fallen kin. Maybe people do need to start asking veterans they know a simple question: "do you feel you have done enough?"

I hadn't come even remotely close to doing enough for you girls when I faced your mother with divorce court. I could see it in your face. You needed her to stop ignoring you. What child doesn't need their mother? I had so much to do to get her out of that rut. She was so focused on taking you away from me, she forgot the fundamental thing she was not giving you: quality time. Taking off with you to Florida wasn't going to fix that. It wasn't going to help her run away from the kind of trouble she was bringing on herself. The arm of the law is longer than she can run. I am so sorry I had to keep a stack of felonies leaning against her head on a constant basis, but it was the only way I could keep her in line. She absolutely refused to give into the fact that you needed both of us. She constantly reminded you that "you don't have to go with your father" from the get go, even when she was court ordered. She didn't care and I am grateful I ended up having time with you when you were young. I enjoyed every breathing moment we shared together even though you didn't share my joy. I am sorry it turned out that way.

Under normal conditions, keeping myself sane during that wait for January 4th, 2004 would have been easy. Your mother had already set me up with that "cousin" routine for my fall from sanity. At first, the disgusting thought of her being with her cousin was just something planted in my head by Satan, waiting for the right moment to set off my alarm clock from her actions. I did not see Satan's man around much, but knew he was in her life. We were far too busy that summer, fall and winter to have time to think about her personal life. The guardian ad litem was truly neutral with our divorce and had only one job, get Satan and me to put things in writing that we agreed on with custody and work out our schedule with "custodial periods."

Every detail of our divorce was agreed upon without much argument or discussion. There wasn't much left of our assets because of bankruptcy court. We had already split up things and anything of value was agreed; I would hold onto them until you go to college and those assets would be sold to help out with college. Most of those assets were just collectables. I had my car and bought her the other one so that was a wash. I kept all my retirement funds and she kept hers because there were no joint retirement funds. There was no issue even with the courts on that. It was a custody thing. Because we were fighting each other over primary custody, and the only solution was joint custody; all three lawyers did their best to handle it the only way possible, leave it blank on the paperwork indicating shared physical custody and let us work out our own schedules. Their hands were tied from district court anyways. The catch 22 was in place by my attorney and because of state involvement, nothing could be put in writing on the divorce papers.

Working the schedule out was a breeze at first. I was the one doing all the work including getting Satan to and from work. I still had more time with both of you girls during the week because I always had to work weekends and my two days off fell on the weekdays; Monday and Wednesday, the two slowest retail days of the week. Satan's lawyer must have finally gotten into her head during this timeframe because she stopped letting me have you sleep in my home every night. She had no clue without a divorce lawyer's intervention that she was being set up to be the weekend parent. She insisted on having me drop you off at her place when I brought her home from work. She didn't like it, but I insisted on only giving her three nights a week. I knew I needed four of the nights to keep primary custody. I would have kept you every night like your mother would have done, but she was motivated by money and wanted child support. I gave her Sunday, Tuesday and Thursday nights only. Eventually, the guardian ad litem leaned on me to be fairer, so I let her have every other Saturday night.

I found a new parent support group with that card the facilitator had given me. It was led by a single man who was a full blown psychiatrist. I was the only single guy in the group. There were only four other members, all were women. Two women were married unhappily I will say, and two single moms. I felt bad for those stand up husbands that were taking care of their family even though they were stuck with wives that badmouthed them behind their backs. One single woman had a baby daddy that was in and out of legal trouble and was a total dead beat. He never payed child support and never spent time with his kid. She was so stuck in her problems, there was no wonder why she was so frustrated about her life. The other one was a wonderful woman that really had her life together. She was finishing up college, working full time and taking care of two sons and an infant girl on her own. Yeah, her only hang-up was three dead beat baby daddies and having no man to take care of her personal needs.

Those meetings got a bit exhausting for me. I went to them during the day when I was off from work and you girls were in daycare. All I would hear for an hour was how horrible men were. All I could do was complain that those were the kind of fathers that gave all of us a bad name and they were the reason why I was going through so much hassle to get divorced. A lot was said behind my back in front of the new meeting facilitator before meetings got started. It wasn't anything bad per-say, but you will find out now that you have an adult life that there is such a thing that is called a "human meat market." Adults have certain biological needs that kids don't have and quite often find themselves looking for a hookup to take care of those urges. Parent support groups are definitely one of those human meat markets. That nice lady I am talking about was looking for a man to take care of her biological needs. That's what everyone was talking about behind my back. She was interested in me for more than somebody to hang out with and the group was trying to help her get to that point with me.

I know you remember her and her kids since they would come over for supper and you would play with the boys. You would play with the boys while she would sit her daughter in the high chair in the kitchen while I cooked everyone supper. Those evenings gave me time with another adult to talk to while I gave you an opportunity to interact with boys the right way. I am so proud of the fact that you took that lesson to heart. I always found it important for you to have friends that were guys to give you an opportunity to learn what boys were all about without finding out the hard way. So often, girls without guy friends fall victim to some charismatic dude that tells them everything they want to hear, just to get into their pants. I was proud that you learned to have balance with that part of your life and make your career goals a priority.

That nice woman had a different priority and that was to get into my pants. I am not going to say that I wasn't tempted, but it was an ethical dilemma for me. First of all, her timing was off. I was in the middle of a divorce, and I didn't want to complicate my life any further than it already was. Second, she was offered a job down south and was moving soon. One thing about sex is that it does create an intense emotional attachment to the other person. I didn't want to create those ties to her. She showed up at my home one day that I had off from work. Her boys were at daycare and her infant daughter got conveniently dropped off at her mothers. There was no question in my mind what that was all about. She was making her move to have sex with me right there and then. She got extremely clingy to me physically and the situation was very hard to fight off, but I did. I made sure she knew that I really wanted to get intimate, but couldn't. We wouldn't see each other once she moved and as I put it to her, "I can't do that to you." I just wanted to show her respect, but that wasn't what she wanted. Needless to say, I didn't see her after that day, she moved away and the group facilitator broke up the group. Don't let anyone fool you, men can stop themselves from having sex with a woman if they respect them. Keep that in mind during your adult life. It's all about respect first, then everything else falls in place.

I did talk to my therapist about the woman. She surprised me that she was kind of leaning more toward encouraging the relationship rather than keep it simple and say goodbye. I really didn't understand this twenty-first century thinking of everyone just trying to get lucky without thinking about any consequences. However, there it is and I just shrug it off, but that doesn't mean that I am going to jump on board with that recklessness just because everyone else is doing it. My therapist did say that it would be an intense long distance relationship; I didn't need any of that, so we simply disagreed with how we viewed that situation. I had more important things going on with the divorce and she was very helpful with keeping my stress level down with that. Perhaps that's what she was thinking about, relieving stress with a hookup for me. Talk about a guy being born in the wrong century.

Work was a bit stressful too. I had to take the demotion and my boss stuck me back on overnights as a clerk. It was very disappointing how political things were in a silly grocery chain. I continued working just as hard as usual, but the hours were killing me. I needed to get back to the day shift or I was going to lose my battle with Satan over custody. My boss was the biggest jerk and I couldn't afford to lose my job. It was almost as if he was in cahoots with Satan to force me to give up my custody. All my lawyer could encourage me to do was to get my rest. I was crafty enough to make sure I had a baby sitter with the twins through the night. I was out by seven in the morning, so it wasn't a problem to get them off to daycare and get back home for some sleep. Satan finally got her car back working again, so I didn't have to worry about taking her to work.

The summer had past, September and now it was the end of October. Satan had gotten standoffish with me and I figured some of it had to do with limiting her conversation with me because we were still in the middle of a divorce. Satan had gotten herself fired from that good job for whatever reason and I figured that had a lot to do with her giving me the silent treatment. She never had a good work history, so I wasn't exactly surprised about that. My bills were pretty low and I only took a pay cut for the exact amount I got for a raise as a manager in training. It was easy to manage my money without Satan dipping into it, so I continued paying all the daycare, my bills and started paying her child support so she wouldn't lose her home. Just because she was being a lazy and not getting another job didn't mean I was going to help her be homeless. I was very serious about both of us being parents, no matter what her shortcomings were. Halloween fell on different nights for our two towns, so there wasn't any argument about that. I took the twins out trick-or-treating in my town and they had a blast.

The only peace I had during that time was when I spent my time at home with you twins. Everything else in my life was just a lot of negative pressure on me. We had a pretty good routine. I already kept up with most of the housekeeping and chores on my own, but we always tidied up a bit when we got home. That would only take about fifteen minutes. It was so much fun back then watching you girls push a broom around or load up the dish washer. Then we would cook together. You could do real simple stuff like help make macaroni, toast and stuff like that. You were eager to learn new things and it was so much fun watching my twins learn so fast. After supper we finished up dishes and then it was homework time. Yes, even at the age of three (going on four) you had homework time. We would read, learn numbers and the alphabet and then color. You would get some play time, then baths and bed. Giving you a good routine is just something half-azzed fathers do for their kids. I don't know if it was helpful, but I did my best. It was definitely different that the disorganized, don't know how reliable things will be kind of life you had with Satan.

Thanksgiving was around the corner and Satan was being extra nice considering we would be having a meeting just

before the holiday with our lawyers and the guardian ad litem.
She would let us know what her recommendation was going to
be for the judge on that day. Satan was just acting extra weird
for her. She was being way too nice. She was even willing to
give up some of her Thursday time with the twins so I got to
have Thanksgiving lunch with them, Satan would have her
celebration for supper. I knew something was going on and
everyone knew about it but me. I was going to find out what it
was all about in that meeting. Even my lawyer knew all about it,
but was afraid to tell me. Everything turned into a big mess as
soon as we sat down and I expected a simple shared custody
agreement with the days already being set, but that wasn't
what was on everyone's mind.

Satan sat quiet the whole time except to answer a few
of my questions I asked her direct. Satan's lawyer spoke first
and talked about "the elephant in the room." "Your wife is
pregnant" she said candidly. I answered her right back with the
first thought that came to my mind. "It's definitely not my

child!" "No, we all know it isn't." My lawyer spoke next as everyone watched for my reaction. "I'm sorry. It slipped my mind to tell you about it. This is my fault for not telling you sooner." I think everyone in the room was going to have a heart attack over my reaction. I wasn't angry, yes I was a bit thrown off, but not surprised that she had already gotten herself knocked up by someone. Everyone was so shocked that I didn't even care and talked about more important things directly to Satan about it. "You have been getting pre-Nadal care haven't you?" "Yes she responded." "I'm glad, because you know how complicated things can get for you during pregnancy." People never really understood me very well and that was one of those moments. I really didn't give a crap what she was doing with her life anymore as long as I got my divorce and my time with the twins.

Everyone seemed relieved that I didn't flip out over that one and we were able to move onto more important things. I looked at the guardian ad litem. "What are you going to recommend for custody?" "I am recommending that your wife gets primary custody. It is better for you to pay her child support than a baby sitter when you have to be at work. " Now that set me off. "I do everything right, support both houses and you are still going to take away my custody. This meeting is over and I will see you in court." I got up and left the room. I was surprised that Satan got up and followed me out to the hallway. I could tell she was behind me so I stopped and turned to face her. "I suppose now that you have another person in your corner to take away my custody, you don't need to go along with what we arranged on our own. I also suppose you won't let me have time on Thanksgiving." "No, I'm not stopping you from having your time. I just want child support."

It was amazing how she could just lose a job any old time she wants and not be held accountable. If I was to lose my job, I would be in deep trouble with the courts. It is such a double standard and very unfair for fathers. We always will be threatened by the immorality of the court system to be blackmailed for money and never see our kids. The thugs could embezzle all the money they wanted, but they were never taking away my twins. Satan was easy to read. She was all about the money and she would get it, but I was all about my twins and I was going to get what I wanted in writing. Satan could not be trusted on her word. Without court orders, I would never see my twins again because she would take off to Florida. She was that mean.

Satan was also pretty slick with how she would slip in an intended lie to a conversation, just to use it for some mischief. She seemed to be in a pretty good mood out there in the hallway, so I asked the question. "So who is the father?" I should have known she was up to something with that big smirk on her face when she told me it was her strong man that got her pregnant. Keep in mind, up to that point in time, the information I had about him was that he was her cousin. All that trauma from DCF and losing the twins had already put a bullet in the chamber of the gun to my head. Satan just pulled the trigger with that lie about getting pregnant by her cousin. She did it on purpose. The grin on her face told it all. I just let it go for the moment because she was pregnant with an innocent child. My lawyer followed us out to make sure everything was o.k. I motioned for her to follow me down to my car. "Did you know she got herself pregnant from her cousin? How am I supposed to be expected to give up my custody to that situation." "Let me handle it" was all she said. I would only see my lawyer one more time before the divorce.

I was in a total panic. The one person that should have been standing up for me seemed too calm about the situation. My attorney had a good reason for being calm; somebody had to be. My back was against the wall and I was in jeopardy of losing my girls again, and for what? Did I do anything wrong? Yes, I did. I was born to be a man and that is always a problem for fathers. We always take a back seat to mothers. Mothers can screw up, time after time, and they are always given another chance at parenting, even if they do something extremely bad. It seemed to me that Satan broke a cardinal rule with our society when it comes to incest, but I was misinformed. Satan told me that lie to set me off and be able to point a finger at me to the world that I was dangerous and not fit to be a father. Even though it would seem on the surface that all she cared about was the money, she cared about something else too, taking my children away from me.

Thanksgiving went very well. We spent our lunch at your aunt's on the other side of the duplex with your two cousins. Do you remember or were you still too young? Your cousins had long since outgrown that swing set she had on her side of the yard, but you liked watching the pine trees sway in the wind as I pushed you on the swing. I guess I was given so much trouble by the rest of the world, I made sure I cherished any moment I had with you. It was a good day and I was at peace because I was with you. I knew you were safe from anything weird that could happen within a questionable living arrangement at your mom's. I did drop you back off and everything was cordial. I asked Satan "how's the baby?" She

said "The babies are doing fine. I'm having identical twin girls!"

I knew she was getting huge, and believe it or not, I really did

care what happened to those kids. They would be your sisters

and that was important to me. I didn't know who would raise

them since I believed that your mom would be in trouble for

that, but they would be important to you and that matters.

Satan could have kept that figurative gun from being

cocked back and fired at my head, but she wanted it to go off.

She knew how the thought of her having an incest baby would

eat away at my mind. All she had to do was tell the truth that

she had moved on and found another man. I would have been

very happy about that because he turned out to be a very

decent man. Keep that in mind as you live your life. You could

have done a lot worse as your mother shopped around to give

you a step dad. He changed dramatically when his twins were

born because something inside him said it was time to grow up

and be a man. He did just that, not for only his kids, but for you too. Remember how much he has always been there for you, because he is all you have now. My time on this earth is done. I have done enough for everyone else, including you. There is nothing left to give and it is time to move on to be with people that really need me around.

It was Thanksgiving night and I was alone. Grocery stores don't stop working for holidays so I had to go in to work that night. I was surrounded by other workers, but I was still alone. I tried to keep working, it was all I had left, but those gears in my head kept turning. Satan had wound me up good with those thoughts of her doing something inappropriate in your presence and it really bothered me. I just wanted you safe. Then it happened as I dropped the case I was stocking on the shelf. That alarm clock went off in my head. I was headed toward a total melt down. I had to get my twins to safety. I told the supervisor I was sick and had to go. I punched out and headed for my car. It was two in the morning. I had about ten minutes before I would arrive at Satan's home. What was I going to do about getting you out of there? There was only one way to do this and I called the cops to meet me down there. If Satan had no problem sleeping with her cousin, I had no way of knowing what would happen to you. I had to get you out of there.

I waited for the cops in the parking lot. They showed up after me, but I waited none the less. They would have to be the ones to go in there, not me. There were two of them in the squad car. They approached me and asked what the problem was. I told them "my soon to be ex-wife got herself pregnant by her cousin and there is no way I am going to allow any of my children to be stuck in that home." One of them knocked on Satan's door to talk to her and make sure you were all right while the other one stayed with me and checked out my court orders. When the other one was done with Satan, he rejoined us. "The children are safe and you will need to go" he said with a big grin on his face. I didn't see what was so funny about it. "So you don't see anything wrong with her sleeping with her cousin?" "What's wrong with that" he asked jokingly? I really thought that the whole world had gone insane, but it turned out to be me. The other cop decided to do his job and keep me calm. "Sir, this is a court matter and there is nothing we can do about it. Why don't you go home and get some rest. Everyone is safe."

The calming effect of those words "your kids are safe" is quite amazing. If you look at every piece of paper written on the subject of human needs, safety comes before everything including food and shelter. You were temporarily safe and that is all that mattered for now. There was nothing left to do but wait until court and fight Satan. It was tricky because I was very conflicted about the whole thing. She was pregnant and there was nothing I would do to harm a child, but I had the legal ammunition to end her parenting with you. I was stuck in a real mess or so I thought. I turned on my engine and drove away without incident. The cops followed me to the edge of town to make sure I went away. I went home alone and straight to bed.

I needed a good night sleep. It can be exhausting to have a mental break down.

The first time it ever happens to someone, that alarm clock goes off in your head "Danger! Danger!" but you don't really know what's going on. It was going off in my head and it was so confusing. I knew there was danger and you were not safe, but it was a false alarm. It would take me years to understand what was going on for real. Had I taken it more seriously, maybe the second time it went off in my head would have happened much differently. Oh, I knew what was going on that time, but when you have a breakdown, things can get real weird. I woke up the next morning in total panic mode. A good night sleep didn't help. It was just a band aid that fixed the problem just long enough to get me to my shrink that Friday. Band aids are great for little cuts, but my whole psyche was pouring out. I needed a serious cure, and my psychiatrist took care of that. She was a bit of a workaholic and it was a good thing for me. We didn't have an appointment, but she was in her office and she made the time for me. It was a good thing I had her watching out for me. There is no telling what would have happened to me without her. We did have many good years together because of it, didn't we? At least I thought we did, but it seems that you didn't feel the same way.

I poured my heart and mind out to my psychiatrist. She listened intently to my story and got real angry at my lawyer when she heard that part of it. The one difference for the second time in my life that came out of her listening ear was action. This was the second time in my life that someone actually did something to help me out. The first time was when the CASA volunteer helped me figure out how to pay for the surgery I needed to help you with. My psychiatrist took my lawyer's number from me and gave her a phone call. She agreed with me that there was something very wrong with my children being stuck living in an incestuous home environment. As a doctor, there was no way she could allow that one to slide. I was helpless with the situation, but my psychiatrist wasn't.

Men don't do well most of the time with just getting a listening ear without some form of action. That is a difference you will find when you decide to have a serious relationship, so keep that in mind. You will be mostly interested with just having someone to listen and not try to fix things for you. Even this half-azzed father understands this about women.

My shrink didn't stop there. She had to fix me too. The best way to do that was remove as much stress from my life as possible so we could work on fixing me. She had the power to put me on medical leave from work and that is exactly what she did that day. She cleared the rest of her day from any distractions to help me. That is how much she cared. I don't think she billed the insurance company for more than a session, but that was not what she was all about. I have never had anyone take it to the distance like that except my real family; fellow soldiers. Not even my blood relatives have ever dealt with my real problems, they don't have the ability to cope with mental illness. I am an embarrassment to the family and that is why you have never seen me be invited to any family occasions other than help them with chores. I hope you will learn to deal with mental illness better when you are older. My shrink took the lead with getting to the bottom of my panic attack and PTSD until my veteran benefits kicked in and they could take over. For that first day, she got me calm and got the paperwork done so I could immediately collect my short term medical benefits from work. The rest of it, she and I had to work on over time.

My shrink kept me out of work way past the court date in January. It was the only thing she considered important for me to face that was negative in my life. She knew that I needed to put closure to my marriage without any more problems added to my plate. She was so right about work. I never would have had all those wonderful years with you, being a part of your life as you grew up if I was stuck in that work environment. This was the first time I had ever taken more than a week vacation from work ever since I was sixteen years old. She was a very talented doctor and knew I would need a lot of rest after the divorce day. She called it decompression time. She warned me, I didn't believe her, but it was true. Your mother had the first two days with you after the divorce date so I had two whole days to rest. I barely woke up during that time. Do not let anyone make you believe that mental health is fiction. Every ounce of your physical health depends on your mental well-being.

I complain about my blood family not being there for me, but that is strictly about my mental health. They are stand up people when it comes to everything else so keep that in mind if you ever get in a jam. Just don't talk about your mental health to them or you will become the black sheep of the family like me. Being on a disability check made things very tight on money for me and your aunt was there for me. She let me play catch up on back rent when I was able to. She wanted me to get through this divorce and took the day off from work to be there. It was a good thing because my lawyer had two other cases in that courtroom on the same day. She was very busy and needed my sister to keep an eye on things so they wouldn't

go bad for me. Everyone involved with my case knew I was in

no mood to negotiate and wanted to battle things out in front

of the judge. They also knew I had documentation of Satan's

crimes of double dipping the welfare system. If I was allowed to

air it out in open court, she would have been arrested on the

spot. The guardian ad litem, Satan's lawyer and mine were all in

fear of me that day with good reason, I had the power to

destroy everyone in my path with the law on that day. The

judge would have had no choice but comply if I so chose.

What nobody knew is what truly was in my head that

day. Yes, I was going to negotiate the best deal possible so my

situation didn't get any worse, but I wasn't going to hand Satan

with the law on that day for one simple reason: your unborn

twin sisters. I didn't know them yet, but I would have a part in

their lives down the road and I knew it. I knew better than

anyone that this life I was put into was all about you girls and I

wasn't putting a roadblock on that. No matter how bad the

future would become for me, this was all about you girls having a childhood together and I was going to protect that to the end. It was my health insurance that paid to have your identical twin sisters be born healthy, not their father's. You won't hear that story from your mother either, but I insisted on doing it. Her idiot lawyer overlooked the fact that she would be without insurance on that very day, knowing full well that she was knocked up. I made her lawyer pencil in a condition to keep your mother on my insurance for two years to buy her time to get her life in order without getting sunk with medical bills. Nobody wants to tell you that story either.

Most of the entire divorce agreement was already typed up by my attorney and it was just minor details that had to be scribbled in between the lines. My lawyer was too busy with other clients to be there for all of that with the exception of looking at it when Satan's lawyer was done with it all. The guardian ad litem sat there silent the whole time without saying anything. The custody arrangement was exactly the way I said it would be, shared custody, and that nonsense talk from the guardian ad litem was a bluff. She was just a neutral party through the whole thing and she never asked for any money. She volunteered! Can you believe that? Satan and I had already worked out the details of custody, shared, I would get Monday, Tuesday and Friday nights each week; we would switch off every other Saturday night and Satan would get Wednesday, Thursday and Sunday nights. I made sure there was a deadline of four p.m. for the latest time allowed for conducting the parental switch. I knew your mother too well.

Because I was on disability, which was the only condition left open ended. I would pay a reduced rate until I got back to full time employment and then the adjustment would be made, my lawyer would forward the information to the judge and he would finalize that condition based on my new rate of pay. I was given six months as a verbal warning to have that completed or would be found to be underemployed. Funny thing how lawyers think they can make medical decisions about a person's life. It's a good thing all that worked itself out within that timeframe because I was prepared to file charges against a bunch of lawyers for practicing medicine without a license. Lawyers bluff but I don't. I may have gone along with this negotiation process, but that was just a delay tactic of my own to get your twin sisters born and in the clear. I wanted a clear shot at Satan without having collateral damage. I was a patient man and was willing to postpone that fight.

We were all ready to present the agreement to Judge Hamster. Even my lawyer finally finished up with her other cases. Hamster did an unusual thing that day, he didn't sit on the bench and let one of his magistrates sit on the bench. He hung back in chambers and waited for us. He wasn't the mean old man everyone made him out to be, that was just a show he put on for deadbeats. He already knew somehow what was really going on with our case and especially that I am a stand up father that didn't have to be told by anyone to spend his money on Satan's household. I guess the guardian ad litem was really doing her job. I was the only one sworn in (by my attorney) to make sure the agreement was "fair" in my mind. For the time, it was, so I lied. I would change things down the road. He looked over the agreement carefully and only commented on three things.

He had no issue talking in a mean tone towards our attorneys. "This is kind of dark, saying in case of death, Mr. Stewart will keep life insurance active" chewing out my lawyer. "Don't you think you could have said it a little different?" "You couldn't leave out the bowling could you?" he said sternly at Satan's lawyer. "Saying both parties will insure children won't miss activities would have been much more appropriate" he added with a disgusted look on his face. He really got after Satan's lawyer for this one. "I've known you for over ten years and you know better than threatening Mr. Stewart with leaving the state. The laws have changed and you better get your nose back in the books and brush up on them. Mothers can't leave with the children any time they want. Mr. Stewart is correct with demanding she must keep a residence within this town or lose all physical custody to him. Divorce will be granted based upon irreconcilable differences unless someone has anything else to add." I picked up my dirt file and was ready to unload it to the judge if anyone spoke up, but nobody dared. "I hereby announce you divorced. Have a wonderful day." Everyone silently got up and began to leave the judge's chambers but me. "Thank you your honor!" "You are most welcome." Now I got up to leave. I was finally free and things didn't turn out so bad for me in court.

I was officially free from DCF now and kind free to spend time with the two of you without anyone interfering, or so I thought. Your mother was tied down to one town and I could live where ever I pleased. She got the money and I got you, it was a fair trade. I would never trade those years I spent with you for anything. The whole next year was filled with mixed feelings because Satan went back to her usual self of ignoring you girls and using me to take care of you during the day if it worked to her advantage. When it didn't work to her advantage, she was always late having you ready to go with me for my custodial periods of time. She has no respect for the law or the father of her kids. My lawyer made me wait a whole year to take her back to court over violating my custody. She gave birth to your identical twins in the spring without any problems. It was her man that explained that he wasn't her cousin, nobody else. It kind of pissed him off that she would say such a thing. He changed dramatically once the twins were born. He no longer viewed me as a threat and got to know the real me, just a half-azzed father trying to take care of his kids. That was our common ground and we built a friendship based on that.

Had Satan, your mother shown the least little respect for my rights to have my custodial periods of time start on time, we would not have gone back to court. I would have let everything go because I got what I wanted out of the deal without hurting her situation; you. But she couldn't let it go and had to do everything possible to make me miserable and the only thing she held on me was you. She wasn't dumb enough to refuse to let me take you home because I would have her arrested for kidnaping, but she was slick enough to always be late. My lawyer finally gave in to my constant complaints and she sat down with me to draw up the complaint to send to the courts. Satan's violation of custody was on top of the list and there were fourteen other complaints, worded perfectly to show that I suspected her of that many crimes.

I didn't just stop with her. I knew I had to get the criminal proceedings moving on her so I made a formal complaint to welfare for her double dipping and they got copies of the evidence. That complaint was time stamped and I added it to my dirt file on Satan. All I could do was wait. Apparently, Satan hadn't been paying her lawyer, so her lawyer never contacted her with the court date. It was her lawyer that was supposed to deliver it to her, not the sheriff and it wasn't my responsibility either. My lawyer's secretary tipped me off that if Satan didn't show up in court, I would win by default so I kept my mouth shut and so did the secretary. I was going after full physical custody and forcing her to pay me child support. Her welfare fraud would give her two years minimum in jail and lack of paying child support would add even more time. My twins had a father and so did your identical twin sisters. We two fathers would have made sure you spent all the time in the world together. You didn't need a mother for that, especially not a fraud. But my lawyer was slick and when we were two days away from court, she grilled me hard to find out if I had told your mother about the court date. I reluctantly said no and she figured out that her secretary was behind the stunt and fired her. She told Satan's lawyer since they were friends and Satan's lawyer told your mother about the court date.

I suppose everything worked out for the best because look at you now! You're in college to become an editor and the Ivy League at that! I was in no mood for negotiating and everyone left me alone to talk with your step dad. He was the only one that had a chance at calming me down. "What do you want out of this" he begged me. After about the fifth time he repeated himself, I saw that he was sincere and worried about the situation. I was seriously rocking the boat and he knew it because of his experience with the law as a gang banger. "I want the fourth day of the week for custody added to my other three and I want her to stop being late, that is all." I said straight up to him. He went back to Satan and the two lawyers, they drew up the papers, had Satan sign them, I signed them and it was given to the bailiff.

Our lawyers didn't want to be there since Judge Hamster was sitting on the bench and he was already in a bad mood. We didn't even need to speak since an agreement was made, but he had a couple of things to say to us. "Mr. Stewart, how are you today?" "I'll be o.k. I suppose your honor." "I'm going to approve this agreement and I hope it makes your day a little better. Mrs. Stewart, I hope you understand the direction we are going here, don't let me see you in here again!" That was all that was said and we left. She took his warning and was never late again. I had gained primary custody and she still kept

half my paycheck. It was extortion I was willing to pay just to be

with you. Even though I was back to work full time with a pay

cut since my shifts were made medically limited to the day shift,

she was still getting a big part of my money. I had gone through

three years of hell to gain peace with my girls. It was worth it

for me, but I don't think you were happy.

It killed me to find out eventually that you didn't want

to be with me, but I gave you up to make you happy. That's

what half-azzed fathers do. I'm sorry I wasn't the dad you

needed, but I tried. I was always deeply wounded over the

tragedy with your twin sister, my double miracle. You always

took it in stride, but I never did. I'm sorry that I made you

miserable over that. At least I have already given you

everything of value on this earth and my death won't cost you a

thing because Fort Sam will take care of that. I'm glad I already

transferred all my copy rights from that silly little book I wrote.

It's doing pretty good and you'll get a cut of the money from those artists that turned it into a cartoon series. You'll get my social security until you graduate from college too. There's nothing else left for money, I transferred all my retirement funds right into your school loans with Sallie Mae so you wouldn't face that debt. I spent my last forty bucks to keep my phone on one last month in hopes of hearing from you. I already gave you my car since you needed it for college and asked me to borrow my camping gear for that summer road trip.

It is a simple thing to kill a hyena. It has to come from the pack, somebody special like a child. Some times when a hyena gets too old to be useful, it is killed by the pack, but most of the time it is left behind to die alone. That's what happened to me. I am no longer useful. I have given you everything you needed and there is nothing left. That tie to me is gone. You never really wanted me in your life and I gave it one last try with that phone, waiting for just one call, text or message, but nothing came to me. Maybe if you had just text me two simple letters, "hi" I might have had the strength to go on, but I am all used up now. I had the phone on for a whole month, and nothing. It died last month and apparently I screwed up again and I will die next. A hyena can survive with just being needed, but when that is gone, the truth of the matter comes out. If the hyena isn't wanted, it will die.

Yeah I screwed up pretty bad. I am two days past sixty five and old enough to collect my social security. I planned everything out so I could take the summer off from work to go camping and then start my retirement in the fall. I didn't need money for those months because I was up here in this tree house I built you, deep in the woods where nobody goes but me. There are always plenty of wild berries in the summer and plenty of trout to fish. I ran out of fish hooks back in August and you have all my survival gear, including the knife I could have carved out hooks with. I trusted that you were going to return my gear to me before you went back to college. I suppose all that college hustle made you too busy to remember. That's o.k.

It's not your fault, I should have at least kept one jacket since I

know how cold it gets in New Hampshire in the fall time. It is

one of those bitter falls this year. I am so cold.

I went down in to town to the VA medical center just to

find a "closed" sign on the door. I guess money is tight all

around and they had to shut it down. I didn't have the strength

to walk the 150 miles to the nearest VA hospital where I would

have gone to now. All I had to say was that I was homeless and

they would have taken care of me until things sorted out. I

barely had the strength to walk back here and climb back up in

the tree to die. People chose many different weapons to kill

themselves; knives, guns, drugs, alcohol or pills, but not the

hyena. A combat soldier knows it's not the bullet that is the

biggest danger, it's the elements. That is the weapon of choice

for so many of us veterans who are ready to die. If you see one

homeless and huddled up against a building, the veteran may

have already made the choice to die. If he or she is convinced

that "I have done enough," it is time to die. I have done enough and it is my turn to join my brothers and sisters who have

already fallen. I am too cold to write any more so I want to just

say a few last things to my Millennium baby, I love you and am

so proud of you. Be happy and safe and if you haven't already,

forget all about me.

Hypothermia set in and the veteran died much later,

alone that night in October. His frozen body remained

unattended up in that tree house for months. Nobody went

looking for him. It wasn't until the following January that the

body was discovered up in that tree house. Another local boy

that had just spent thirty years as a ranger was finally home to

enjoy his well-earned retirement. He was enjoying a cold, but

sunny day of snow shoeing when he spotted the tree house in

the distance. Anyone would have been curious like he was to

discover a tree house in the middle of nowhere, so he took off

the snow shoes and climbed up in to check it out. The tree

house was well built and not a flake of snow found its way

inside as the ranger veteran peeked his head up through the

trap door. The ranger tossed his back pack in through the trap

door off to the side as he looked around. He saw the frozen

body curled up in a fetal position on the floor. He hopped in

and read the name on the dog tags hanging on the dead man's

neck. He didn't know the man, but recognized the army patch

and rocker on the dead veteran's BDU shirt.

He wrenched the diary out of the dead man's hand. He

wasn't being disrespectful to another veteran's privacy, but he

had the need to know how to get ahold of the next of kin. The

retired ranger sat down and read through the diary. He wasn't

in a rush, there were still hours before it would get dark. When

he finished reading what he needed to see in the diary, he

tucked it safely into his cold weather coat. There was a jar of

pennies sitting on the floor, so he put that in his back-pack, as

he took out a blanket and rope from it. He used the blanket to

wrap the dead veteran and the rope to lower him down from

the tree house carefully. He climbed down himself and put back

on his snow shoes. He picked up the dead veteran to carry him away and back into town. "C'mon brother, let me take you

home."

www.ingramcontent.com/pod-product-compliance
Lightning Source LLC
Chambersburg PA
CBHW071154250626
47159CB00001B/79